SNOWFLAKE IN A BLIZZARD

John Buehler

Vantage Press
New York ● Los Angeles

Some of the names of characters in this book have been changed to protect their privacy.

FIRST EDITION

All rights reserved, including the right of
reproduction in whole or in part in any form.

Copyright © 1991 by John Buehler

Published by Vantage Press, Inc.
516 West 34th Street, New York, New York 10001

Manufactured in the United States of America
ISBN: 0-533-08880-1

Library of Congress Catalog Card No.: 89-90549

To Mary, Queen of Love and Peace

Contents

1. Where It Began	1
2. Heavenly Ireland	14
3. "It Is an Illusion!"	20
4. The Tour	24
5. Mirth and Melancholy	33
6. Tales and Reminiscences	41
7. The Life and Culture of Eire	54
8. "The Three Musketeers"	58
9. Scholars and Storytellers	63
10. Miss Switzerland, Miss London, Miss Copenhagen, and Mr. Universe	70
11. At Bunratty Castle	73
12. Blasket	75
13. England Ho!	78
14. And Again England	83
15. Normandy—the Ones Who Remain	86
16. At Peace in the Alps	88
17. From Waterloo to Amsterdam	90
18. The Little Mermaid, a Big Storm, and More Electricity	98
19. Statues that Almost Breathe	103
20. Back in Inch	108
21. Reunion . . .	111
22. . . . And Return	126
23. Dr. Aquarius and Her Son Jonathan	129
24. In Russia You Sit Where You Want	135

25. Snowflake in Russian Is Che★nhka	142
26. Leningrad—a Five Star City	150
27. Off the Beaten Track	153
28. Smitten by Blasket	160
29. The Leather Connection	163
30. Tatoo!	165
31. Café Society	169
32. Memories in Tangier	175
33. The Wealth of Portugal	188
34. Once an Activist, . . .	202
35. On the Beach	226
36. Romance and Complications	235
37. I Find Myself in Greece	244
38. The Bliss of Being with Dr. Aquarius	251
39. Heat Wave from Hell	255
40. Among Gods and Goddesses	260
41. Eli and Isabel	263
42. Crete	267
43. Christmas in the Holy Land	270
44. New Year in Berlin	272
45. Getting to Know the Universe	281
Epilogue	292

1 / Where It Began

When I arrived at the famous "White House" in Kalamai Bay, Corfu in Greece on October 1, 1988, I knew I had found the perfect place to complete my manuscript.

In 1938, Lawrence Durrell, the English novelist invited Henry Miller to the White House for a long visit which changed Miller's life.

Fifty years later I would also experience a dramatic transformation in my personal lifestyle.

My Odyssey began on November 20, 1984, when my plane touched down in Dublin, Ireland.

This was the beginning of what unexpectedly would be almost five years of living in Ireland, Portugal, Greece, and Germany.

During this period of time I would travel throughout Europe and also visit Russia, Israel and Egypt.

I had been to Ireland with my family very briefly in 1964 and I will talk about this later.

Now I was going to live on this Irish emerald island for one year and perhaps forever.

While flying across the Atlantic Ocean on the six-hour Aer Lingus flight I reviewed the pattern of my life and what brought me to the decisive point of leaving my wife, family, friends and everything!

It is amazing how in such a brief period of time, while crossing the Atlantic to a brand new lifestyle, my mind was rapidly reviewing the main events of my life.

I had to wonder, "What does it all mean and where will this journey end?"

I was born in Bayonne, New Jersey, and I always felt very special living in the small peninsular city so close to Jersey City and New York City. My mother, Veronica, was an Irish Catholic and my father, Clarence, was a Salt Lake City, Utah, German Mormon.

Some years later I would learn in a late evening argument between my mother and father that I was illegitimate.

My father married Veronica when she was two months pregnant. Of course, she could have had an abortion, but then I would not be telling this fantastic story.

Despite the fact that I was born out of wedlock, it never interfered with my love for Veronica and Clarence.

Seven years after I was born, my brother Warren legitimately entered the family picture and three years after Warren came our sister, Florence, to complete the family circle.

As I grew older I was never sure about my parents' relationship because there was very little conversation and even fewer outward signs of love and affection.

My mother spent many hours of the day and night working out schemes to "hit the numbers." She was a compulsive gambler at the very lowest level of gambling.

I will never forget the most violent fight my mother and father ever staged.

Every day she would buy the New York *Daily News* to find the three winning numbers from the previous days' horse races. On this particular day she learned she had won five thousand dollars.

I remember she paced up and down the rooms of our small, rented home like a caged animal anticipating the arrival of my father and her five thousand–dollar prize.

It was my father's daily responsibility to play my mother's numbers with a "bookie" on the railroad where my father was employed. I never discovered the reason why Clarence did not play the numbers that day or if he ever played the daily list of numbers Veronica so earnestly slaved over morning to night.

The explosion from our house rocked the entire neighborhood. Veronica's screaming and shouting rage and Clarence's sympathetic excuses were to no avail. Finally he had to agree to take out a railroad loan to calm my mother's fury. In her mind she had already spent the five thousand dollars and now she was convinced her luck was running in her favor. A few years later she won ten thousand dollars on the Irish Sweepstakes and she became a gambler for life.

In the 1930s, the depression years never seriously hurt our family since my father's job as a mechanic on the railroad was never threatened.

I especially remember Christmastime when there was always a toy under the tree which I knew other families could not afford to buy for their children. I recall how sad I felt and somewhat ashamed that I could be so fortunate while so many other children were so unfortunate during those difficult years of fear and unemployment.

My father, like most workers, was a big supporter of Franklin Delano Roosevelt and his "New Deal" for America. How happy I was when my father allowed me to stay up late in the evening to hear the president's "fireside chats" with the American people.

It was the first time I realized that Democrats were the working class and Republicans were the big business managers and owners.

I know now that this was my introduction to the democratic principles as the party of the majority. How this has all changed since the election of Ronald Reagan in 1980, followed by George Bush in 1988.

I also know that because Bayonne was a classic "melting pot" city representing every nationality, race and religion, that my personality and character were molded in this unique democratic environment. Whatever feelings and aspirations I have for humanity were born in the openness of the city of Bayonne, New Jersey.

My classmates and friends in our neighborhood came from every corner of the world.

If Oscar Handlin, the noted historian who wrote *The Uprooted* about the life of immigrants, had lived in Bayonne, he would have understood why I was so happy to be a small part of this great experience.

Growing up and being educated in Bayonne was to understand the full meaning of freedom, independence and equality.

After my parents and grandparents, whom I will talk about later, my fondest memories are of my school years in Bayonne.

I was left back in the first grade because my teacher said I could not read well enough to be advanced to the second grade.

Of course this was the first shock of my young life as I watched all my classmates move on to the higher grade.

I suddenly felt older and not so smart.

Only years later when I received a college scholarship did I understand my early failure.

Neither Veronica nor Clarence had a high school education.

The only reading material in my home was the *Daily News* and the *Bayonne Times*.

I never saw my mother or father read a book in their entire lives.

I know how proud they were to see the first member of the family attend Cornell University in Ithaca, New York.

They were also very happy that I never gave them any serious problems while growing up and becoming a man.

Looking back as though it were only yesterday, I remember the first outstanding teacher I ever had. She played an extraordinary role in my life as a young teenager.

Mrs. Vreeland, my eighth grade English teacher, was one of the special breed of professionals who could recognize the potential of all her students.

By the time I left her class to go on to high school, I had become the class president, starred in two school productions and was an honors academic student.

My classmates and I would move mountains to make her smile because we knew she wanted us to be happy and successful.

Now that I have been a teacher for many years I realize the overwhelming influence of a truly dedicated professional teacher.

The Irish pilot was jokingly informing the passengers that we were in the mid-Atlantic and had reached the point of "no return!"

Everyone laughed while enjoying a fine Irish meal topped off with a great Irish coffee.

A few weeks before I left America there were unpleasant family discussions about financial arrangements, future contacts, et cetera.

It is difficult to understand sometimes what happens in a marital relationship of more than thirty years especially when five children are involved in a family upheaval.

It is not easy to rationalize and say that all the members of the family are grown up and independent.

I can only say in my personal defense the words of Henry David Thoreau in his classic book *Walden Pond*, "that every person has a drummer in their head. They must listen to the beat of the drummer and march to the tune which makes them happy!"

All my life I had a burning desire to travel the world and I could not deny this ambition and remain true to myself.

One of the reasons why I am telling this story is so my children and grandchildren will understand that the unpopular decision I made to leave America was not an insane judgement, but a most compelling force which gave me no other choice.

Before I left the United States I made one final effort on behalf of Senator Alan Cranston of California who in 1983 was one of the candidates running for the democratic nomination for president.

I had carefully reviewed the backgrounds and positions of all the democratic candidates and I was convinced that although I did not know Cranston personally I liked what he stood for on the important issues of the 1980s.

Senator Cranston's agenda called for a nuclear freeze and full employment for all Americans.

With the exception of Jesse Jackson all the other candidates sounded typically political.

I contacted Cranston's Washington office and informed his staff that I was a former state senator from New Jersey and I was anxious to work for the senator as a volunteer speaker and organizer.

Two days later I received a call to proceed to Old Orchard Beach staff headquarters in Maine.

I was also informed that I would receive my assignment from Maggie, a California staff director.

I arrived in my 1977 Classic Caprice Chevy in a blinding snowstorm.

I will never forget my first impression when I entered the compact staff headquarters.

Maggie was anticipating my arrival, but she was up to her eyeballs in staff work.

The command post was a summer cottage jammed with brilliant young men and women who were all from California and they were working like hell!

The headquarters was alive with ringing telephones, issue papers, schedules and Maggie was clearly in charge of everything.

I looked around and saw papers everywhere, Coke cans stacked in the shape of pyramids, and pizza boxes looking like the Empire State Building.

Maggie, observing the astonished look on my face, inquired, "Don't they do it like this in New Jersey?"

Everyone laughed, and when I asked if anyone drank coffee you would have thought I uttered a dirty word.

Maggie, nevertheless, took recognition of my age and political experience and handed me a key to a private suite close to the command post right on the beachfront.

She also handed me my first assignment. I was to speak for Alan Cranston at a national conference of gays at the University of Maine in Orono the following evening.

Cranston was detained in Washington and would arrive in Manchester, New Hampshire, in a few days.

As I was walking out the door Maggie handed me a recently published book about the life of Alan Cranston.

She also gave me a very large issues packet which she knew I would study to familiarize myself with all the policy statements made by Senator Cranston.

When I turned the key to my suite I had the feeling that Maggie and the young staffers, who were all on the campaign payroll, were impressed with a man who had traveled almost one thousand miles to work without receiving any financial reward.

Very early the next morning I was awakened by the strange sound of horses running on the beach.

In fact, they were trotters getting an early morning workout even while the snow was falling on the white sandy beach.

My spirits were soaring!

New England primary weather can be rough on even the toughest political campaigners, but especially on suntanned Californians.

By late afternoon, as I prepared to leave for the University of Maine, I encountered a full-blown New England blizzard.

To make matters worse I made a wrong turn and became lost in a blanket of white snow.

By the time I arrived at the university, the car parking lot was jammed with many cars and also many state and local police security officers.

As I made my way to the massive auditorium I was greeted by a very tall woman wearing an "I am a lesbian" button.

I was the last arrival and she would escort me and my campaign button, "Cranston for President," to the speakers' platform.

She politely reminded me to confine my remarks to ten minutes as the other candidates were also informed.

Senator Hollings was speaking and I observed Gary Hart, Mondale, Jackson and John Glenn all looking very subdued and serious.

As always when I am campaigning I was alive with energy and intense feelings.

After Senator Cranston's telegram of regret was read I was introduced as a former state senator from New Jersey who had volunteered to speak on behalf on Alan Cranston. "Friendly applause!"

For me a prepared statement is always a crowd loser and so taking a deep breath and remembering Cranston's record in a state with the highest gay population I launched into my speech.

Alan Cranston received the highest number of votes in California history even exceeding the votes received by Ronald Reagan in his 1980 victory over Jimmy Carter.

I knew what Cranston would say to a national audience of gays, but coming from a man who traveled from New Jersey, I wanted to sound even stronger.

I quickly realized I did not disappoint the conference.

They were on their feet before I reached the five minute mark in my presentation.

They were too young to know that I had prepared this speech before they were old enough to vote. In 1960, I had campaigned for John Kennedy on the same issues of human rights, justice and freedom in our democracy.

Many of them were not yet born in the infamous era of Joseph McCarthy when even I, as a teacher, was questioned about my outrage against witch-hunting and countless violations against human rights.

They would never know that since my childhood something very deep inside of me was sensitive to the question of fairness and equality.

These were not Senator Cranston's thoughts alone, but it was my personal philosophy of life, and Alan Cranston was the voice of my sincere belief in the American

Constitution's legal protection of the rights of all its citizens.

When I had reached the dramatic conclusion of my statement I reminded the audience that not only in California, but in Washington as well, Alan Cranston stood head and shoulders over everyone in his fight for human justice for every American.

The applause came like thunder! Everyone was on their feet and since I was the final speaker two women wearing their emblem escorted me off the platform to a widely cheering crowd.

I knew I had hit the mark for Cranston!

The following morning Maggie received a personal call from Alan Cranston telling her he had several calls, all highly complimentary, regarding my address to the conference.

Maggie also had many calls requesting me to speak at other meetings around the state.

She asked me what happened and I told her it was easy to campaign for a person you could get excited about.

The very next day I had new marching orders to proceed immediately to Manchester, New Hampshire.

The first national primary contest was in New Hampshire and Cranston had to be in the top three.

He had not done well in the Iowa caucus and so all the stops had to be pulled out in Manchester.

It was decided that the centerpiece of Cranston's campaign in New Hampshire would be an all out appeal for support from the veterans of war.

Cranston was the chairman of the Senate Committee of Veteran's Affairs and was also the champion of legislative action for the VietNam vets who were suffering from "agent orange."

The staff decision was a good one. Cranston was on

solid ground with more credentials than any other candidate.

My assignment was to assist in organizing a huge veterans' rally to be held at the peak of the election.

We would bring out vets from all over New England concentrating on New Hampshire leadership veterans.

I was introduced to a middle-aged couple with one son who had a home located on the Merrimack River.

They were all avid supporters of Alan Cranston and would be happy to invite me to live with them during the campaign.

I was flying!

Bob was a professional photographer and his wife, Kitty, was a political activist. Robbie worked with his father and also enjoyed his motorcycle.

They made me feel like a member of the family. It was wonderful!

I immediately began to visit every post commander in Manchester.

I can say with some authority that New Hampshire enjoys more veterans' organizations than any state in the nation.

When you enter a vets' hall the first thing you must do, no matter what the time of day, is have a beer with the post commander.

By the end of the first week I was staggering!

Word came back to the headquarters that Buehler was making big strides for Cranston but his stride was not always straight and forward.

It quickly became one of the big jokes of the campaign, especially with the young soft drinkers who were always deadly serious.

It was not always work!

One Friday afternoon I left one vets' hall with a World

War II legionnaire who had invited me to address a group of his friends and neighbors.

When we got into his 1964 station wagon I commented on the peak condition of his car.

He laughed and told me one of the movie directors for *On Golden Pond* spotted his old car and wanted to borrow it for their movie scenes.

He was given two hundred and fifty dollars a week during the filming and also had his car totally renovated.

The wagon was used by Henry Fonda who was making his first and final film with his daughter Jane Fonda.

When he learned that I was given a light weekend campaign schedule he offered me his wagon and the keys to a cabin on Squam Lake where the fabulous Fondas filmed *On Golden Pond*, which won many Academy Awards.

If I ever return to New Hampshire I will head for Squam Lake where at sunset hundreds of loons descend on the lake with their enchanting songs of love and beauty.

The first time I met Alan Cranston face to face it was electric!

When I gazed into his penetrating deep-set blue eyes it felt as though his piercing look could see into the very depths of my soul.

His eyes never could be captured by the television viewers who only saw a baldheaded gaunt shallow-faced man with little personal attraction.

But it was his knowing eyes which made me feel good to be with him in New Hampshire whether in victory or defeat.

The agony and ecstasy of politics is unlike anything you can ever experience unless you have been there personally!

I was given the special privilege of introducing Senator Cranston for President at a very exciting veterans rally.

My naive heart told me it was possible for him to win in New Hampshire, but it was not going to happen.

The day after the election Cranston called a staff meeting and announced that he was withdrawing from the race and would return to Washington to continue his responsibilities as the senior Senator from California.

There were many tears in the room and the sad expression in Cranston's eyes showed his great disappointment.

Gary Hart moved up to challenge Walter Mondale and the rest is another chapter in the history of American politics in 1984.

2 / Heavenly Ireland

As my plane approached the runway at Dublin airport I was smiling at the heavy rainfall, so well known to every visitor to the green island.

Zeff and Mimi Lawless, friends of my oldest son Warren, were at the airport to welcome me to the shores of Ireland.

Their modest but comfortable home in Killester was on the outskirts of the capital.

I enjoyed several days with the young Lawless family and I especially loved getting acquainted with their two children Zeke and Jessica.

It was also my first moment of nostalgia and I knew it was going to be difficult to be so far away from my family during the Christmas season.

Zeff's father Kevin and I became good friends from our first handshake. His love and knowledge of Dublin was fascinating.

Our long walks throughout the city were like the pages of Irish history as seen through eyes of James Joyce and Brendan Behan.

He also introduced me to his golfing partners and to his favorite pubs.

Kevin's Irish sense of humor was staggering especially after a few pints of Guinness special beer.

He grinned from ear to ear when I told him I had decided to live in County Kerry on the west coast. When I asked what was so amusing he replied, "The Kerry men are the best footballers in all of Ireland. They are also the most intelligent, shrewdest and wittiest people in the nation. They also will always answer a question with another question. If you remember what I am telling you then I am sure you are going to enjoy County Kerry."

Before I left Dublin, Kevin introduced me to a used car salesman and two days later my 1977 Van Gogh Yellow Renault #5 was serviced for my journey to many exciting places throughout Ireland and Europe.

How can I tell you that my magnificent car, which cost me one thousand dollars has been my constant companion for almost five years. Without this astonishing car, which is an object of curiosity wherever we are traveling, my story could not be so amusing as you will see in our journey of over 100,000 miles.

Zeff supplied me with salt and fresh water fishing equipment and Kevin gave me some canvas and many art supplies which he knew I would enjoy. Kevin also reminded me about our conversation regarding the Kerry men.

"Well now!" he said, "you take the pipe and a plug of tobacco on your first visit to your local pub. I will leave the rest up to your imagination."

Mimi said she and the family wanted me to spend my first Christmas with them and enjoy the festivities of this special season of joy and music in Dublin.

The morning I left Dublin for the Dingle Peninsula, Kevin rode with me to the city limits. He said I had a full tank of gas for the seven hour trip and I should enjoy my first experience of driving on the left side of the road playing with a stick shift on the right side. "Good luck and I will see you for Christmas" were his parting words of cheer.

One hour later the clouds turned black and the sky

opened up one of the heaviest rain storms I had ever witnessed. It was at that moment I realized that the most important part of a car in Ireland is the windshield wiper.

I was overjoyed to learn that my Renault had two speeds: fast and faster. What I was not so happy to discover very quickly was that the car was starting to act funny.

Suddenly, in the middle of nowhere, the car shuddered and then stopped. Several attempts to start the car failed.

I spotted a lonely farmhouse a few hundred yards down the road and in the pouring rain I prayed that this solitary beacon of hope would get me to Kerry before darkness.

A middle-aged farmer politely invited me to come in out of the storm while I explained my problem.

A short time later he was opening the hood of my car and asking me to start the engine. In a few moments, drenched to the skin, he leaned into my window and turned on the ignition switch.

Very calmly and in a soft voice he asked me when I last put petrol in the car? I remembered Kevin's words of Kerry wisdom and I replied with "How far is the nearest petrol station?"

When I offered him five pounds for his help he refused and suggested I buy him a pint at his local the next time I was in the neighborhood. Visitors to Ireland are always taken aback by the warmth and hospitality of the Irish, who are the most friendly people on earth.

By late afternoon the sky became clear and the sun was brilliant casting colorful rainbows over the green mountains of Killarney.

I was already getting the feeling that in Ireland there is a unique spirit which fills the air. It is everywhere! The changing dramatic colors of the sky! The magnificent kelly green landscape! Puffs of smoke pouring out of chimneys with the aroma of ancient turf from the bog.

Above all this, you need but wave at any Irish stranger and your wave will always be returned with smiles of friendship, even love.

I was heading in the direction of Dingle where Zeff had made contact with Michael O'Sullivan, a local entrepreneur.

Before I could unload my car Michael invited me to his home to meet his charming family. His wife had just baked some cookies and we quickly became acquainted over a pot of tea and a warm fire.

Dingle Bay in former times had been a principal fishing harbor and while it is still active it is no longer so important as a fish market. It is famous, however, for the vast number and variety of pubs which are enjoyed by countless tourists from all over the world.

Another outstanding attraction of this amazing place is the well-known, controversial film *Ryan's Daughter* which was directed here by David Lean in the late 1960s.

I decided on my first night in Kerry Co. I would not unpack my bags. Instead I wanted to write to my family to tell them about all the events since my arrival in Ireland and to let them know I was already missing the family.

The next morning I asked a local fisherman for directions to the post office. "Is it a stamp you are looking for?" he replied. When he asked me why I was laughing, I said, "And of course you are a mind reader, are you not?" He smiled and directed me to the stamp house!

This is the way it would be for over a year so you can understand how happy I was to be a part of the Kerry life.

Later that first morning I enjoyed one of the most spectacular drives I have had in my traveling experiences. Driving very slowly to capture the awesome scenery,

I was impressed by a feeling of moving between the mountains on my left and the Atlantic Ocean on my right.

The sky was as blue as any sky you will ever see, while the gathering white clouds, moving slowly in the breeze, added to the vivid sharpness of contrasting colors which surrounded me at every turn on the narrow winding road.

My destination was the incredible beach at Inch which was the opening scene in *Ryan's Daughter*.

Bob Mitchum was returning from a teacher's conference in Dublin and Sarah Miles, his former pupil, was walking on the beach anxious to welcome him back home.

David Lean's setting for this opening scene was poetic. It was also one of the romantic reasons why I had come to Ireland after viewing this film in New York.

When I approached the final turn before the beach I had to park my car to capture the fullness of beauty which I knew would become my home.

The sandy beach is framed by a three mile stretch of sand dunes with the highest snow capped mountains of Ireland standing silently in the background. A crystal clear, blue-green sea is crashing against the shoreline while the rays of sunlight are reflecting unimaginable colors in the crest of each new falling wave. My heart was filled with unbelievable joy and peacefulness.

The Strand Hotel sits on a bluff overlooking the beach and is owned by Tom and Eileen Toumey. They, along with their son Shawn, would become three of my closest friends in Ireland.

Tom is a pipe smoking retired sea captain who had traveled to all of the leading seaports of the world. His slow, winning smile and relaxed countenance immediately put you at ease.

Eileen is another story. A former Tralee beauty she

would soon impress me as one of Ireland's most severe critics.

I ordered a pint of Guinness and told them I would be living in Ireland for some time and would be very happy if I could locate a small cottage in Inch.

Tom, with his wonderful old pipe clenched in his teeth, exchanged glances with Eileen and before I could finish my beer Eileen was taking me to meet her neighbor Mary O'Shea. This special day I will always embrace as one of the happiest times of my life.

Mary and Dan O'Shea had built a second dream house overlooking the fabulous beach of Inch. Perched high on the side of the mountain, facing the ocean and mountains of Killarney, was the home of my dreams.

The view from picture windows in the living rooms and master bedroom could not have been designed better by even Frank Lloyd Wright, the famous American architect noted for environmental construction.

Three more bedrooms and a massive kitchen completed the interior with comfortable furnishings throughout the house.

I had to sing for the joy which was pounding in my heart. To be in Ireland and to live in Inch was much more than any person could ever desire. I had it all!

3 / "It Is an Illusion!"

The next day I informed Michael O'Sullivan that I had found a place in Inch which had everything I was looking for in a permanent home. Knowing Inch, Michael was very understanding and told me not to forget to visit him and his family in Dingle.

Throughout the period of time I lived in Kerry, Michael and I had a very good relationship. I would find out later that Michael O'Sullivan was one of Kerry's most ambitious businessmen.

In addition to the apartments, he also owned the local youth hostel, a stable of riding horses, the local movie theatre and numerous other activities in Dingle. His wife once confided in me that Michael's only problem was that he wanted twenty-five hours in every day. Every time I went to his movie house when he was there he would not let me pay for a ticket.

By the time I returned to Inch, Dan had delivered a cord of turf for my living room fireplace and Mary had arranged flowers in my rooms to add more color to the splendid surroundings.

The first night the O'Sheas invited me to their home for a roast beef and a get acquainted evening. Of all the relationships I have been blessed with in almost five years of living in Europe, my relationship with the O'Shea family has been the most gratifying. They not only welcomed me into their family, but they taught me the things I came to Ireland to learn. It was then and still is today a lesson in knowledge which helped immensely to change the direction of my life.

Their unreserved friendliness and simplicity made me realize why I had left America. My decision to come to Ireland was not going to be an exercise in futility.

Everything about Dan O'Shea can only appropriately be described as big! Broad shoulders, powerful arms and a smile as wide as all outdoors. When he laughed or sang an Irish song his face was so pleasant to see and his curly reddish blond hair under his cap gave him the look of a mischievous child.

In New York or California Mary O'Shea could have been a cover model. Her face is so alarmingly radiant that you are seized with the impression that you are looking at a beautiful painting. You are dazzled by her sparkling blue eyes and warm smile with perfect glistening white teeth. Her chestnut brown hair shining in the sunlight is unnerving.

I have never seen Mary in pants or jeans. She is always looking stylishly feminine in the most attractive and natural manner.

The inner light which I felt on my first night with the O'Shea family only increased with each passing month. We had become very quickly the best of friends and we were always exceedingly happy when we were together.

The O'Sheas were blessed with three children: Kevin, Theresa and my favorite, little Mary.

Mrs. Clifford, Mary's widowed mother was an integral partner in this close knit family circle. We also became very good friends and I cannot recall ever meeting a more dignified woman than Mrs. Clifford.

After our first dinner together and light conversation Dan invited me to his local while Mary and Mrs. Clifford got the children ready for bed and organized the kitchen.

Since I had anticipated a trip to the pub I brought my pipe, tobacco and a small pen knife. Following a perfect day and evening I was in rare form and decided to make the most of it.

Dan ordered two pints of Guinness and after greeting all his friends we sat by the turf fire to relax. I could feel all the eyes of Inch trying to figure out who Dan's new acquaintance was.

I peeled off a small plug of tobacco and carefully lit my pipe. I could see Dan smiling out of the corner of my eye.

After some minutes, while waiting for the Guinness to set-up, we approached the bar. "Dan," said I, "*Slonca*" (good health and a long life). We raised our glasses and touched them before drawing our first long drink.

I looked down the bar again and with my glass raised high I said to Dan, "This is the finest beer in the world, isn't it?" The reaction in the pub was slow, but it gradually turned to outright laughter. I had made my first American impression and I could see by the look on the faces of the men that they enjoyed my sense of humor.

After a second Guinness Dan took me by the arm and told me he was taking me over the mountain to the most popular pub in County Kerry.

Dan Foley's Pub in Annascaul is Dan Foley. The national post card with a colorful picture of Dan's pub is known throughout Ireland. The famous pub card reads "It is an illusion!"

Dan used to be a professional magician and he is still making magic behind the bar of the friendliest pub in the nation.

Dan O'Shea was also in rare form and when a young man entered the pub with his guitar there was suddenly a crack! In Ireland, a crack is a spontaneous, unrehearsed, unplanned party of beer and music. Dan's gifted Irish voice rose to a crescendo inspiring everyone to join in singing those songs I had traveled so far to hear.

It was an exceptional night to always cherish in my memories of Ireland! When I finally closed my eyes that first glorious night in Inch, I could still hear Dan's clear voice over the waves pounding on the beach below my new home.

A week after I had written exciting letters to my family and friends, I told Mary and Dan I was going to drive a complete circle around the Irish coast. I would return to Inch before the New Year of 1985!

The O'Sheas had never had any desire to travel in northern Ireland and I could see they were apprehensive concerning my safety in Derry and Belfast. My driving plans were to leisurely travel on the coastal roads and ultimately arrive at the Lawless home before Christmas.

Looking back now I can say it was one of the greatest experiences in my four and a half years of travel. My Odyssey, which began in a tiny village of 100 farmers in Inch, would culminate in a small, well-hidden cove called Kalamai Bay, Corfu which had a population of five Greek families.

4 / The Tour

The first day's drive was to Tralee, Limerick and a town I will always have difficulty pronouncing and so will you. Ennistymon will always be remembered as the place where a river is rushing down the side of a mountain crashing right through the center of the town. Also Ennistymon is only a fifteen minute drive from the dramatic Cliffs of Moher.

I wanted to arrive at the Cliffs before sunrise on my second day and the reward was a musical and artistic performance of thousands of sea gulls soaring over the sea and magnificent cliffs.

It was a breathtaking sight which signalled the start of a brand new day. The diving gulls and their excited voices in early morning flight were unbelievable.

Walking alone for some time on the precarious cliffs, I was reminded of the ancient Celtic history and imagined the feelings experienced by the first settlers to witness the wonder of Moher.

Leaving the Cliffs I pointed my bright yellow car in the direction of Galway. I found myself singing "When Irish Eyes Are Smiling." My mind and heart were feeling the rhythm of Ireland.

I enjoyed an Irish stew lunch in a small Galway pub and was advised by the publican to spend the night in Roundstone directly on Ballyconneely Bay. "There is a famous pub on the waterfront where they are making the finest fish chowder in all Ireland," he called to me as I started to leave.

The hours I spent traveling from Galway City to Roundstone could easily have been many, many days. My eyes were dazzled by the color and magic of this region called Connemara.

Men and boys in hip boots were standing in rocky streams fly casting for trout fish. Wild Connemara ponies were grazing in the fields and sometimes running across the empty street directly in front of my slow moving vehicle.

It was a scene of serene peace and rare natural beauty.

It was also the area where John Wayne, Maureen O'Sullivan, Barry Fitzgerald and Victor McLaughlin made the classic film *The Quiet Man!*

When you are traveling and you find such a place as Connemara, it is difficult to say "good-bye."

Arriving in Roundstone before sunset I remarked to myself that I had not seen more than ten cars on the road. The traffic was terrific! Yes, driving at this time of year was a tremendous pleasure and it continued like this all the way to Dublin.

I am also thinking how nice it is to write about this traveling story. Perhaps I can put you, my reader, in my fantastic car and share with you the many pleasures I have known.

Roundstone comes at you very suddenly following a winding road which terminates at the sea coast. Just like a post card, your eyes are capturing a panoramic picture of sea and sky, small fishing boats in the harbor and men sitting on the wharf repairing their nets for the next day's catch.

It is as though the clock of time has ceased and you

are allowed to enter a moment of eternal bliss never to end. Ireland is like this!

I must say I was not disappointed by the delicious fish chowder. Many times I would return here with friends and naturally I became very friendly with the owner of the pub called Fish and Chowder.

In the evening I walked along the wharfside to watch the men working on their boats. I also came to see the sunset!

For me, my happiest times of day are the peaceful hours of sunrise and sunset. The universal forces from dawn to dusk stir my emotions and heighten my awareness of how small I am in the cosmic scheme of life.

Returning to my room overlooking the village, I studied my map and decided I would move on to Castlebar, Sligo and renowned Donegal.

Passing through Sligo and Ballyshannon I observed fields sprinkled with light snow. This reminded me that now Vermont and Zermatt, two of my favorite snow places, must be receiving many American and European ski enthusiasts.

By the time I reached Donegal many snowflakes were landing on my car, but not enough to use the windshield wiper.

There are many stories and songs about Donegal, its historic castle and even more historical life.

Living so close to the sight and sounds of British border patrols reveals the sad, tragic picture of a story which is still unfinished. It is a story of the folly of young men in uniforms carrying weapons. It is also the insane failure of a government who puts the men in this uniform.

The following morning I crossed the border at Derry! The English map calls it Londonderry! There was no traffic at the security check point and my DZN308 (Dublin plate) with an American driver made for an interesting fifteen minute discussion with the patrol guards.

Having lived with my family for one year in Great Missenden, Buckinghamshire reassured the officers that I was not a risky traveler. Nevertheless, I was very uncomfortable! I am always terribly unhappy with the sight of uniforms and guns.

The main roads in Northern Ireland are extremely good and before I realized it I was passing Portrush and moving down the coast to the port of Larne. The following year I would return to Larne to take a ship to Scotland. When I return to Larne I will tell one of the funniest traveling stories I have ever experienced.

Since it was still daylight (I never travel at night) I continued south to the city of Carrickfergus, which became one of the highlights of my Irish tour.

I registered in my first small hotel only because it was facing an ancient castle jutting out over the sea.

All my traveling days in Ireland always culminate when I arrive at a bed and breakfast. For all my American and European readers, who I encourage to visit Ireland, I hope they will take advantage of the incomparable Irish traditional bed and breakfast. Thousands of Irish families offer inexpensive bed and breakfast accommodations for their guests.

After traveling in over forty countries of western and eastern Europe and driving coast to coast in the U.S.A. and Canada, I can say with some authority and passion that the Irish bed and breakfast is the finest stop in the western hemisphere.

From the moment you enter an Irish family home you are welcomed as a guest and a friend. Even before you unpack your bags you are usually invited for tea, coffee and homemade cookies.

Your room will be spotlessly clean and comfortable.

Without a doubt the morning breakfast is something to talk about. Unfortunately, many European travelers are not in tune with the enormous Irish morning starter.

The Irish morning banquet opens with oatmeal, cereal and juice. This is accompanied by tea, coffee and stacks of toast. There is a brief moment to relax and talk with other guests before the arrival of the main course.

The main event includes ham, bacon, eggs, fried tomatoes and sometimes potatoes or fried toast plus more bread, butter, jam and usually an extra surprise.

When you are able to handle this enormous breakfast delight your Irish hostess will be smiling.

There is a saying in the Irish bed and breakfast community that "a hearty breakfast is the beginning of a perfect day for touring." Moreover, the Irish family will welcome your informality and be happy to assist you with suggestions of places to visit on your day's program.

I must also add a personal belief that while Ireland is an ideal country with countless attractions, for me it is the Irish people who will leave you with the fondest memories.

No day in Ireland is complete without a visit to a local village pub. There was a time in Irish history when the church was the center of social life and activity.

Today this in no longer true! If you want to know about the farm crops, the sheep population or who is going to marry a foreigner you must visit a pub. The publican can give you more information about what is happening in Ireland than the village priest.

The pub is the most significant social institution in Ireland and most Irish men or women will confirm what I am suggesting.

A visit to a pub is to feel the pulse of the country and

singing voices continued into the street and my waiting Renault #5.

But, this time there was no pushing or shoving for positions. I would learn that on one of their trips to the W.C. (toilet), the nurse who looked like Sophia Loren had won the prize. ME!

After I drove the other two nurses home, Sophia directed me to the Castle and a secluded spot on the beach front. Before I had turned off the ignition key she was all over me like an electric blanket.

In response to such an unforgettable night I could sing one of my favorite ballads, "Once in a Lifetime This Moment Is Mine."

Fortunately, I have lived many lifetimes and the words always sound very good.

Even at Christmastime Belfast is looking very grim, sad and hostile. Large painted letters on buildings saying "Brits go home!" were everywhere and much, much worse.

British soldiers were walking on every street carrying automatic weapons held in the ready position. Armored trucks and tanks were standing at every major intersection of the city.

The whole scene reminded me of a battleground ready to explode at any moment.

I was feeling very ill all over and could not wait until I reached the city limit and got on the road to Armagh. I was choking for need of fresh air and an end to fear and terror.

Armagh was one of the main reasons I came to the north. Brian Boru and his son are buried on the ancient cathedral grounds in Armagh where so much Celtic history was made.

Brian Boru who has been poetically referred to as

"The Lion of Ireland" was actually the first and only King of Kings of all Ireland.

In 1004, Brian Boru drove the Vikings out of Ireland and was successful in uniting Ireland under one rule.

At Tara he was recognized by all the kings of Celtic Ireland as the true "King of Kings." Like King Arthur in Camelot he was successful in bringing all the kings together at the roundtable to establish peace and order in a land which today remains torn by ignorance and insanity.

I remained rooted to the site of their grave for some time, contemplating the life of this Excalibur giant of strength and honor. I wanted to remain longer in Armagh but I knew Zeff and Mimi were expecting me in Dublin two days before Christmas.

When I arrived at their home in Killester they were like children prodding me with questions about Inch, Kerry County and my surprising trip to the North of Ireland.

5 / Mirth and Melancholy

It was like a home coming only I was three thousand miles from my home and that night in bed I cried for the first time. It was thirty-two years of being with my family at Christmas that suddenly fell on me like a ton of bricks.
    I wondered what they were feeling in New Jersey. From Thanksgiving in November to Christmas and New Year's Day was the most special time in the life of our family in New Jersey. Even the selection of a very large Christmas tree which would almost fill a room was a very big event.
    When the children were very young my wife and I loved to watch the children race down the stairs from their bedrooms to see what Santa Claus had left them under the carefully decorated tree.
    The sight of the blue lights on the tree in the early morning hour and all the gifts nearly took their breath away. It was such a warm and loving feeling on this day when Christ was born.
    On Christmas Eve after we had finished our job as Santa Claus, Claire and I would sit by our roaring fireplace with a glass of wine. We had a very special love and we did not have to talk about it.
    On New Year's Eve everyone knew the Buehler's had a tradition and they never left their home or children to attend the many New Year's Eve drinking parties.
    My wife always prepared a very delicious buffet table

for any of the neighbors who would stop by to wish us a Happy New Year!

Our children always went to bed very early on New Year's Eve because they knew we would wake them up in time to see "the big ball" drop in Times Square, N.Y.C., signaling the end of one year and the start of another brand-new year.

They all had "noisemakers" and enjoyed running out on our porch to wake any neighbors who had fallen asleep before the big event.

There are things in your life which are set in stone and can never be dissolved. Such was this magnificent time of our life together!

Dublin on Christmas Eve is something everyone should experience once in a lifetime.

While I had purchased gifts for Zeff's family when traveling in the North, I had not found the special gift for little Jessica, aged three. I knew Jessica loved animals and Zeff had already told me he did not want any animals in his home.

Before I left Killester for the short fifteen-minute train ride to the capital, Zeff gave me a very unique map.

Every tourist coming to Ireland quickly learns about the "Ring of Kerry." Few tourists, however, know about the famous "Ring of Dublin."

Zeff jokingly pointed out the ten most well-known pubs in Dublin and then he numbered the route I should follow to complete the famous ring on my initial foray in the city of music and laughter on Christmas Eve, 1984.

Mimi, meanwhile, had been listening to Zeff's instructions and tactfully reminded me that I had promised to take her to midnight mass while Zeff was playing Santa Claus. I assured her that ten pints in ten pubs was not such a staggering challenge and I would not disappoint her.

I remember telling Dan O'Shea about my delightful "Ring of Dublin" story when I returned to Inch. He laughed and said, "On my wedding day I had put away seventeen pints before Mary admonished me. 'Remember, Dan, I am Mrs. O'Shea now and I want a sober husband on our wedding night!' "

I was not surprised that my first two pubs, which were located on the same street, were in full swing when I arrived at 10:00 A.M. I wisely decided to have an early lunch of Irish stew and bread to prepare my stomach for the afternoon assault on pubs three, four and five.

By now the shopping streets were crowded with many enthusiastic celebrators. There was music and much laughter everywhere!

The late afternoon air was cold, but there was not a sign of snow which would have made it a perfect day! I wisely decided to search for Jessica's gift before I reached pub number six.

By this time the decoration lights of the city had come alive and you could feel the mood of Irish Christmas spirit.

Pub number six was packed with a raucous singing crowd of young men and women standing five deep waiting for the publican's attention.

A great fire was not all that was warming the pub. The broad smiling faces and close-knit bodies made everyone lighthearted and happy to be there in the famous pub of James Joyce.

Pub number seven was impossible to enter. People were spilling out into the street and you could not see the bar.

I was remembering Mimi's final words and also I realized I had no wrapping paper for my gifts. I glanced at my watch and realized that pubs number seven, eight, nine and ten would have to wait for another day.

Grafton Street was a sight to behold. Hundreds of last minute shoppers were rushing in all directions while dozens of vendors were shouting their holiday prices in a language I had never heard before.

Standing on a busy corner I saw a small girl of perhaps nine or ten waving brightly-colored wrapping paper and shouting the words, "Christmas wrapping paper—ten pence." Her bright blue eyes were glowing like candles in the night when I handed her a brand new one pound note and asked for ten sheets of gift paper.

For reasons that are difficult for me to explain, I was captivated by the vigor and energy of this young Irish child hustling wrapping paper on Christmas Eve. I observed her running very excitedly to her mother who was standing on the opposite corner also selling wrapping paper.

The exchange was very brief and after the woman had taken the money she waved the girl back to her post. I could not move from the place where I was able to study her more carefully. She looked like a character out of Charles Dickens' *Christmas Carol*—only she was real.

Observing her more intently I noticed she was wearing a very plain dress which was clean but obviously well worn. Her knee length stockings had fallen down and were hanging lifelessly about her thin legs and ankles.

Her skin was red from the cold night chill, but she remained very animated and continued to scream, "Christmas paper—ten pence."

I also saw that she was staring at an old man holding a small air machine and blowing up huge green and red "Merry Christmas" holiday balloons. I realized she was fascinated by these colorful balloons! She could not take her eyes away from this picture.

After some minutes, I had the man blow up a great green balloon which was then attached to a long stick.

When I handed it to her and said, "Merry Christmas," I could see her mouth drop open.

Rushing into the crowd I turned to watch her approaching the balloon man. After a brief exchange of words she handed him the green balloon for her favorite color red which matched the color of my eyes as I ran to catch my train back to Killester.

A few days after I had returned to Inch I wrote a long letter to my oldest daughter Wendy describing my Christmas Eve experience.

Wendy and her husband Bruce had tried unsuccessfully for more than two years to have a baby. Finally, after they had gone to their doctors, Wendy was told that she could never conceive a baby by natural methods.

All Wendy ever wanted out of love and marriage was to have a family like her mother. The tears and emotional pains of anguish were terrible.

Only Bruce and his enduring love for Wendy held her together during a most difficult time in her young life.

When I wrote my Christmas letter, many months after Wendy's regrettable condition, I hoped that she would interpret my words in a most positive way.

On February 12, 1985, Wendy called to tell me that she and Bruce had adopted a baby boy named Bradford!

Every Christmas day, I learned, Zeff Lawless is like Leonard Bernstein conducting a symphony. He has a full program which includes two days of eating, drinking and endless surprises in entertainment.

Many of these surprises are better than you would find in any first class Manhattan night club and this is no exaggeration. I will never forget the late hour featured performance.

Very early on Christmas morning I could hear Zeke and Jessica knocking on Zeff and Mimi's bedroom door.

They were so impatient to see what Santa Claus had left for them. Even I was excited to see Jessica's eyes when she opened my present to her.

Before long we were all assembled in the living room huddled by the coal fire and surrounded by many colorful gifts and a fresh-smelling blue spruce tree. It was another magic Christmas day!

When Jessica finally came to opening my gift to her I could see she had found her favorite toy. A small soft furry white mechanical puppy started to move across the room. Finally it stopped and then standing on its hind legs it began to bark.

Jessica was overjoyed! She would not leave her puppy the entire day and of course "Snow-white" had to go to bed with Jessica late that night.

It takes Zeff one year to prepare his special vintage homemade brew. This "grog," as he calls it, is a cross between Kentucky moonshine and white lightning, and the effect can be absolute madness.

I cannot recall all of the events of the party, but I remember much sumptuous food accompanied by too much liquid and extraordinary live entertainment.

It was three or four in the morning when Zeff reached up on the living room wall and came down with his guitar. By this time, many relatives, friends and neighbors had joined the traditional Christmas festivities. It was wild and it would become much wilder!

I think it was somewhere between 11:00 A.M. and high noon when Mimi and her two younger sisters were bustling about in the kitchen preparing an Irish breakfast.

Now if you have a good imagination and you are capable of reading between the lines you will know that an Irish Christmas party is no ordinary holiday event. It is a spectacular extravaganza!

Several days later I was prepared to return to Inch for the New Year. I also wanted to give Zeff and Mimi more time to spend with their family and friends.

Before I left Zeff had many questions about my family but especially Warren. He had received a letter from Warren telling him that he and Cindy were divorced, but Warren never explained the reasons why they had split.

I tried to explain to Zeff and Mimi that my wife and I never interfered with the lives of our children once they had come of age to make their own independent judgments.

We knew Warren was crushed by the divorce and he was attempting to pick up the pieces of his life and get it all together again. He knew we would be there if there was anything we could do to help him. That was the most important matter and the gory details were not so important.

I had two surprises waiting for me when I returned to Inch. I could never have anticipated the first surprise nor did I enjoy it.

Driving in the early evening darkness was dangerous and I was extremely cautious. As I approached the final turn in the road before the Strand Hotel, I quickly realized that the sharp curve was playing on my front left tire. In what felt like slow motion, before I could regain total control, my car began to climb the embankment and turn over.

The impact with the ground was terrifying. The crash broke my windscreen and the windows on the driver's side. I was left sitting on the ground and feeling very ridiculous.

After checking all my vital parts for a few minutes, I climbed out the front window and in a short time two cars appeared.

Two young men insisted on taking me to the local hospital in Dingle until I convinced them that only my car needed medical attention. The three of us had no trouble in turning the car right side up and pushing it down to the beach and clear of any passing vehicles.

When I offered them a beer at the Strand Hotel they simply looked at one another with very puzzled expressions and politely declined my invitation.

One week later, John Joe Dorgan, one of the best auto body men in Kerry, had my Renault #5 back on the road.

Of course, there is much more to this story and if you ever come to Inch, everyone will give you their versions of what happened to the only American living in Inch from 1984 to 1985.

Two weeks after my accident, there were two new road signs. One announced "Dangerous Curve" and the second sign outside the street entrance to my home said "Welcome to Inch."

The second surprise after I left the Strand Hotel and walked up the hill to my house was an elaborate display of Christmas and Happy New Year decorations throughout the house.

Dan had also delivered another cord of turf and left a note to join him and Mary for a New Year's Irish coffee.

Mary and Dan O'Shea had succeeded in making my accident as trivial as a minor headache. Once again, I was reminded of how very fortunate I was to be living in such a wonderful place.

6 / Tales and Reminiscences

The days and nights of my first winter in Ireland rolled by like the constant pounding rhythm of the waves hitting the beach. I realized that this was one of the most peaceful periods of my life and I was loving every moment.

Dan would stop in to see me several times a week to see if I needed anything, but I knew he was very happy I was living in Inch. Our weekly discussions covered a wide range of subjects and I know we both gained a great deal of knowledge from them.

More importantly, we were drawing closer in a relationship which can only be described as "Brotherly Love!" We both realized our friendship was as permanent as the ancient sea we were so fond of gazing into.

Dan knew I wanted to learn everything about Celtic history, the Book of Kells, the fairy stories, the mysterious Druids, everything. Dan was fascinated by American life, especially the Western region of America. He fancied himself a cowboy. He would have loved to own a ranch and cattle.

When I told him the story of Brigham Young and my father's Mormon ancestors crossing the plains in covered wagons to settle in Utah, he was sitting on the edge of the chair like a schoolboy.

Of course, we were both very good story tellers and we were equally prone to exaggerating. The contest was very enjoyable.

Mary had once confided in me that there were only

"old men" left in the village before I came and she felt Dan was sometimes very lonely for male companionship. She also told me how happy Dan had been since my arrival in Inch. If I had left one family in America, I had gained another in County Kerry, Ireland!

There were many cold winter nights when the powerful winds off the Atlantic would whistle through the mountains and heavy rains and hail would pelt my roof making it impossible to sleep.

On nights like this I would often leave my bedroom and go to the living room fireplace and gaze out the window to the sea and mountains and sometimes I would wonder, "What am I doing here?" An awful fear would seize me and I would ask myself the terrible question, "What if something serious happens to my family while I am on the other side of the world?"

It was always during these periods of depression that I reflected on my past life and tried to recall only the best times. As in a dream, my childhood and teenage years never left the corner of my brain reserved for my youth.

Dreamily, I would sit for many hours enjoying the pungent aroma of the fire and smile with pleasure over those happy days of growing up in Bayonne.

Bayonne had a population of over sixty thousand people and was divided into two major divisions simply called Uptown and Downtown. At the mid-point in the city was our very large high school.

Uptown was very close to Jersey City while downtown was a short ferry boat ride to Staten Island, New York.

The uptown area had a park fronting the Newark Bay and was mainly residential. Downtown was predominately commercial, but with many large apartments and housing developments.

My uptown crowd was only interested in two main

activities: sports and girls, in that order. If you were not an athlete you did not belong to the group that I grew up with.

There were four seasons of nonstop, around the clock sports activities. All were unorganized games which produced city, county, state and national champions.

We were all dedicated to perfecting our own abilities and talents in the competitive world of sports. Smoking, drinking and drugs were unheard of diseases with all of us.

I was three or four years younger than many of the young men and therefore I had a tough time holding up my end. I grew up with many local sports heroes who I looked up to in our neighborhood.

Jerry Scala was already sixteen years old and in the eighth grade with thirteen or fourteen year olders when he landed a contract with the Chicago White Sox baseball team.

Another hero, who was a great all-around athlete, was Bill "Turk" Hanlon. Turk was six feet, three inches of perfection in body and mind power.

I still remember with some pain the day Scala wanted his favorite protégé, Smokey Davidson, to have a fistfight with me. Turk knew I was not a fighter and he told Scala I would fight Smokey, but first Scala would have to battle with the Turk. It was the last time Jerry Scala suggested a Buehler and Davidson bout.

To this day I have never had to engage in a fist fight with only one small exception. In "boot training" in the U.S. Coast Guard I was matched against a young man from Wisconsin.

Before the three round match he told me he was a professional boxer and I should not make him angry. For the entire three round fight I danced like our former heavyweight champion Muhammad Ali. I even did a few backward shuffles. He hardly laid a glove on me for the entire bout.

One day in 1941 our neighborhood youth was gone. A handful of younger boys and I were saying good-bye to men who were marching off to war.

It was the kind of shock which made me realize how terrible war could be to everyone. I could not believe that our young men were being sent to the other side of our world to fight and perhaps be killed. It was impossible.

Only later did I realize how painful it was for the mothers, the sisters, the wives and lovers of all these young men from Bayonne.

One terrible day the first infamous telegram arrived in our neighborhood from the War Department in Washington, D.C. Harry was a young Jewish scholar who had graduated first in his high school class. He was killed in action on an island in the Pacific.

Harry had not been interested in sports or girls. His ambition was to be the first surgeon in his hard-working, corner grocery store family.

There were many stories about Harry's childhood. How he worked in the store helping his father and mother. How angry his father was one day when he discovered Harry had prepared special gift boxes of food from the store to give to the most needy families at Christmastime.

When Harry was gone his mother and two sisters never sang anymore. His father lost his fiery temper and his great sense of Jewish humor. Our neighborhood was never the same after his senseless and tragic death on the battlefield of insanity.

In the summer of 1942, I told my father I wanted to get working papers so that I could take a job on the railroad. As unhappy as I know Clarence was to have me exposed to the difficult and dirty work on the railroad, he, nevertheless, managed to get me a "war-time" position as a mechanic's helper and laborer to fill in for the young men who had been drafted into the military service.

I quickly became a "jack of all trades," dipping rail rods into chemical tanks to check for imperfections and "gandy dancing" which is too difficult to explain here. What I can smile about though was a popular song of the day called "Rosie the Riveter."

Women were vitally needed in all essential war plants and also on the railroad. We had a "Rosie" in our rail yard who had an incredible face and figure. She could stop men from working by simply walking through the yard. She was something else!

Near the end of the summer season my grandfather, Bill Harding, always rented a large cottage on the beach in Point Pleasant, N.J. Since I was a small child I always looked forward with great anticipation to these summer vacations at the Jersey shore.

The excitement in our family at this time of the year was like the joy we knew at Christmas time. My wonderful grandfather would put money aside each pay week for the family holiday.

Arriving in Point Pleasant, which was only sixty miles south of Bayonne, was the biggest event in my early childhood and teenage life. The fresh smell of the ocean air and the feel of the warm evening breezes while walking on the boardwalk were intoxicating.

Always, Bill would give the children spending money for games and boardwalk amusement rides. Point Pleasant has always been a family resort, but it is an especially joyous place for young children.

My grandfather was always the first one to wake up in the morning. He would enjoy a long walk on the beach to get his morning newspapers and many bags of fresh baked rolls and buns. How we all loved this generous man! Only now do I realize this fabulous era of family life has virtually disappeared from the American scene and I am sorry to say I am part of the reason why it has changed.

When I was only fifteen, in the summer of 1942, there was another song which was very popular in America and was played over and over again! "They Are Either Too Old or Too Grassy Green" was the song of the wartime women who were left behind. I was one of the "grassy green" in the summer of '42.

I had met a young teenager on the beach and we quickly became close friends. Before the summer vacation had ended she introduced me to her older sister who was much, much older than I was. She was an ancient twenty-three!

One night, for reasons I did not fully understand, she accompanied us on our nightly walk on the beach. Later, when we arrived at their cottage to say good night, I politely kissed the younger sister, but then the older sister also embraced me and introduced me to my first "French kiss"!

By the end of the summer of '42 I was no longer so "grassy green." When I returned to high school in September I was well tanned and well kissed!

I had always been very fast in running and so I decided to try out for the school cross-country team. In my first race I placed in the top ten and by the end of the season I was leading our team to the County Championship.

During the winter indoor season and spring competition, Bayonne High School was winning county and state recognition. In 1943, which was our junior year, we became national celebrities.

George Buttner may not have been recognized as one

of the top coaches in the nation, but as far as our team was concerned he was the main reason why we became national champions. He was the most dedicated coach I had ever worked with and I would always remember the tremendous influence he had on all of us.

We were all approaching our seventeenth birthdays which is always a difficult age. It was even more difficult because we had to decide whether to enlist in a branch of the military service at seventeen or wait to be drafted into the army at eighteen.

At lunchtime, while other male students were enjoying the social activity in the school cafeteria with music and girls, we were eating "wheat germ" with our coach who was always preparing us for our weekend competition. He not only taught us how to train, but, more importantly, he taught us about the self sacrifice and hard work that is necessary in order to achieve a goal! We never forgot this lesson!

Of course our team had many private jokes about our "crazy coach." Privately, we admitted that he was a fanatic!

Our coach was tall, trim and practically bald. Occasionally, he would train with us and while he was over fifty he could still break one minute for the 440-yard run.

Like a doctor, he gave us one hundred "no no's" for perfect racing conditioning. In addition to our terrible diet rules, of course, there was no smoking, drinking or drugs.

The list included no bike riding, jitter-bugging, masturbating, et cetera. All of the normal teenage activities would take the sharp edge off our performance.

I will always remember one afternoon when we were celebrating a one mile relay victory and he happened to spot us coming out of a high school "hangout" ice cream parlor.

When we saw him we instinctively hid our ice cream

cones under our high school team sweaters. It was ridiculous, but ice cream was also on the no list.

George Buttner also owned a few race horses and he used to joke about how easy it was to train horses. When we asked why he replied, "I always know what they are eating and where they are sleeping at night."

Our relay team always received invitations from the girls to attend their many parties. The football players were always smoking, drinking too much beer and only wanted to "make out" with the girls.

Lou Junker, Eddie Burger, Jack Lynch and I were like "The Chariots of Fire." We were in great demand and we all enjoyed our "class style" of living and our discipline.

We all had steady girl friends, but we were never very serious. My girl friend was an Italian cheerleader who had an attractive face and a gorgeous figure.

Henrietta also had a pleasing personality with an infectious smile. I always loved to sing and so I changed her name to Candy because this was the title of one of the popular songs of the 1940s and she was as sweet as her song.

Whenever the team and our girl friends traveled together I was requested to sing my Candy song. I had developed five different versions of the song, but everyone enjoyed my "rock and roll" Candy best of all.

On November 23, 1944, our cross-country team traveled to Clifton Park in Baltimore, Maryland for the National Championship of American Schoolboys. It was a very cold and snowy morning and our team had been named as one of the favorites by sports journalists and coaches alike.

Each team entered eight competitors with the first five finishers qualifying for team places in the final count across the finish line after completing the two and a half mile course.

Over two thousand runners were assembled at the starting point with each team lined up with the number one man first, the number two man behind number one, et cetera.

It was an incredible sight and when the starter's gun went off all the tension which had built up by arranging the runners in team order suddenly vanished and we were moving.

Harry Keith, who was not a member of our one mile championship relay team, but was an exceptional long distance runner, was right behind me at the start of the race.

We began the race on a football field but very quickly we reached our first steep hill leading to the main course route which was well-marked with flags and many judges. After reaching the summit of the hill we came down a dangerously narrow path. There was much pushing and shoving to obtain a comfortable position.

Most of the runners wore a special cross-country spiked shoe and I thought, as the cold wind was bringing tears to my eyes, how awful it would be to fall on this narrow path with so many runners coming from the rear. No sooner had this terrible notion entered my mind than I heard cries and much commotion coming from behind me.

I did not realize that at that moment our own Harry Keith had been pushed and had fallen into the oncoming traffic of spiked-shoed athletes.

I crossed the finish line followed, seconds later, by Junker, Burger and Jack Lynch. Where was our number two runner Harry Keith whose finishing place was vital to our final team score?

After a few more seconds we heard many cheering

voices from the large spectator crowd. Harry Keith, blood streaming down his torn leg and obviously in severe pain, was finishing the race as our fifth man to give us the lowest team score and the National Championship of America. An ambulance had been standing by and when Harry was being rushed to the hospital for nineteen stitches in his leg we could not but smile at the proud look on the face of our coach. He had succeeded in helping to mold young boys into young men!

That same winter I decided to enlist in the U.S. Coast Guard. My grandfather's brother Harold was a commander in charge of Coast Guard transportation. He encouraged me to talk with my relay companions about enlisting with me to represent the U.S.C.G. in track competition.

Jack Dempsey, the former great heavyweight champion, was the sports director for the Coast Guard and a major recruiter. Eulace Peacock, a former Olympic and world record holder in the long jump, was the track and field coach.

The incentive was so strong that Junker, Burger, Lynch and I traveled to New York City with my uncle to collectively volunteer our services. We were astonished to be welcomed at the recruiting office by the Admiral of the Coast Guard and a host of reporters and many photographers.

We were even more astonished when we learned that the Coast Guard public relations and service moral department wanted to use our National Championship reputation as a campaign slogan to encourage enlistments for young men of seventeen. Our photograph would be placed on billboards from coast to coast.

Suddenly we had become national celebrities and we were only seventeen. Our coach George Buttner was visibly upset when he heard about our plans to join the Coast Guard.

We were all seniors now and we had a full winter indoor season and spring outdoor season before we would graduate. He also knew that we were all going to celebrate our eighteenth birthdays before graduation and we did not want to go into the Infantry division of the Army.

The American government was awarding military diplomas in cooperation with American high schools to all young men of seventeen who enlisted in the military. The die was cast!

We had all signed the official enlistment documents with our parents' consent and were advised that we would be notified very shortly about taking the required military physical examination. We were also training for what would be our final race together as high school competitors.

Seven outstanding, one-mile relay teams from high schools in New Jersey and New York were invited to compete in the annual Milrose Games at Madison Square Garden in New York City. It was one of the most thrilling nights of our athletic careers.

The greatest track and field competitors in the world were performing. Gil Dodds, holder of the world record for the indoor one-mile race, was going for the first indoor four mile. Bill Vessie, the world's leading indoor record holder in the high jump, was also competing and many, many more from all over America and the world.

While the four of us were warming up on the banked, board track it was obvious that we were all very nervous. I remember thinking to myself, "We are not boys anymore!" After this final high school race we would be young men and there would never be any turning back.

Now the starter was calling for the invitational one-mile high school relay race. While we were lining up the Garden announcer called for the attention of the athletes and spectators.

"The four runners from Bayonne High School, N.J.," he announced, "are all National Cross Country Champions. Tonight they are competing in their final race as high school performers. The next time you see them, they will be running for the U.S.C.G."

As if on command seventeen thousand people rose to their feet and went wild with enthusiastic applause. It was a night we would cherish for the rest of our lives.

Eddie Burger was our fastest sprinter and our coach always used him as our lead-off runner. When the pistol went off Burger immediately shot into the front position and we were going for the gold.

Coming into the final turn, before handing the baton to Lynch, he momentarily glanced over his shoulder to see where his opponents were. In that reckless split second he broke a cardinal track rule, that is, never to look back at your opposition.

While leaning in on his turn to the finish line he lost his balance and the crowd gasped as we watched him crash to the Garden floor. He quickly recovered and rose to his feet, but now we could see he was in deep trouble.

When he hobbled across the line to hand off the baton to Jack Lynch we were in last place. Lynch ran a strong second leg to bring us back in the race and by the time I handed off to our anchorman, Lou Junker, we were in fourth place.

Junker ran one of the best races of his career and gave us all a bronze medal and third place. The crowd also gave us sympathetic applause for our effort!

Moments later the Garden announcer was saying that Emil Von Elling, the New York University doctor and trainer, had given medical attention to Ed Burger who had suffered a broken ankle. Once again, the entire Garden rose on its feet, only this time the coaches and athletes were all applauding Burger's courage and determination to complete his race despite a broken ankle.

Such was the memory of our last race together. One week later we went to New York for our physical examination, only Burger was walking on crutches.

A few hours after a very intensive examination the doctors gave us staggering news. Lynch had vericose veins in both legs and was medically disqualified.

Lou Junker, it was discovered, had what was diagnosed as a slight heart murmur. Ed Burger, of course, was still suffering and it would be several weeks before he could resume normal activity.

On February 6, 1945, I alone left my high school and reported for boot training at the Manhattan Beach Coast Guard Station in New York. With the "grassy green" days behind me I was prepared to face the countless days of young manhood and much, much more in the years yet to come.

7 / The Life and Culture of Eire

If I had come to Ireland to commence work on a manuscript I now discovered I was too absorbed in the life and culture of a country about which I had much to learn. Instead, I found myself writing very long letters to my family and friends telling them everything I was feeling and experiencing in my life in Kerry.

I also invited everyone to visit me in Inch but only my brother Warren and his wife Eileen were able to make their first trip to Eire. How we all enjoyed those two marvelous weeks touring all the places they had wanted to see.

Only once did their guide give them the keys to the Renault #5 when they told me they wanted to travel to the place where the famous Blarney Stone is located.

Since I had not been there, my brother and his wife gave me a detailed picture of how they had to hold each others' ankles while they leaned into the well where the famous stone is found. After kissing this "magic stone," you are not only endowed with the special gift of Irish gab, but you are also protected for a long and happy life.

My brother, who is six feet, four inches tall and weighs 220 pounds, managed to put his foot through the floorboard of my car and laughingly told me on their return to Inch that I should consider buying another car. That was in 1985, when the rusting problem caused by the sea air was only one year old.

Some weeks later I had John Doe Dorgan weld a steel plate where my brother's foot had gone through the floor of my car. You can only imagine the condition of this car in 1990, but we are still on the road.

After Warren and Eileen left Ireland I spent a day in the County Library in Tralee. I was amazed at the vast collection of books which were available to me as a new member.

While my knowledge of Irish history was above average I soon found out that I had only scratched the surface and if I wanted to really delve into the archives of Celtic experience I would have to spend all my rainy days and nights reading the whole story of Ireland's great and tragic life as a very small island nation.

No matter where you go in Ireland you are stumbling over a piece of ancient history and so my thirst for new understanding became unquenchable.

On those exceptional days when the weather allowed me to enjoy the outdoor beauty of Ireland's natural green environment I would walk in the lush mountains with sheep and wild goats all around me. I also particularly relished my long treks through the three-mile stretch of sand dunes on the beach of Inch.

When you have time in your life to truly observe the countless wonders of nature, then you begin to realize the full meaning of life. To lie in the sand dunes for many hours and observe the majestic flight of white gulls, as they play in the wind and then suddenly dive directly into the sea for their afternoon meal, is really something to behold.

To leisurely sit under an old tree on the side of a mountain, watching a spider spin a web with such speed and patience, makes you wonder at the scientific and engineering skill which is involved in this work of art and survival!

Tell me when you have had enough free time to see a bird meticulously and arduously build a nest for the as yet unborn baby egg which will rest in this house high in the tree facing the sun and sky. When you have done this then, I must say, you have become one of nature's millionaires and perhaps your wealth will be everlasting.

One Saturday morning Dan came to invite me to his bog in the mountains. He wanted to teach me how to cut the turf out of the side of his mountain bog. He even brought an extra Irish cap for me to wear so that I would not look like a tourist.

He showed me how to use the special long-handled shovel which is used to slice into the bog, but he began to laugh when I made my first cut. "No, no," he bellowed, "first you must spit on your hands and then take your shovel." He took many photos of me slowly plodding along the straight bog line attempting to imitate his performance until I finally collapsed and happily joined my six pack while Dan jokingly said I had passed my first real Irish test.

Cutting the ancient turf in the bog fields is a popular weekend social activity. All over the Irish mountain landscape you see endless small turf fires with large tea pots steaming.

While the men are busily cutting and stacking the turf to dry in the sun, the women are chatting and preparing a midday picnic. Children are chasing butterflies and there is such a lighthearted spirit of music in the air that you cannot avoid the peacefulness and joy which is surrounding you everywhere. How I loved this silent Irish melody!

There were other evenings around sunset when Dan would come scampering up the mountain with his long gait to check on his sheep and cattle. One night he saw me wandering down the side of the mountain and he called to inquire if I was out for exercise.

"Do you think I can make the 1988 Olympics," I replied like a true Kerryman. We both laughed long and loudly realizing how much we enjoyed sharing this Irish-American fellowship.

We stood for some time watching the sun disappear behind the mountain. Dan turned to me and, gazing into my eyes, he asked me if I had ever seen a place like Inch in all my travels.

"Dan, I have visited many places I would like very much to see again. But nowhere on this earth will I ever see or feel as I am experiencing at this moment. Dan, you have it all!" I could see the tears filling in his blue eyes and he turned away and started down the mountain ahead of me.

"Dan," I called to him, "one day I would like you to build me a great one-room, thatched roof home right on this spot." "Well now," he answered, "when that day comes I do not want to be old and gray and toothless." We were still laughing and singing when we reached the bottom of the mountain.

In Ireland, as in Portugal and Greece, many people do not own a car or do they have telephone service. Luxury transportation and communications are never considered big problems.

I am sure there are some of my American friends and some Europeans who will be surprised to hear this, but in the Eastern world they will smile and say, "Is that all they are missing!"

The Irish people, in particular, are not shy about hitching a car ride from village to village. In fact, it is one of the enjoyable pleasures of Irish life and, for me, it was a remarkable introduction to many people I might otherwise have never had the pleasure or opportunity of meeting.

8 / "The Three Musketeers"

On one very special day I decided to go to Cork City which was celebrating its 750th anniversary. I was smiling at the thought that my country was not yet 200 years old.

It was a sunny morning although the weather forecast was not very encouraging. I wanted to stop at Youghal, which is a coastal town selected by John Huston as the location for Herman Melville's classic story, *Moby Dick*!

You enter Youghal on Main Street, which becomes very narrow. Then, you must pass under an old clock tower and small tunnel. It is a very picturesque welcome to this ancient fishing village. It was not difficult to find the well-known Moby Dick Pub. Standing on a corner facing the sea it is like a beacon to all seafaring men who enjoy the scent of the ocean along with their draft beer.

When the owner heard I was from America he proudly brought out his album of personal pictures which he had taken during the months of filming of the Academy Award winning film. Gregory Peck and John Huston were in many of the photos along with local fishermen who, as extras, played themselves.

He also insisted on showing me the small quarters above the pub where Huston lived while directing the film. He told me it was one of the most exciting times in Youghal history and everyone was employed in some aspect of the film production.

When I had my second beer I opened my wallet, but he refused to let me pay for my drinks. He was still beaming over his recollection of the hundreds of California film people who lived in their great city.

Finally, it was time to get back on the road to Cork City and a very pleasant surprise!

Now the sun was not to be seen, only dark clouds and an occasional clap of thunder. A storm was approaching and I began to wonder why I left Inch.

Hadn't I lived in Ireland long enough to pay attention to the daily weather forecast? The weather report called for late afternoon showers, but now it was coming down in buckets.

A solitary young woman with an umbrella was standing on a bus stop corner. I slowed down to ask her if she wanted a lift into the city. Almost before I concluded my question she was opening the door and sitting by my side.

Looking at her I imagined she could have stepped out of the cover of *Vogue* magazine. She wore a very wide brimmed rain hat with a matching ankle length coat and leather boots that came to her knees.

Behind all these garments I also imagined there was a voluptuous figure. I was not mistaken!

When we reached the great city she invited me to her favorite pub. It is sometimes obvious when two people meet they want the moment to last a little longer and this was the case with Naive and me.

This night we were meant for each other regardless of all other circumstances. After she had finished her drink she excused herself to go to the W.C. (toilet).

When Naive returned I learned she had called her girlfriend to break an engagement that same night. She had two tickets to the ballet.

I invited her to have dinner if she could recommend a good fish house. Everything was settled for the evening in less than five minutes. This night in Cork belonged to the both of us and we were happy!

I have found that the most fabulous women I have encountered have not been afraid to let their guard down. They have been confident and know exactly what they were searching for. More than this they have not been embarrassed to go for the things they desire.

Returning to Inch the next day I was flagged down by a young woman who was in a big hurry. She was an actress from Tralee and she was late for a rehearsal.

Could I please drive a little faster? I was already smiling to myself and thinking, is there anything else you want me to do?

It was a very short trip and when we arrived at an old warehouse she handed me a ticket for the opening performance, opened the car door and said "ciao!" We did not even have time for introductions but, of course, I was there for her performance.

Studying the program and seeing three main characters on the stage when the curtain opened, I knew her name before she would know mine. The play was about a hilarious love triangle and Sharon was the third party.

After the performance Sharon invited me to join her friends at a small pub in Tralee. Her best girlfriend Carol, who was later selected for an All Ireland acting award, was also looking extremely good.

An hour later I was driving them to the small village of Camp which is also on the road to Annascaul and Inch. They shared a small apartment near Camp. They asked me if I wanted to have a beer and listen to some good Irish music at Ashes Pub also located in Camp.

The three of us quickly became "The Three Musketeers." They drank two Harps to every Guinness that I drank and their singing voices could only remind me of angels who had fallen from heaven and landed on my lap. It was starting to look very promising!

I glanced at my watch and it was now 10:30 P.M. Just enough time, I thought, to arrive at Dan Foley's for closing and after that who can tell? They both knew Dan Foley very well and were delighted that I suggested his pub for our nightcap.

Arriving at Foley's only ten minutes before 11:00 P.M. was cutting it very close. When I entered the pub Dan's facial expression was very discouraging, but seeing the two young actresses, whom he knew, seemed to revive his senses.

He confessed that the Garda had hit him with two fines in the last three months and the next one could close him down for one week and cost him a heavy fine to boot.

Precisely at 11:00 P.M. he pulled the curtain down for the night and his patrons, knowing his problem, quickly departed. He knocked off the lights and invited us to his private quarters for a drink on the house.

As a former performer I could see how delighted he was to be able to talk with the actresses about the problems of the performing arts in Kerry and, in fact, all over Ireland.

No one was in a hurry to go anywhere and I was very content to sit by the fire and listen to their animated acting performance. After all, I had a private viewing and what more can one ask for?

At midnight we were enjoying small sandwiches and drinking Dan's special Irish Foley coffee deluxe. I was floating on a cloud at one A.M. when Sharon leaned over and whispered in my ear.

"Carol said you are gorgeous and she thinks you like

me better than her but she wants to share you with me."
It was the finest proposal I had ever received in my life.
I did not need my electric blanket in Inch on that cold and
rainy night of pure bliss!

9 / Scholars and Storytellers

In February, 1985, I was very happy to receive a reply to a letter I had written to Senator Alan Cranston requesting his assistance in arranging a grand tour of Europe and the Soviet Union.

I want to share with you some of Senator Cranston's thoughts about his aborted campaign for the presidency and also tell you why he was so important to my work as a writer:

> "As the 1984 democratic nominating process enters its final days, I look back on my presidential bid with an ever-increasing feeling of accomplishment.
>
> While I wanted to win, the experience has not in any sense been a loss for me. I feel stronger and wiser as a consequence of the race for the presidency. Moreover, I entered the race for the Democratic nomination for one primary reason. I have a strong sense of urgency about the need to end the arms race; a sense of urgency which I felt then and feel now must be a major focus of the 1984 campaign.
>
> I shall continue to push with all the force of my being the urgency of arms control and the defeat of Ronald Reagan. I shall not let up the pressure on either my fellow democrats or our adversary in the White House.
>
> I cannot hide my disappointment that I won't be the Democratic nominee for the president. But I said

from the start that I was running in two races. One was the race for Democratic nomination for the presidency. That race is over now. The other more important race, is the one to banish nuclear weapons from the face of God's earth. I'm in that race to stay.

For all you have done for me in Maine and New Hampshire, I thank you. For all you will continue to do in the cause of economic opportunity, individual rights and human dignity, compassion and peace, I commend you and urge you onward."

These ideas have been a constant inspiration for me in my writing because they are the essence of my own personal views and ambitions for the future of mankind. Senator Cranston also included in his correspondence to me two letters of introduction to all American ambassadors in Western Europe and a personal letter to our former American ambassador in the Soviet Union, Arthur Hartman.

In March I also received another welcomed letter from my friend in New Jersey, Senator Bill Bradley. Senator Bradley had written to former U.S. Information Director, Charles Wick, to ask him to assist me with my traveling plans in Europe and Russia.

Needless to say, the influence of two of America's most respected Senators was an invaluable asset to me in whatever nation I was visiting.

As time was passing I found myself spending most of my time in Ireland reading instead of writing, which had been the main reason why I came to Europe. I had made friends with the staff in the Tralee library and if there were books they did not have on hand they would contact the bigger libraries in Cork and Dublin.

They were extremely helpful to me and my research

efforts in obtaining many important books by outstanding authors. To increase my knowledge and understanding of Irish life in County Kerry during the nineteenth and twentieth centuries, I was advised to read two books which I enjoyed immensely.

Maurice O'Sullivan, who was raised and educated on the famous Blasket Island off the west coast of Dunquin in County Kerry, wrote *Twenty Year a Growing*. Peg Sayers, who was born on the mainland, came from a typically large family and was sent to the island as a young teenager.

Her father had managed a wedding arrangement for his young daughter so that there would be one less mouth to feed in his big family. Much later Peg Sayers wrote a book called *The Reflections of an Old Woman* which is on the required reading list of every Irish student.

In her well known story she gives a vivid account of the difficulties and hardships which had to be endured by the islanders, especially the long winter days and nights when the islanders had to survive in total isolation from the mainland. Her personal story of raising a large family under such adverse conditions is told with passion and even ironic humor.

She became the island storyteller and many nights the young children would gather around her warm fire impatient to listen to her spell-binding tales of fairies and legendary characters of Irish history.

In one very dramatic chapter of her book she describes the tragic day when one of her young sons fell from a high mountain cliff to the rocks and sea below. When his small battered and unrecognizable body was recovered she could only cry from deep within her own tortured body and soul over the death of her son and the fate of her island.

Peg Sayers describes how the winter storms cut the islanders off from the mainland for days and weeks at a time. There were no priests or doctors on the island and so it was impossible in time of emergency to seek out help.

Even when islanders had died they were unable to have a proper mainland burial service until the sea had become calm enough for a mainland church service and a graveyard ceremony. It was another tragic truth which was a terrible part of island living.

On the lighter side of Peg Sayer's great story telling were the tales of Irish ghosts. When the cold wind was howling all over the five-mile mountain and the stormy sea was crashing against the cliffs, Peg delighted in telling hauntingly shocking tales about the legendary characters who still roamed on the Blasket mountainside.

The children were so frightened by these tales that they would refuse to leave the warmth of Peg's home fire to race across the island hills to their own homes.

Peg Sayer's reflections are undoubtedly some of the most moving human documents I have ever read.

I was compelled one day to take the small ferry from Dunquin to the Blaskets to walk in the village where she had lived for so many years. I was so fascinated by my brief experience on the island that I decided to return for one entire summer and I will talk about this wonderful experience very shortly.

In the meantime, I had learned some very interesting facts about the resourcefulness of the Blasket Islanders during Ireland's worst potato famine in Irish history. This sad and tragic Irish story that took place in the late 1840s and early 1850s forced countless thousands of Irish people to sail to America while untold millions were dying of starvation unable to get help from any nation including England, its next door neighbor.

During this crisis in Irish history the Blasket Islanders were so resourceful that church records in Dingle and

Dunquin illustrate an increase in the island population during this period of famine and starvation.

The thirty families, numbering between 250 and 400 people, survived on fish from the sea, birds and birds' eggs from nests on the sides of cliffs and goats' milk. Many of the sheep that grazed on the fertile mountain were part of their diet and provided their wool clothing as well. Also, the bog section of the mountains gave the islanders sufficient turf to keep their fires ablaze throughout long winters.

This inspiring story only ended when it became apparent in the 1950s that too many young men and women were leaving the island for new opportunities on the mainland. Maurice O'Sullivan describes this moment in Irish history very vividly as I recalled from his book *Twenty Years a Growing*.

The old Blasket Island men, huddled together enjoying their pipes and the warmth of the fire, were very silent while reflecting on their life and their future. One of the oldest and most respected men turned to the group and suggested that soon there would be no one left to bury them.

It was that simple yet poignant scene which forced the last of the Islanders to abandon the Blasket forever. It was the end of a very proud and courageous chapter in Irish history.

Today, only the ruins and the grave of Peg Sayers, lying in peace at Slea Head, remain.

In anticipation of my trip to the Soviet Union I had been searching for a special book concerning Russian history and life which led up to the Revolution of 1917. I was already an avid student of Russian history and two of my favorite books were Robert K. Massie's *Nicholas and Alexandra* and John Reed's *Ten Days That Shook the World*.

These books and my discovery of Leo Tolstoy's *Confession* in the Tralee library were to play a very significant part in my travels from Moscow to Leningrad in the spring of 1986!

Leo Tolstoy was not only a great writer but he was also a brilliant scholar. In 1877, after completing his work *Anna Karenina*, he turned his attention to an exhaustive study of religion.

He was only forty-nine years old and his intellectual powers were at their zenith. He could be content and very happy with the knowledge that he had been acknowledged as an international celebrity for his great work. He was also happily married with a family, much property with many working peasants, horses, everything.

It was at this high peak in his life that he began to seriously contemplate suicide. It became a daily obsession only he admitted he lacked the courage to do it.

Instead Leo Tolstoy wrote the famous *Confession*, which has been compared to the confession of St. Augustine!

For seven long years he dedicated himself to the sometimes very painful study of every religion known to mankind. Not only did he read every scholarly work which was available but he consulted religious leaders, scientists and historians. Always, his search was for the meaning of his life.

He was convinced someone was playing a cruel joke on him and he was driven to the point of trying to decide how he could end this nightmarish joke! So intense was his desire to find the answer to this question of life and death that, at the age of fifty, he taught himself the Greek language in order to study from the original manuscripts of the Holy Bible.

Tolstoy left no stone, not even a pebble, unturned in

his long quest for the answer to the most vital question ever posed to a man. His finished work was immediately banned in Russia. While attempts were made to suppress his book, it nevertheless was circulated clandestinely in hectographed copies which were smuggled out of Russia.

So powerful was his denunciation of all institutional religion that he was finally excommunicated from his Orthodox Church in Russia before he died at the age of eighty-two in the year 1910.

Later I will discuss my visit to the Soviet Union and the importance of Leo Tolstoy and John Reed during my fantastic tour of Russia.

10 / Miss Switzerland, Miss London, Miss Copenhagen, and Mr. Universe

On April 10, 1985, after living in Ireland for almost five months I decided to celebrate my birthday in Dingle—a superb Irish fish dinner washed down with exquisite French white wine and later a call to Shawn O'Flatherty's singing pub. How could I know how fabulously my birthday would end?

Standing in the center of the pub surrounded by a group of handsome young singing Irishmen were three of the most cheerful foreign women I had ever seen in the pub. Minutes later with my Big G. in hand I joined the merrymakers and by closing we had all become great friends.

When I learned they had not yet made plans as to where they would spend the night, which was not unusual for this light tourist season time, I offered them my four bedroom castle on the side of the mountain. Now they were even more cheerful.

During the drive to my home I decided we would be called "The Four Musketeers" from Dumas', "one for all and all for one." We all laughed and started singing our new song! "We are all for one and one for all time!"

I also told them I would be calling them by their national names: Miss Switzerland, Miss London and Miss Copenhagen, who was a writer and the funniest of all four of us.

The next four days and nights were raucous in the most delightful way you could ever dream about. We only had one house rule! The first one up in the morning would put the coffee on for our wake up time.

The women decided that since I was the host and their guide they would do all the cooking and house cleaning. I jokingly asked them to stay forever!

I balked at their idea of calling me Mr. America and suggested Mr. Universe was much nicer. Our breakfast conversation each morning was hilarious.

We would look up to the sky before we made a decision on where we would spend our day together. A rainy day meant indoor sight seeing including visits to famous pubs and a sunny or cloudy day meant outdoor picnics and also visits to more famous pubs.

They liked the aroma of a good pub, especially when there was Irish music filling the air.

Our nights together were also very special moments to remember. Late each evening when my petite yellow Renault rolled into the driveway it was always rumbling with peals of laughter. No one wanted to say "good night" or leave our roaring fire and discussions about everything.

It was the best of times and we knew it would not be easy to say good-bye. We were very happy together!

Before they left Inch they all gave me their addresses and telephone numbers and I made a promise to visit them during my summer tour of Europe.

I think we all realized when we were finally saying good-bye that my visit to their home countries would be even more intimate and intense than our April in Inch. And so it was!

My western European travels to London, Switzerland, Copenhagen and other experiences dramatically changed the direction of my life. But now, once again, I was alone in Kerry!

11 / At Bunratty Castle

Mary and Dan O'Shea were always a part of my escapades in Ireland. Dan especially enjoyed the "comings and goings on" which he found more amusing than a barrel of monkeys in the zoo!

In May, I surprised Mary and Dan with an anniversary invitation to the very famous "Bunratty Castle Banquet." They knew about the extragavant dinner and entertainment at Bunratty but this would be their first visit to the ancient castle.

Entering the castle you are greeted with "piper's music" and also a large glass of glorious "Mead" which is a rare mixture of many interesting ingredients which all remain highly secretive.

All the ceremony and rituals of an eighteenth century banquet are enjoyed including the best harp music and singing you will ever hear. Also you discover there is no silverware used for eating in this castle banquet and that is fun.

I could see Mary and Dan were thoroughly enjoying their eighth anniversary party! Dan was in rare form!

Taking Mary's picture sitting on the Queen's throne, with one hand clutching his ever-present glass of Mead, he was a big part of the entertainment.

By the time we were leaving the castle for a nightcap at the equally famous Dirty Nellie's Pub, Mary was already suggesting that she should drive the car back to Inch which was two hours away. Dan had no objections! He was flying!

While Dirty Nellie's is a tourist hot spot, that night the music and singing were all Irish and I never heard Dan sing so well and with such emotional feeling. He had been tremendous in the castle, but in the pub he was sensational.

Mary could not suppress her joy and laughter and I knew how much love they had between them. It was a perfect night!

The O'Sheas knew that I had planned an extensive summer tour on the continent and they were happy when I informed them that I would send cards from every country where I was traveling. Today their fireplace has over fifty cards.

12 / Blasket

In June, I went back to the Blasket Island for a few days of seclusion and relaxation. I wanted to prepare my summer itinerary and write some letters to tell everyone where I would be traveling and the special places I wanted to see on my great tour.

My car had been serviced and was pronounced fit for an extensive drive. Shawn Evans, my mechanic in Annascaul, assured me that the Renault engine performance would not fail me for another thirty thousand miles of traveling throughout Europe.

Crossing the choppy waters of the Atlantic, while bobbing up and down, I could barely see the island through the rain and heavy Irish mist.

When we landed at the crude rocky port I saw a small group of men erecting a huge antenna at the end of the island. Also, a young Irish couple and their small son had come to spend the entire summer living on the island.

Mary and Paul were both Blasket Island enthusiasts and had been granted permission and a small stipend by the government to be of service to the visiting tourists. While there were only limited facilities and an outhouse for tourist convenience, Mary and Paul decided to prepare tea and light snacks for anyone desiring to camp on the island or simply spend the day walking the mountain.

We enjoyed some tea and cookies sitting at an outside table now that the rain had stopped and a brilliant sun was shining directly over us. They told me the men who were making a small campsite were ham radio operators from Belgium.

They had received permission to erect the first radio station on the island and they would be sending and receiving calls from all over the world. It was all very interesting and exciting.

The Blasket Island was considered the last parish before reaching North America and naturally ham operators were anxious to make contact with this lovely outpost in the Atlantic.

When I walked to their station I was fascinated by all the activity. Dr. Luke was a physician from Lokeren, Belgium and his three assistants were college professors and one was a T.V. and electronics expert.

Ham radio operations was their hobby and a very important part of their lives. I could not believe the exotic calls they were receiving from Japan, the Soviet Union, Canada, everywhere. Also, I was astonished to learn, they all spoke several different languages, including perfect English.

In the next few days Luke and I became very good friends. I quickly learned that he was an extraordinary man. In addition to being a physician and a ham radio operator, I discovered we had a common interest in Irish-Celtic history.

Several years ago he came to Ireland and built a home overlooking the Shannon River. He also was a boatman and kept his craft docked in the Shannon.

One night, sitting by his camp fire drinking fine wine which he always carried with him, we exchanged life stories which is very unusual for me.

He was sixteen when the Germans invaded Belgium. He left his home before the Germans arrived and joined the Belgian resistance. Luke's wartime resistance against the Germans won him national recognition.

We were both public officials and naturally, we also talked about politics and government. He was a conservative at this time and I am always a liberal democrat. Of course we both enjoyed this exchange very much and left the subject equally convinced that we had won the debate.

He was very sad when he told me his wife had died shortly before his home in Ireland was completed. It was supposed to be their retirement home and they both eagerly looked forward to the time when they would be living on the Shannon River.

After his wife's death he adopted a second family of Vietnamese children and I will talk about this later in my story.

One evening a few young German campers descended on the island and joined our small party at the fireside. I discovered Luke also possessed a great sense of humor.

After the young German men had introduced themselves, Luke responded by saying, he enjoyed the company of German men provided they came in small groups and were not wearing uniforms. Everyone laughed, but hidden behind the smiles there was some sadness.

Reluctantly, I had to leave the island and head for the port of Rosslare from where my car and I would leave for our trip to England. Miss London was anticipating my arrival and she managed to rearrange her schedule so that we would have two weeks to tour her country.

She knew I had lived in England for one year and so we could plan our trip together to visit our favorite places, especially in the south of England.

13 / England Ho!

In 1963, a presidential committee of ten persons in Washington, D.C., selected a group of teachers to represent the U.S. government in a Fulbright Exchange program. Fortunately, I was one of the proud recipients of this outstanding honor.

For many weeks before our departure for our new home in England, there was great excitement in our family. We had been successful in renting out our large home to a family from Ohio who would be relocating to New Jersey.

My wife had much packing to do and assured many relatives and friends that we would stay in contact during our one year in Great Missenden, Buckinghamshire County. Warren was then eleven, Wendy was ten and Laurie would be starting school in the small village called Ballenger.

Our friends and neighbors gave us a huge outdoor farewell party which I will always recall because everyone finally decided they wanted to come to New York City to see us leave on the illustrious S.S. *United States* ocean liner. The fine crossing on this magnificent ocean liner would be one of the truly outstanding events of our year abroad.

The children would never forget the three thousand mile cruise across the vast Atlantic Ocean. They would realize what it was like in the last century when the millions of immigrants came to America in small ships which took many weeks and sometimes months to reach the new world of North America.

Our new home, in the Chiltern Hills of Great Missenden and Ballenger, was perfect. The owner was an English film director who was making *Lord of the Flies* in Africa.

The realtor from Pretty and Ellis came to see my wife the day after we moved into the house. He had a thick diary of every article in our seven-room house. My wife had to spend an entire day going through the inventory list from aprons to washboard. This procedure was repeated when we were leaving.

In one year we had broken two glasses and one small plate. The damages cost one pound. While very time consuming and expensive the English renting system protects everyone!

Before the opening of the English school term I took a ship and train ride to Wolfsburg, Germany, to buy a new V.W. The fabulous "Beetle" carried us over twenty-five thousand miles.

We would make long weekend trips to every corner of England, Wales and Scotland.

On long school holidays we covered every country of Western Europe. Our family year of living in England and traveling throughout Europe was obviously one of the most memorable years of our lives together.

The highlight of our year in England was the birth of our fourth child, David Charles, born on March 29, 1964, in the Chalfont St. Giles nursing home.

When we left N.J. Claire was already two months pregnant, but she did not want to alarm our parents with the surprise of an English birth. My wife was then and remains today a very unique woman.

Arriving at Aylesburg High School for the opening day, I learned that I was the first American teacher in the school's history.

There are not enough pages in this book to tell you how fantastic this special year was for everyone. Even when the English students were "Sir"-ing me to death I was loving it all.

Only the tragic B.B.C. program interruption announcing the assassination of President John Kennedy on November 23, 1963, shook my family's foundation. To be living in a foreign country at a time of national disaster can be a very unnerving experience.

When I came to school the "Union Jack" was flying at half staff. At this moment, while I write these words, I can feel a lump in my throat.

Yes, John Kennedy was not the greatest president in American history. But no president in American history ever inspired a nation or a world with such intense emotion.

Kennedy was a man for all seasons. His intelligence, Irish humor and his fresh clean looks won the hearts and minds of millions.

We may never see this great flame of life pass this way again!

My family had been invited to the American Embassy in London for Thanksgiving. It was the saddest Thanksgiving Day of my entire life.

I had actively campaigned for John Kennedy and for me he was the first president who made me feel proud to be an American. I must also add that, after John Kennedy, no American president has been successful in reaching the pulse and heartbeat of humanity.

Since Kennedy, his brother, Robert, and Martin Luther King have been assassinated, "the recipe for the cake" has been destroyed.

After the tragic and unexpected Kennedy assassination, something snapped in my mind. Only a few people have had a direct influence on my thinking and on the direction of my life. John Kennedy was one of these persons.

Kennedy's inaugural charge, "Ask not what your country can do for you but what can you do for your country," was more than a political phrase. For me, it meant an invitation to speak, to work, to learn and yes, to strive for a more ambitious level of human compassion and understanding.

In addition to my teaching in Aylesburg, I also volunteered to lecture throughout England. The American Embassy had many requests which I would accept.

My success and enthusiasm led to my selection as the American representative to an International Congress to discuss the future role and outlook for education. Very big topic, very small results!

The elaborate conference was held at Ditchley Park which had been Winston Churchill's wartime hideout. Because I was the lone American representative I was honored to have the Churchill suite for my stay at Ditchley.

I was not accustomed to being served coffee on a silver tray by a butler nor had I ever gone to the stable for a horse ride before breakfast.

You can plainly see that this was no ordinary "bullshit" teacher's conference in Atlantic City, New Jersey, or Washington, D.C. This conference had a "touch of class" which always concluded with a seven course dinner with so many crystal wine glasses and so much silver cutlery that I was always watching someone else to avoid making any serious mistakes.

The best times of the conference were the late evening informal discussions held in the famous Churchill "Smoking and Brandy" room with a roaring fire in the background. I will always feel very warm and excited whenever

I recall those days and nights of splendor in Camelot, England.

After the birth of our son David Charles Buehler, we received an invitation to meet the Queen Mother at St. James Palace. There are always great events in all our lives and for us meeting the Queen Mother was an extraordinary event.

The Queen Mother's lady in waiting had informed the queen that Mrs. Claire Buehler had a son born in Chalford St. Giles, the famous village where a blind John Milton wrote *Paradise Lost*.

After the formal introductions, the Queen Mother asked my wife if the baby was born American or English style. When my wife proudly announced that David was delivered by a midwife you could see a queenly smile light up this face of royalty.

For me, standing in the background and listening to two mothers talk about life in England was "the delicious icing on top of the cake!"

14 / And Again England

Miss London and I enjoyed two brief love affairs and one was with England. We decided to spend a week sightseeing in the south of England.

Every region in England has its own history and signs of beauty are everywhere. Devon and Cornwall are well known attractions for English vacationers as well as for foreign tourists.

Even the names of these places in the south sound very romantic. Tintagel is the mythical site of King Arthur's famed roundtable and the glory that was Camelot!

Tiny seaside villages like Clovelly and Polparra can never be forgotten. Walking down the ancient cobblestoned main street of Clovelly you are able to stretch out your arms to touch the many shops with your two hands.

Of course no cars, et cetera, are permitted in Clovelly.

One cloudy day when we were traveling through Dartmoor, which is very popular for countless wild horses and much open space, we came upon an old stone house with a small sign inviting tourists to enjoy a "tea and cream scones."

The small group of young women and men inside the house were all very busily engaged in numerous handicrafts using wood and metal.

While enjoying our tea and Devon cream scone and jam we fell into a conversation with one of the young workers. Their story is one I had heard before, but I always enjoy listening to this special tale of happiness and success.

Several young couples decided to leave their high paying professional jobs in London to experiment with a brand new lifestyle in the wilderness of Dartmoor! More than big city competition and professional pressure is causing this new social phenomena.

Young people especially, but many older people also, are getting fed up with the "rat race life in the frying pan of futility." Life on the outside lane is becoming much more attractive than the insanity of being on the inside lane.

Take a good look all around you and ask yourself what is the good life for you, for your character, for your individual personality?

How encouraging it is for me, after almost five years of traveling and meeting thousands of people, to learn that we are in the midst of a major social upheaval.

When we were returning to London by way of Bath and Stonehenge I invited Miss London to one of my favorite pubs in London. She had never been to The Prospect of Whitby although she knew it was one of the most famous pubs in all of England.

It reminded me of the many New Yorkers who have never taken a boat ride to Liberty Island to see the famous woman who is always smiling and welcoming people to Manhattan, the greatest city on the planet earth.

Located directly on the Thames River you must first find the Tower of London and then search for old Whopping Road in the factory district of London. When you think you are lost you have found it!

Like an oasis in a desert the Prospect of Whitby is a unique wharfside gem with a great cheese board and special draft beer which is neither bitter nor mild.

Leaving Miss London with a great smile on my face and a happy, singing heart, I was on my way to Dover and the crossing to Calais, France.

15 / Normandy—the Ones Who Remain

I have been to France many times but on this trip I wanted to spend one day at Normandy. Everyone should spend a day at Normandy, especially all the political rulers, generals, high priests of religion and young men who enjoy, even today, still wearing uniforms and carrying guns!

Twenty-five thousand small white crosses decorate a field of immaculate green marking the final resting place of young Americans between the ages of eighteen and twenty-five who never left the beaches of Omaha and Utah in Normandy, France.

Silently walking alone through row upon row of fallen Americans I was also recalling a time in my youth when my heart and mind were shattered. I was eighteen and I was in training to become a third class radio operator.

Our school in Atlantic City was a former hotel which had been taken over by the coast guard. There were also dozens and dozens of large hotels which were converted into military hospitals serving mainly as rehab. centers for thousands of young men who had lost their arms and legs and everything in the D-day landing at Normandy.

Why is it that my eyes cannot wipe out the picture which sometimes drives me wild with rage?

On the boardwalk in Atlantic City, N.J. in 1945, months before the war had ended, thousands of women from all over America came to visit the living dead men who survived Omaha and Utah beaches.

Mothers, sisters, young wives and young lovers were all in Atlantic City to wheel their helpless loved ones on the famous boardwalk of living death. I cannot forget the painful and tragic look in the eyes of those helpless men who were crying and praying for a death which avoided them.

Unfortunately, the father of one of these young men I knew told me, one tearful night, that he could no longer visit his son! His twenty-one year old son was a "basket case!"

He had lost both arms and legs but after many, many months of great pain and untold agony, day and night, he had only one desire—to kill himself. He finally mastered the technique of hand manipulation through the use of artificial limbs. He constantly urged his father to bring him a revolver so that he could end his tragic life.

How men in the countdown period of this insane century can continue to wear uniforms and carry guns is what this story is really all about!

16 / At Peace in the Alps

Traveling across France on my way to Basle, Switzerland my mind was still very heavy with sad thoughts which were not pleasant for my reunion with Miss Switzerland. Sometimes I regret having a very vivid imagination and, even more dangerous, not being able to close my eyes to reality.

My visit to Switzerland was very brief because my friend, who is an active member of the European Green party, was highly involved with a large group of demonstrators who were planning a massive protest against the Siba-Geigy Chemical Company.

The Rhine River was being polluted by a toxic chemical which was having a devastating effect on several European nations. My timing on this part of the trip only encouraged me to learn more about my friend and the growing greens of Europe!

Miss Switzerland was not only physically attractive but her mind was also fascinating. She was one of the leaders of the planned demonstration and ironically, she was employed in Basle by the Siba-Geigy plant!

Her friends were happy to learn that I was no stranger to demonstrations. I had been involved in several anti-nuclear demonstrations in Europe and as a state senator and candidate for governor of New Jersey I led a few demonstrations for human rights.

I was then and will always be an activist for world peace and justice for humanity!

On the evening before I left Basle, Miss Switzerland

took me to her favorite garden restaurant where they serve the best fondu and finest white wine in all of Europe. There was magic in the garden air and for the first time our eyes were exchanging glances which were more meaningful than our first meeting in Dingle, Ireland.

Once more I was on the road again and my soul was at peace. The Alps can do this for you!

In 1964, Innsbruck, Austria, was hosting the Winter Olympics. My family and I planned a winter holiday in Austria and Switzerland immediately after the games were over.

We were all laughing and singing the songs from *The Sound of Music*! Zermatt, Switzerland, was our favorite stop. Relaxing in our chalet in the shadow of the Matterhorn was something else.

Zermatt is another environmentally perfect Swiss village which does not permit cars or motorized vehicles. The awesome silence of "the crooked white mountain giant" is one of the European wonders of natural beauty.

Of course I must tell my European readers that the American and Canadian Rocky Mountains are equally spectacular and one must be careful not to get a "Rocky Mountain High!"

After saying good-bye to Miss Switzerland my Renault #5 was looking north to Germany, Belgium, Amsterdam and Copenhagen!

17 / From Waterloo to Amsterdam

Dr. Luke had returned from the Blasket Island and had invited me to spend some days with him and his ham radio operator friends. Arriving at his home in Lokeren I was impressed by the admiration and respect he received both as a doctor and as a politician.

Luke and I were operating on the same wave length in many things, but especially our mutual interest in art, history and good food with rare wine! He wanted to show me everything he knew that I would enjoy!

One day it was Waterloo where Napolean had suffered a terrible defeat. It was not only the military aspect of Waterloo which excited Luke!

He wanted me to walk around the battlefield and to examine some of the more intimate details of the surroundings which included an old barn which had been used as a hospital for the wounded soldiers.

His eyes would light up at any new revelation that he believed would heighten my interest. Luke is like this! If he can make another person happy then he is feeling great.

Earlier I mentioned he had adopted a Vietnamese family of displaced persons. One member of the family was in her early twenties.

Observing her total devotion toward Luke opened my eyes for the first time to the Oriental woman.

On the first night we returned late from a call he had to make at his hospital. When we entered his home he winked at me and, as if to say "watch this," he offered me a beer and we flopped in our chairs.

Thaou was a very slender woman with an exotic face which was at once very arresting. Her movements, especially her hands, held my attention. She was as graceful as a ballerina.

Once Luke had been seated she removed his shoes and replaced them with comfortable slippers. Then I watched her gently and very naturally massage his neck and shoulders while he was relaxing from ear to ear.

Of course, I was thinking how chauvinistic all this personal attention was, but then I realized that I would not have minded being in his chair.

Before I left Lokeren, Luke and Thaou invited me out for a typical Oriental dinner. Thaou had a young woman friend from Thailand who would be my escort for the evening.

It was my first eastern experience and I am still somewhat bewildered by her natural signs of affection and this chauvinism I am feeling.

Amsterdam was very much on my mind when I left Belgium. I had been to the "city out of control" before, but now I was coming to see Vincent Van Gogh!

On Christmas morning at the Byways in Ballenger, Great Missenden, England in 1963, my three children gave me one of the finest gifts I had ever received. It was a very large book containing the major works of Vincent Van Gogh, the famous Dutch impressionist.

My children knew how much affection I had for this sad, great painter. But now I am standing in the center of the world's largest collection of work by Van Gogh, in his art museum in Amsterdam.

Vincent's sometimes furious brush strokes covered more than 875 known canvases and uncountable sketches.

When I arrived at the museum I had been shocked by the large red painted letters on the front wall reading "Fuck Vincent Van Gogh."

If I live to be one thousand I will never understand this behavior especially to a monument of a man such as Vincent Van Gogh.

Inside, however, was another story. Intelligent curators had arranged Vincent's work in chronological sequence so that you were easily able to follow the progression of his art as well as his life.

The year 1990 marks the one hundredth anniversary of the death of Vincent Van Gogh at the age of thirty-seven. Few artists in human history are as well known and are as loved as Vincent, the man they write songs about.

Although his brother Theo was an art dealer in Paris, Vincent was only able to sell one painting for $240. After his death his work was internationally acclaimed!

Recently his *Sunflowers* sold for a record-breaking forty million dollars and today his paintings are in treasured collections throughout the world.

As a young man he began by following in the footsteps of his father who was a village pastor. Vincent was sent to a small coal mining town where he quickly learned the many problems he would be facing as a young pastor.

Perhaps this brief period of his life reflects the story of a man whose love for humanity knew no boundaries.

During his brief tenure as a pastor, Vincent would descend into the mining pits to see the horrible conditions and dangers which the miners had to endure. He was appalled at the level of poverty in the village and gave his clothing and few possessions to help the most needy families.

Even his modest salary as pastor was used to buy food for those miners' families who were unable to work any longer. He found it impossible to prepare an optimistic sermon every Sunday when he saw the sad, grim-looking faces in his parish.

One day he was paid an unexpected visit by his church leaders who were appalled by his simple dress and deplorable living conditions. He was unworthy to serve as a pastor.

Vincent's short career as a parish priest must have had a profound influence on his later years of artistic genius. For him, it was not so important to clothe himself in regal robes of great elegance, but to teach the word of God.

He saw the true humanity and later he was able to capture this face in one of my favorite Van Gogh masterpieces. The *Potato Eaters* for me, more than any other painting, is the mirror of Vincent Van Gogh's heart and soul.

A small, impoverished family of four persons is sitting at their very modest living room table set for the evening meal. A large steaming bowl of potatoes is sitting at the center of the table along with a pot of tea.

The faces of this farming family are illuminated by a dim kerosene lantern suspended over the table. Van Gogh's dark colors and brush strokes highlight the sad but proud faces of the peasants.

The gnarled hands of the working man and woman give evidence of their devotion to the land which is giving them their daily sustenance. It was this famous canvas which conveyed Vincent's deep sense of humility!

This great artistic genius was a man who worshipped humanity. He could feel the pain and inner anguish of his numerous models and was able to capture their emotions on his canvas.

Vincent also suffered much personal pain over the fact that his younger brother Theo was his only lifeline enabling him to continue his ambition to paint.

Other great impressionists like Cezanne, Monet, Renoir, Degas and even Paul Gauguin were able to make a living from their work. Vincent always had to rely on Theo for everything.

Despite the fact that Theo was an art dealer he was unable to sell his brother's work. Nevertheless, Theo's unflinching confidence in Vincent's talent is related in many letters which the brothers exchanged over a period of turbulent years.

Every month Theo sent Vincent money and art supplies to keep him at his canvas. There came a time, however, when Vincent became very emotionally and mentally distressed.

Theo had married and his wife would shortly give birth to a son. Vincent was obsessed with the feeling that he was a terrible burden for his brother and his family.

He sometimes wrote desperate letters telling Theo he could not continue to receive help when he knew Theo had many family responsibilities.

Theo, equally emotional, continued to urge Vincent to paint. He knew one day his brother's art genius would be recognized and he was able to persuade Vincent to persevere and not be concerned over financial problems.

The voluminous pages of their correspondence reveal one of the greatest love stories ever told.

Some months after Amsterdam I traveled to the south of France to where Vincent would paint many of his great masterpieces. In his famous "yellow house" in Arles he would work with Paul Gauguin for many tumultuous months until his nerves gave way under the pressure of personal conflict.

One night, following a terrible argument, Vincent took a razor and cut his ear off in a fit of rage. Later, he voluntarily admitted himself into a mental institution where, after some months, he was permitted to resume his painting in the garden.

I also traveled to Auvers where he painted seventy canvases in seventy days. He knew he was losing his control and was working at a furious pace.

One afternoon, in a state of depression, he walked into the fields where he had been painting and shot himself. One year later his brother Theo also died.

When I visited the church in Auvers immortalized on canvas by Van Gogh, I also walked to the small cemetery where Vincent is buried side by side with his brother Theo. It was a very emotional moment for me to stand alone at their graveside.

There are two small grave markers simply reading: "Vincent Van Gogh, Born 1853, died 1890." "Theo Van Gogh, Born 1857, died 1891." Covering the two graves is a very special ivy flower plant entwining both grave sites.

Close by is a small simple plaque from the people of Holland. The plaque reads: "As they were always joined in life so in death may they rest side by side forever."

Vincent's genius was not only his masterful brushstroke or his ability to mix brilliant colors for his canvas which would capture the natural beauty of the landscape.

Once he had written an impassioned letter to Theo telling him how much he loved to paint portraits. He said it did not matter if it was the postman, a doctor or a whore from the street.

In all these characters he could find love and human understanding.

The greatest living monument to Vincent Van Gogh for me was his great enduring passion and love of humanity.

I recall the story when Kirk Douglas was preparing to make the academy award-winning film portraying the life of Van Gogh. He had traveled as I did to all the places where Vincent had lived and worked in his short life of thirty-seven years.

Douglas wanted to know and understand Vincent in order for him to bring Van Gogh alive in his *Lust for Life*.

While making the film Douglas received a surprising phone call from his good friend John Wayne. Wayne was very upset and angry with Kirk for making a film in which he was playing the role of a weakling.

Perhaps John Wayne's problem was a sign of the times. Perhaps there is not any time left for humanity!

Before leaving Amsterdam I had to visit the home where Anne Frank and her family were imprisoned during the German occupation of Holland in World War II. I had read Anne Frank's diary several times before arriving in the small attic rooms where she had lived and wrote her diary.

Hidden in an attic provided by friends of her family Anne would grow and mature from childhood to young womanhood. She would write of having her first period and of her hostility towards her parents whom she blamed for the condition of her life.

She would speak so sadly about peeking into a tiny crack in her window to observe other children her age going to school in the morning, playing street games and everything. Only her intelligence and her love of reading could conquer the growing fears which constantly became more and more threatening.

Her vivid imagination would sometimes take her out of the attic prison to attend dances and parties with people her own age. She could write about her feelings of love, her first kiss and romance. She could dream about the kind of mother she would be to her children who she knew she would never see.

When the end was near, the reader of her diary can easily trace the dramatic transition from childhood to young womanhood. Anne Frank was a SNOWFLAKE who was caught in the ugly web of man's insanity and for this crime the world lost a vital part of its soul forever.

18 / The Little Mermaid, a Big Storm, and More Electricity

My next stop was Copenhagen. Since my summer travel plans were flexible I had no planned schedule. When I arrived at Miss Copenhagen's apartment I learned from her neighbors that she had not been home for several days.

Her mother had taken ill and my friend had gone to the village outside of Copenhagen to be with her. Her neighbors did not have her address nor did they have any idea when she might be returning home.

There are times when you are overwhelmed by hospitality!

Miss Copenhagen's neighbors were a young couple with two small children. When they learned this was my first visit to Copenhagen they insisted I stay with them.

They wanted to show me their city which is one of the most attractive cities I had visited in Europe. Eric was a great companion and also a good beer drinker. We had a wonderful time in his famous city where a naked woman is always sitting on a rock on the seacoast.

I left a note for Miss Copenhagen explaining my regrets concerning her mother's health and I hoped we could catch up with each other at another time.

There are some events which occur in your lifetime that you have very little control over. On my unusual return to Germany I could not know what fate had planned for.

A terrible storm was raging in the Baltic Sea and by the time I reached the port to return to Puttgarden the wind velocity had reached gale force. It was the first time in over twenty years that they had to cancel the ship's crossing. It was early September and many Germans were returning from summer holidays in Scandinavia.

At the harbor there were many lines of stranded cars. I observed that most of the cars had German plates. There was only one car with Dublin, Ireland plates!

We soon learned that we would have to spend the night in our cars. When you are over six feet tall sleeping in a Renault #5 can be very unpleasant.

I was not looking forward to an enjoyable evening until I observed a single woman sitting in a big red station wagon. Her car was parked in the next lane and not too far from where I was staying.

I had already observed her walking in the rain sheltered by a hooded raincoat. Even in this crazy outfit she was looking sensational. I began to entertain thoughts of grandeur.

I also observed many people, obviously acquainted with the port, were leaving their cars and walking in the same direction. I followed the crowd and when I spotted a small grocery store my prospects for the night brightened.

When I left the store I was carrying much wine, cheese, crackers and everything required for a great party.

Returning to my car I was singing in the rain until I saw a small boy entering the big red station wagon. My heart dropped and my spirits also.

It was going to be a long, lonely and stormy night. Also it was impossible to find any sleep when I could still see the outline of the woman in the wagon.

The following morning it was still very stormy. The

ship's captain, speaking over a loud speaker system, announced that there would be a long delay in making the crossing to Germany, but he invited everyone to come on board for coffee.

When I reached the ship I noticed the woman from the red wagon was also approaching the entrance to the ship.

The wind was still blowing hard and I graciously held the door open so that she could easily enter the ship. She smiled and thanked me in German. Then realizing I was an American, she accepted my invitation to join me for coffee.

From the first exchange of introductions, our eyes were locked in a loving embrace. We would always remember that fateful September storm which brought us together for the first time and also how we almost lost each other some hours later.

When the captain finally announced our departure, I was sitting in her wagon exchanging addresses, et cetera. Since her car was in one of the first moving lanes, I realized I would not be on the same ship with her. I also discovered I had left my traveling map in her car and now she was gone with her address written on my map.

Hoping she would wait for me on the other shore, I purchased a duty-free bottle of perfume as a small surprise gift.

Sometime later, my car was on the second ship's crossing and I had a sinking feeling that perhaps we would not see each other again. After the ship docked, I could not see her or the red wagon.

It was still raining very hard and after driving a few hundred yards I gave up any thoughts of meeting her. Then I spotted her standing in the rain waving to me as my car approached her.

Our second meeting was electric! We both realized something very wonderful was happening to us and we would never deny the excitement of this feeling, which had already become very intense.

After we happily exchanged my map for a bottle of perfume we laughed in the rain for the first time. More than two years later we would be dancing and laughing in the rain and then it was even more fantastic than Puttgarden Showers.

I promised to visit her in a few days but my heart was already racing to her home. Some weeks later I knew she also had the same feelings for me.

When her first treasured letter reached Inch I was overjoyed. She had written, "When you opened the door for me on the ship that stormy day in September you also opened the door to my heart. From the first moment my eyes met yours I fell in love with you."

When I arrived at her home it was obvious that we were both out of the storm and the sun was shining very brightly on both our faces.

Her smile though was the most sensuous mouth I had ever wanted to kiss. A few days later it would happen! That same night we made love for the first time.

There was warmth and tenderness but there was also great desire and passion. We both knew that we had entered into a relationship that neither of us could control nor did we want to control.

The following morning I was standing in disbelief as she was first asking me questions and then telling me I must leave her.

We had been together for several days becoming better acquainted. I realized there was a bridge between us but I knew that we did not build this bridge and, for my part, I wanted desperately to be able to cross this bridge. I had the feeling she also knew we could cross it together.

Five years later we are still asking each other the same question only now we have become lovers.

Leaving her home I was very sad, confused and disillusioned! What had happened to us?

Perhaps it was over and I would never understand the reason nor would I ever see her again. I must confess my emotions were in very bad condition.

I had to stop thinking about her and concentrate on my next stop in Italy and my ultimate return to Inch. But maybe our meeting was wrong from the start and we became involved in an impossible relationship.

19 / Statues that Almost Breathe

Before arriving in Italy I returned to one of my favorite places in Europe. Vaduz is the capital of Liechtenstein, one of the smallest countries in Europe.

Vaduz is in a valley surrounded by the magnificent beauty of the Alps. Sidewalk cafés in Vaduz are delightful, especially when you are enjoying cappucino with an interesting woman.

Jill was from Sydney, Australia. She was a professor of economics but now she was in Europe for some months to lecture and exchange ideas with other universities.

She was flying to London the next morning, but before leaving she took my address in Ireland. Jill had never been to Ireland and would enjoy seeing me again.

While we were enjoying our coffee I could not take my eyes off our waitress. I was not the only one attracted to her ebony face and fantastic figure.

I observed men and women smiling admiringly at her perfect black mini skirt and transparent white shirt. She was a stunning knockout!

After Jill left for her hotel to pack and prepare for her speaking engagement in London the next day I decided to have a second cappucino.

When the waitress served me she smiled and asked where my friend had gone. No one ever needs to hit me over the head with a hammer in order to give me a message.

Dolcina would be leaving the café shortly and I would meet her with my car a short distance away.

I purchased a six pack of beer and we drove into the mountains to wait for the sunset. No sooner had I parked the car to find a secluded place when I observed Dolcina unashamedly stripping and lying under a giant evergreen tree.

The bright late afternoon sun was streaming through the branches shining on her body. I handed her a cold beer and thought to myself that her black body was glistening under the sun's rays and was looking like polished marble. She was magnificent!

After some minutes of enjoyable silence she turned to me smiling and asked me if I wanted to make love with her. I did not answer for a few seconds and then I replied, "What ever gave you that idea?" We were both laughing!

It was such a marvelous feeling to unwind on the side of the Alps in Vaduz.

For me Italy is one of the most exciting countries in the world. When you are in Rome you are reminded that the Roman Empire extended into every country of Western Europe.

You must also be impressed by the cultural upheaval brought about by the Renaissance period. In Florence, I had come once again to stand in awe and marvel at the work of Michelangelo.

For me to stand before the marble statues of David and Moses is to recall the genius who created this monumental work of art.

While I had been admiring the statue of David for some time I became engaged in conversation with a young woman from Paris. She also was a very enthusiastic admirer of the work of Michelangelo.

When I told her I had a young son named David who

could have been the perfect model, she smiled and told me she would like to meet my son.

My David is now twenty-six and is standing six feet, three inches of perfect body structure. His handsome face and curly head gave me the uncanny feeling in Florence that I was looking at my son.

Michelle could see how excited and astonished I was by the likeness and she had many funny jokes about how popular I would be in Paris.

I invited Michelle to join me for a good Italian dinner and some fine Chianti but she regretted having to take the evening express train back to Paris the same evening. We exchanged addresses and she was gone but you will find Michelle and me together quite frequently as my story unfolds.

Michelle is Paris and Paris is the most beautiful city in Europe! Our relationship is one of the most pleasant experiences I have ever known.

There are so many places to visit in Italy that it is mindboggling! No tourist can see Italy on a summer holiday.

Italy must be taken in small stays and it will take you a lifetime to appreciate everything this great country has to offer the foreign visitor.

Now I am in the Vatican standing in front of the most amazing work of art I have ever seen in my life. Michelangelo's white marble statue of the Virgin Mary holding her dead son Jesus Christ on her lap is a miracle.

I had seen the *Pieta* in New York many years ago and I would travel anywhere in the world to see it again. It is an emotional feeling you will experience unlike anything you have ever felt.

To study the lifeless figure of Christ after he has been

removed from the cross had to be an inspired artistic work at the highest level of achievement.

Only a true master could have reached such perfection of form and expression.

Tom Toumey, the owner of the Strand Hotel in Inch, had suggested I visit the small famous village of Loreto on the Italian Adriatic Sea. Before arriving in Loreto I had traveled south to Naples and Pompeii. I spent one day walking through the ruins of the city which had been buried by a volcanic eruption from Mt. Vesuvius which is a short distance from Pompeii.

When you are in Pompeii you feel as though you are walking through many layers of ancient history. You are also made aware of the total devastation which occurred immediately after the terrible volcanic eruption.

Back on the Adriatic Sea, Loreto is only a short distance from the famous seaport town of Ancona. Perched high on the side of a mountain is the cathedral I had come to see.

Arriving at the church I was happy to find a very small and intimate hotel just opposite the "miracle site!" I checked in with a young hotel manager who was the son of the owner of the hotel.

I was very delighted to be staying in a family-run and owned hotel. I was also very pleased by the delicious smell coming from the kitchen where the owner's wife was making special tomato and garlic sauce for the evening meal.

While I was having a conversation with the young man telling him my reason for coming to Loreto he knowingly smiled and said, "Here comes the priest from the church!"

Sure enough, for the next half hour the priest, speaking perfect English, answered all my questions concerning Loreto.

"Yes," he replied, it is authentic and it has the seal of

approval from the Pope. Centuries ago, he continued, a wealthy Italian from Loreto had visited Israel and had traveled to visit the home of the Holy Family.

Fearing that this sacred home could be destroyed, he was able to purchase the home of the Holy Family. Then after numbering all the stones, he had everything shipped to the location where you will find it today inside the cathedral.

He told of many miracles which have occurred in connection with the Holy Family shrine. Before he returned to the cathedral, he invited me to attend his evening mass in the Church of the Holy Family.

After enjoying a sumptuous macaroni and cheese banquet washed down with homemade vintage red wine, I crossed the street to the famous cathedral. Entering the cathedral, I immediately saw the small, simple stone dwelling which was the home of Mary, Jesus and Joseph. It was an overwhelming feeling to realize that I was about to enter the Home of the Man who would change the course of human history.

Inside I was joined by nineteen very old women who were covered in black from their heads to their feet. The diminutive priest had already started the mass and as he was speaking in Italian, I was only able to follow the principal parts of the sermon with which I am familiar.

I observed all the women going from wall to wall kissing the stones in such reverance that I was deeply moved. It was not a very large home which housed the Holy Family, but then everything about the life of Jesus Christ was marked by simplicity.

A year later, I would be in Israel. I would attend mass in the Church of the Nativity in Bethlehem on Christmas Eve. I would also visit Jeruselum and walk in the footsteps of the Savior as He walked with His cross to be crucified.

20 / Back in Inch

It was October, 1985 and I am back in my home in Inch. Mary and Dan invite me for dinner. They want a blow by blow account of all my European travels. It was good to be back in County Kerry enjoying all the Irish treasures that I loved so much!

There was a small stack of mail with postmarks from everywhere. The letters were from my family who were anticipating my flying home for a brief Christmas and New Year holiday.

I was reminded by these letters that I was approaching the end of my first year abroad. I also was wondering about the kind of reception I would receive from my wife and family after one year's absence.

There were also many letters from my friends in Europe. Letters from Jill, Michelle and Dr. Aquarius in Germany all of whom were looking forward to visiting me in Ireland. It would be their first trip to the emerald island and they were all very excited.

I had a telegram from Dolcina which simply read: "Urgent, please call immediately!"

The telegram was already one week old. When I called at the number she had given me, I was advised that her summer contract had expired. She left an address in Lisbon, Portugal, where I could reach her if the telegram did not get to me in time.

A few weeks later, she answered my letter, telling me she had wanted to come to Ireland to live with me. Sometime later we would meet again, but then she would be living with a German.

The last time I had entertained three women in my home in Inch, we were like a family, but this time it would be very different. Fortunately, I was able to arrange all arrivals and departures at convenient intervals from late October to mid-December when I would be flying to New York.

I was very excited making elaborate plans to visit all my favorite places which I knew they would appreciate. Mary and Dan O'Shea were almost as anxious about the arrival of my guests as I was.

One night at Dan Foley's Pub, Dan O'Shea jokingly teased me about how I could keep up the fast pace. I told him my secret! Peanut butter and honey! Also, to get to bed early. Dan laughed so hard he had the entire pub in laughter.

Jill, Michelle and Dr. Aquarius are all successful, professional women of the world. They represent the very finest character of women who are in total control of their lives. Only Michelle, who has a lover in Paris, does not have children.

All three are world travelers who visit places where they can learn about the people and the culture of the country. They are not tourists and this is why I enjoy their companionship.

There was never any doubt in my mind about how much they enjoyed their first Irish experience. They all fell in love with the Irish people, their country and yes, they were even able to make great jokes about forecasting Irish weather.

Before I left Ireland to return to New Jersey for the holidays I received treasured letters from all three women. Dr. Aquarius invited me to her home for her birthday in

February and Jill sent me a letter expressing her feelings about Inch and County Kerry.

I want to share a part of this letter with you because it is the intense feelings of a woman who fell in love with Ireland:

> Old stone walls dividing fields of aqua-green mountains blue and misty in the early morning light. The steel-gray sea streaked with breakers silver white. Seaweed on the beach above the waters glossy sheen. Red fuchsia in the hedges along the narrow lanes. The bleat of distant sheep and the song of mountain streams. Clouds suddenly divided where a shaft of sunlight beams. Russet colored hillsides washed by gentle rains.
>
> The aroma of the turf from the embers of the fire. The warmth inside the cottage setting high above the sea. Those clear blue eyes smiling down at me. The shining inner light of our awakening desire. Blinding with the murmur of the endless waves below. The joy of making love in the candle's golden glow.

21 / Reunion . . .

When my Aer Lingus flight left Shannon Airport and began the 3000-mile trip across the Atlantic, I was already in deep thought. It was just over one year since I had left my family and while I was anxious to see everyone, I realized that we had all changed. Nothing would ever be the same again.

My mind was drifting again into my past life. My children enjoyed the story my wife told them about how we met. "When I was 14," she said, "I slipped coming out of church one snowy Sunday morning. Your father ran to me and lifted me off the ground. Six years later, on March 24, 1951, we were married in the very same church where I first met your father."

I know now that you can only experience one perfect honeymoon in a lifetime.

We both came from hard-working middle class families and our modest wedding reception gifts from relatives and friends provided six hundred dollars for our week in Canada. I still had one year to go before university graduation while my wife, Claire (who I call Buzzy), was working in Manhattan as a secretary.

When my wife's boss learned that we were taking a Greyhound bus to Canada, he offered his new car as a loan/gift for our honeymoon trip.

After a late start from the wedding reception, we reached the small town of Liberty, New York. We checked into a small hotel with "ours" and the first bottle of red wine we ever drank. "Ours" were two copper mugs we had purchased for our first drink together as husband and wife.

When we were awakened by a loud crowing rooster early the next morning, we were still virgins. "Ours" were sitting on the table alongside an empty wine bottle. Later that night in Ithaca, New York (Cornell University), we consummated our marriage.

Early the next morning, after observing the condition of the bed sheets, we made a hasty departure for Niagara Falls. We stayed at the Brock Hotel, which was facing the gigantic Canadian horseshoe falls. Because we were looking like honeymooners, we were aware of the special treatment we received.

Our suite was perfect with flower arrangements, fruit and a view to the falls. When we arrived for our evening meal, we were led to a window table with a spectacular view of the falls.

At night, from the dining room, special colored lights illuminate the falls while the misty spray from the powerful falls is hitting the ceiling-to-floor window pane. It was a touch of class! There were flowers, candlelight, soft music and we were very much in love.

Returning from Canada, we moved into a small walk-up flat which became a love nest for the first year of our married life. The honeymoon continued and we became even more intense with each new awareness in our relationship as man and woman.

It was very beautiful! I would arrive home before my wife every evening and prepare our dinner table with flowers, candles, et cetera. It was always exciting to stand at the railroad station waiting for her train to arrive from New York.

Always when we saw each other, at that moment our

hearts would beat a little faster. Weekends were always the happiest days when we could wake up making love which we continued from the night before. We were like Adam and Eve in the garden of paradise wanting to explore each other with every fiber of our bodies.

Every Saturday morning, I would go to our friend Lillian who had a small flower shop. She waited for me as though I were the small boy she had always wanted. I would hand her a quarter and sometimes fifty cents when I was flush. She would give me my small bouquet for my wife whom she also was very happy to see.

We had all become such close friends that one weekend Lillian invited my wife and me to come with her to a small cabin she owned in the mountains of North Jersey.

Lillian was already in her seventies and she had a nervous condition which my wife and I found to be both maddening as well as hilarious.

During this unforgettable weekend vacation, we had an opportunity to observe Lillian close up for the first time.

Lillian was convinced that she was the best driver in New Jersey and that everyone else on the road was dangerous. Traveling at great speed, Lillian would suddenly be seized by a violent body movement which caused her foot to hit the accelerator so forcefully that the car would jump forward at race driver's speed.

Motorists in other cars would panic in their efforts to escape into another lane when they saw her coming. All the while she would scream at the other drivers for getting in her way.

Lillian also had false teeth which she must have outgrown when she was fifty. Every time she became nervous and started to shout out the car window at other drivers, her loose fitting teeth would fall away from her gums.

The result of this was a cackling, choking sound which

produced uncontrollable laughter from Buzzy and me. Undaunted, Lillian would also begin laughing at our amusement. The entire two hour drive was better than a day at a monkey farm. There was no question that we all loved one another even in heavy traffic.

My wife was an Irish beauty. Both her mother and father came from large Irish families. Her beauty for me was awesome and often I felt inadequate standing in the shadow of her radiance.

Working in Manhattan, she was always dressed with great taste. Form-fitting clothes with tight skirts falling just below the knee were fashionable in the early fifties.

Her long dark hair fell majestically on her shoulders. Her face was flawless with the clearest pale· blue eyes I have ever seen.

But her figure was the most alluring and arresting feature and could drive a man wild. No matter what she was wearing, she could never conceal the the full ripeness of her womanhood. I would daydream in my college classes for hours anticipating seeing her at the end of each day.

Shortly after we were married, I taught Buzzy how to drive. We had managed to save fifty dollars and we found a 1935 canvas top Plymouth.

We had more fun with our first car than anyone could ever imagine. The car can only be described as a bomb and today I know it would never pass inspection in any country.

One day, shortly after we had purchased the car, we went for a drive through our local park. Dark clouds opened up with such a heavy downpour on our canvas top roof that we were afraid it would cave in.

Then it happened! The water started to drip into the car until finally we realized we would have to carry an umbrella in the car whenever it was raining. Also, there were missing floor boards and if you hit a hole in the road, water would splash all over your feet and legs.

The used car dealer had warned us not to take any long trips because the engine was burning up more oil than petrol. We did not believe him.

Buzzy's brother, Billy, had invited us for a weekend in Boston, which was a four hour drive from New Jersey. A short time after we were on the New York–New England Thruway, our car became engulfed in a huge cloud of black smoke. Passing motorists were looking back at our car in utter disbelief. Other more concerned motorists would pull alongside of our slow moving bomb to warn us that we were on fire.

I had wisely purchased a five-gallon can of oil which the car consumed before we had reached Billy's home in Boston. By the time we returned to Bayonne, we both realized the bomb had to go to the graveyard.

While we were at Billy's, I realized my first marriage shock. In the middle of our first night, Buzzy began shaking very violently in our bed while she was sleeping. Alarmed, I went to get her brother who was a nurse.

When we came back to her, she was having an epiletic seizure. I stood by helplessly watching her beautiful face change into a grotesque and tortured mask of agony.

For weeks and months I could not forget the horror of that first nightmare in Boston. Every time her body would make a jerking movement in bed, I was alert and horrified.

I began to hate myself for feeling this way, but I could not control my fear of seeing her in a seizure. Even after she had seen a medical specialist and was taking drugs to control the problem I could not overcome my anxiety.

There were nights in bed when she would begin to shake and she would ask me to hold her very close to support her trembling body. It was nerve-racking for the both of us and she was only twenty-one.

One month before graduation from Seton Hall University where I earned a B.S. degree in political science, I signed a contract to teach the fifth grade in a school at the Jersey shore near Asbury Park.

Before leaving Bayonne, we decided to take a short vacation in the Maine woods. For several years I had been receiving a Strout Catalog listing homes and vacation spots in New England.

Buzzy and I laughed when we read the Maine listing: "Pappy Morell's Cabin on Lake Molunkus, boat included, $25 per week." When we arrived at the Molunkus bus depot, Pappy Morell looked astonished to see a young couple all the way from New Jersey coming to the wilderness of Maine.

I told him I was a big fan of Henry David Thoreau who had lived in the New England wilderness for two years. His famous book, *Walden Pond*, had inspired me to follow in his footsteps for one week.

Pappy apparently did not appreciate my New Jersey sense of humor. Looking directly at my wife he said, "This is bear country and the hunting season begins in two weeks."

He also advised us that our lonely cabin on the lake was over ten miles from the nearest neighbor and shopping center. We asked him if he could drive us to a market where we could buy supplies for our vacation week.

When we arrived at our isolated cabin, Buzzy cooked a large turkey which would be our special diet for a relaxing week of boating, swimming and watching out for bears.

It was like having a second honeymoon. Each morning after breakfast, we would pack a big picnic lunch and then we would take turns steering our small motorboat to secluded places on Molunkus Lake. Buzzy was looking very gorgeous in her tight fitting, pink bathing suit which I had tried unsuccessfully to get off her for a nude swim party.

One day we were in the center of the giant lake when suddenly a violent storm erupted. Of all times to develop engine trouble.

The calm, placid lake was looking like an angry ocean of waves and pouring rain.

We spotted a man in the distance waving us in the direction of the cabin. We were moving with the current and rowing to his shore cabin was not too difficult.

He had a warm fire in his cabin and we could see big Maine potatoes and salt pork cooking in his old iron stove.

During our great Maine lunch the storm had worsened and he invited us to spend the night with him in his comfortable lodge. He assured us the storm would be over in the morning and we would be able to cross the lake to our cabin after he had looked at the engine problem.

He told us his grandfather was a full blooded Penobscot Indian and that he had inherited his love of nature's wilderness from Indian ancestry. His strong love for the loneliness of the woods and wildlife was a retirement dream and brought him to his cabin every year at this time.

We had been very fortunate to meet this wonderful descendent of the Penobscot tribe who enthralled us with his interesting stories of the lifestyle of the Maine Indian tribes of former times.

My wife and I had often talked about moving to New England to enjoy a more peaceful living environment in a part of America that has incredible natural beauty, especially the rugged Maine Atlantic coastline.

When we returned to our new apartment in Asbury Park, New Jersey, we were both relaxed and prepared for the next important chapter in our lives together. We had no car but I was able to take a twenty minute bus ride to my school in Wanamassa.

Buzzy was expecting our first child in November, 1952. We were very happy to learn that the school doctor was also a wonderful baby doctor who would become one of our best friends.

Dr. Donald Bowne was an extraordinary man. He knew the medical problem which my wife was suffering from but he reassured her that the pheno-barbitol and diolanten which she was taking would control her during labor.

When the day arrived for her delivery he remained by her side throughout the day holding her hand to give her comfort and security. He was like a father in his special gentle manner.

When Warren was finally born he was happy for the three of us. Fourteen months later Dr. Bowne delivered our first daughter and he immediately called her Wendy to go with Warren.

And so it was! Wendy was born with such long jet black hair that the nurses tied a large red ribbon in her hair immediately after she was born.

My first teaching contract was for $2,500 per year. At this time teachers were paid once a month. My net take home pay was $208 per month.

I was able to find a job tutoring disabled students after school. I also sold encyclopedias and Wearever pots and pans on weekends.

Several evenings every week I also had a job in a supermarket. We would never forget those first years of struggling to make ends meet but always, at the end of the month, there was a search for pennies to buy something that was urgently needed.

If our love was not so strong we could never have

laughed at those early years of month to month struggle. I also recall the countless nights of getting up at all hours to give Warren and Wendy their bottle of formula milk when they were infants.

My wife and I were afraid of the serious consequences of her having a seizure while feeding the baby after waking up from a dead sleep. There were some days while I was teaching when I could hardly keep my eyes open and I would wonder how long I could keep up the pace.

Likewise, Buzzy had to raise two small, very active children and maintain a comfortable home and handle many other responsibilities about which she never complained.

She loved to watch me rolling on the floor playing with the children every night before we would put them to bed. We both knew how fortunate we were to have such a wonderful family.

I was teaching children between the ages of ten and eleven during the first years of my twenty-six year teaching career and I enjoyed every year of my relationship with thousands of young students.

Looking back on my first years of teaching I can still see the bright young faces of students who loved to be challenged into discussions about the history of America.

While I wanted them to appreciate the greatness of our democratic system I also wanted them to think in an objective and critical manner.

When we entered into serious discussions about the tragic demise of the American Indian and the barbaric treatment of the American slave I could see the sadness in their young faces. I would remind them that too often American history books ignore the cultural history and lifestyle of the American Indian and the African slave.

I assigned every student to research particular Indian

tribes as well as their tribal leaders. They were always astonished by their discovery and were always eager to report their research findings to the class.

Why was the white settler pushing the Indian off his land? Why did the pioneer destroy the buffalo which was the very life of the Indian family?

Why did we import thousands and finally millions of black Africans to be sold into southern plantations? Who were the abolitionists and why did they want to free the American slaves from human bondage?

Their parents could hardly wait to meet this new teacher who was monopolizing their dinner conversations with probing questions from their children.

Underlying all these discussions I had employed the whole concept of the American Constitution and the significance of protecting and defending the rights of all human beings. If the American democracy is perfect then it must guarantee justice, freedom and equality for all its citizens.

These were the important principles and values upon which I reminded our students our government must either stand or fall, as the case for human dignity and respect moves forward.

My popularity as a teacher of academic freedom was impressing countless students and parents and they were concerned with the board of education members who had to decide whether or not to grant me tenure as an educator.

By the mid-fifties I had moved up to the eighth grade graduating class working with young teenagers. It was a very exciting and challenging time in my teaching career.

Senator Joseph McCarthy of Wisconsin was on a national witch-hunt for communists in America. I had assigned my students to do a critical research comparing the social, economic and political structure of the U.S.A. and U.S.S.R.

I advised the students to write to the American and Russian embassies in Washington for current information. The students were inundated with books, magazines, pamphlets, et cetera, from the Soviet Embassy while at the same time there was a poverty of information from the American Embassy.

Many of my students' parents were employed at Fort Monmouth military installation in our county. Senator McCarthy was investigating communist infiltration at Fort Monmouth.

My students' parents made frantic calls to the school administration and board of education complaining about my research project. They were worried about their children receiving mail from the Russian Embassy but also they were in a panic concerning their jobs at Fort Monmouth.

It was one of the worst periods in American history. When the infamous work of McCarthyism could reach into a small classroom I knew America was in trouble. Also, because I had refused to change my views on total academic freedom during this critical period, I became a controversial teacher.

In 1958 Laurie, our second daughter, was born. The same year we bought a new car and our first small Cape Cod home. I had earned my Masters Degree at Rutgers University and my teaching salary was being increased every year.

During the summer I worked as a swimming instructor and camp counselor. The 1950s and 1960s were years of professional growth and family happiness.

After our return from England in 1964 with our fourth child, David, we were back in our second home on the lake in West Allenhurst where we would remain for many years.

On July 26, 1967, our fifth and last child, John, was born. Also, I was elected as a councilman in our township of thirty-five thousand citizens.

At this time I was also the supervising teacher with a staff of twenty teachers from the junior and senior high schools. My star had risen and my family life was in a state of bliss.

We have an expression in America which says if you are climbing too fast be careful "your big bubble may burst!"

Returning to New Jersey after an enjoyable summer educational grant at Dartmouth College in New Hampshire, I was advised by the board of education that my position as supervisor was terminated.

In September, 1967 I would return to my former job as an eighth grade history teacher. The board of education, with the advice of their attorney, said I could be fired the same as a football coach who had a bad season.

It was not necessary to give any reasons why I was fired and since I only had tenure as a teacher I could be returned to my old position. I had other ideas but first I wanted to discuss the matter with my family because I knew it would be a difficult time for all of us.

My oldest son Warren broke the ice! "You have always encouraged us to fight for our rights and for justice."

It was not so easy for me to oppose the entire board of education when I knew my family would suffer from the press publicity as well as a long legal battle in the courts. I went to my friend Charlie Frankel who was regarded as one of the best attorneys in Monmouth County.

After we publicly announced that we would fight the

board's decision we were on page one in all the local and county newspapers.

The state teacher's organization joined the battle as well as the state board of education. We were challenging the high court to determine whether I could be fired without specific charges.

Some years later I would learn what the charges were from my colleagues in the teaching profession.

The rumors were that I had an affair with a board member's wife, I had raped a student and that I was a homosexual alcoholic, et cetera. It was terrible and some of these vicious lies reached the ears of my family and personal friends.

My personal opinion was that I was an outspoken liberal Democrat and I was removed by a Republican conservative board of education. I wanted to take my case to the people and let the chips fall where they may.

There are nine members on the board of education and every year three members must stand for re-election. In the first year of my legal battle, three of my personal democratic friends defeated three republican members of the board.

In the second year of my slow-moving case, three more democrats defeated three republican board members. In the third year the State Superior Court ruled that my position as a supervisor of teachers was equivalent to the position of football coach and could be terminated without cause.

My democratic friends defeated the final three old republicans and quickly voted me back to the position of supervisor of the department. My family, my students and I rejoiced over this exercise in democracy.

Something else had happened to me during the three year battle to win justice. I became a well-known name and face in my county and in the state of New Jersey. This would help me later when I decided to run for senator.

Our Irish flight attendant was reminding me to fasten my safety belt as we were approaching J.F.K. airport in New York. My youngest daughter Laurie had invited me to stay at her home in Point Pleasant during my brief holiday in New Jersey.

For reasons I will explain later Laurie was the only member of my family who seemed to understand why I was living abroad. She was also the only one who faithfully continued to write to me during my years of travel around the world.

I knew that Laurie was missing me and for this reason she has a special place in my heart always.

The whole family was invited to my daughter Wendy's home in Little Silver, New Jersey, for the Christmas Eve dinner celebration. It is impossible for me to explain why I was feeling uncomfortable in the presence of my own family. It was as though I did not really belong there.

My wife and I exchanged friendly glances but we both knew that we could never return to our former relationship as husband and wife. My three sons Warren, David and John were all in good form as were my two sons by law Bruce and Larry.

They were all happy with my gift of handmade Irish knit sweaters and will always think of me when they wear them.

My new grandson Brad was celebrating his first Christmas and he was the star attraction. When the party was over I was already contemplating my return to Inch.

It was obvious to me that in one year I had become a stranger to my own family, and of course, I had to admit to myself that I deserved it.

My wife had not worked all the years she was raising

our family but now she was employed by National Cash Register. She had gone to a school training program in Dayton, Ohio and while competing against young college graduates she finished number one in her class.

This was no surprise to me. My wife is not only attractive, but she is extremely intelligent.

Buzzy was, is and always will be the pulse and heartbeat of our family. My children all love their mother with a devotion and loyalty that makes me very proud and happy.

Everyone in my family had plans for New Year's Eve. My wife was doing what she liked best of all. She was babysitting with her grandson Bradford.

I invented an invitation to be in New York with Aphrodite and Nefertiti. Everyone smiled indulgently!

Actually I had run into an old friend in Point Pleasant who was a young nurse. Maggie had no plans for New Year's Eve.

We dined on lobster and fine white wine and danced until the magic hour of 1986. We spent the rest of the New Year celebration in a speechless embrace.

Later in the spring of 1986 Maggie would make her first trip to Ireland. In 1988, when she learned that I was very sick in Greece, she rushed to my bedside.

Maggie is another snowflake with her own special story that is so familiar to so many women who are disappointed with twentieth century men.

22 / . . . And Return

I must admit I was relieved and delighted to be back in Ireland! I had left my car with Joe and Kitty, two of my closest Irish friends who live near Shannon airport.

When you walk into Kitty's kitchen there is always a large pot on the stove with the most delightful aroma you can imagine.

Joe and Kitty have a very large family and many grandchildren. They also have many friends and a very popular B&B home.

After a great Irish stew, I invited everyone to Dirty Nellie's Pub for a nightcap. When we entered the famous pub standing in the shadow of Bunratty Castle we were greeted by a large group of singing Americans.

Men dressed in green and holding small martini glasses were hanging over a piano player who was blaring "Oklahoma." I was totally disgusted!

They had spent a small fortune to come to Ireland to drink martinis and sing to the strains of Oklahoma! Joe and Kitty, knowing me all too well, observed my reaction.

There are two small side rooms in the pub with warm turf fires. Also you always will find Irish entertainers with an accordian or a guitar.

I told them if they could drown out the sounds of Oklahoma for the rest of the night I would buy their drinks! In five minutes the sounds of American music became a whisper. The raised voices of Irish music was pure magic and quickly turned the pub into an Irish Guinness delight.

Joe and Kitty were laughing! Kitty was saying, "John, it is so good to have you back in Ireland."

Yes, it was very good to be home in Eire once again. After a few beers I told Joe why I had to return to Europe!

Perhaps I should have been a nineteenth century American. Like my Irish Catholic and German Mormon ancestors I would have loved their challenge.

It was a time when millions of immigrants were lured to the American shore. We were a nation of struggling foreigners who had the muscle and vision to move America forward.

My country has grown complacent and self-indulgent trapped in a tinsel society of illusion. We are somewhere between "Dallas" and "Dynasty" with Rambo leading the pack.

This kinder and gentler society is waving Star Wars into the face of the twenty-first century and no one is even thinking about it.

"Joe, my life is too precious to be wasted on Sunday afternoon N.F.L. football games or violent and sadistic news reporting."

There is much more in Europe and in the Eastern world to awaken in me the spirit of another lifetime. For me, this is a twenty-first century challenge which I welcome with all my heart and soul.

When you remove America's nuclear missile power and stare into the face of a government that owes over 100 billion dollars in debts at home and 200 billion dollars in foreign trade debts, then you are looking at a marginal nation. I will welcome the day when the American people wake up and return to humanity and reality.

The American people will get no help or find no sympathy from the parasites in their government or in their religious institutions.

23 / Dr. Aquarius and Her Son Jonathan

In February, 1986, Dr. Aquarius invited me to visit Germany and celebrate her birthday. She wanted me to also spend some time in Berlin where I could observe the lifestyle on both sides of the infamous wall.

I was very excited to see her again and for the next three years our relationship became very intense and sometimes bordered on disaster.

Her holidays away from her family and the hospital where she worked were spent with me in Ireland, Portugal, Greece, Turkey and Egypt. Aquarius was very active in her profession and sometimes I followed her to Austria and Switzerland where European medical conferences were being held.

We would have time to ski in the magnificent alpine air, take long walks in snowy forests and even enjoy a unique snowball fight in bed.

On the long winter evenings we enjoyed sitting by the fire, dining on fondu and French white wine. It was the best of times for both of us.

When she drove to Berlin I could feel her vibrations of nostalgia even before we reached the apartment where she had spent the early years of her life. Her building was one of the few surviving structures that remained after the Americans and Russians had leveled Berlin at the close of the war.

Taking me on my first visit to the Berlin Wall, she recalled the terrible day when Russians hastily constructed the wall.

Friends, neighbors and even relatives would be separated in that tragic moment in history. The madness and insanity of World War II continues with no end in sight even as we approach the twenty-first century.

She also remembered the historic day President John Kennedy came to West Berlin to make his famous speech telling the world that he also was a "Berliner."

On our second day in Berlin we went through the East Berlin security check point. She invited me to the well-known Three Penny Opera House.

Before the performance we had time to tour some parts of the city and to stop at a small bar for a drink. I had already felt her tension when we entered the eastern sector, but when I became engaged in a conversation with a communist she became very nervous and even angry.

"You will never understand Berlin and you will never understand me," she said and then turned away and left me standing in the middle of hell! It was our first argument and I did not know what had happened.

Later, we sat silently in the same theatre where Adolf Hitler frequently was entertained, and even after we arrived at her apartment, there was only confused and painful silence.

During the long drive back to her home the following day, I contemplated the fact that no American cities were ever bombed in world wars! No American child had ever experienced the horrible fear of an air raid.

Perhaps I was asking too much in telling Aquarius to put the past behind her. Maybe it is impossible to change our lives or to reverse the course of history.

I thought also that our personal relationship might

not survive. And yet, there was, from our very first physical contact, an attraction which transcended personal differences.

We also shared many intellectual interests in art, music and especially literature. Aquarius was, for me, the saddest and happiest person I have ever known and for these reasons I could never leave her.

She was only three when the American bombers were unloading their deadly bombs on Berlin. She recalled those childhood years of a turnip diet and her daily search for a piece of coal or wood for the apartment fire which was never warm enough.

But, there were worse things than childhood fears, hunger and poverty. Aquarius was one of the countless victims of the worst war in human history. Her sensitive youthful awareness of what had happened to her and her country was something she could never forget.

One day, we were engaged in a serious political discussion and I could see tears filling up in her sad brown eyes. "I am not proud to be a German," she had told me.

Just as I had visited the attic prison of Anne Frank, so also had Aquarius painfully been compelled to visit this place.

Several times she would travel to Israel. Her mind was constantly tormented and tortured by an event she was unfortunately born into and could never escape. There was absolutely nothing I could do to relieve her pain.

Her son Jonathan had been patiently awaiting our arrival from Berlin. He was anxious to talk with me and learn about my opinion of the city, the people, everything.

Jonathan was also very intellectual and extremely sensitive. He even had his mother's facial expressions. He knew his mother and I had many differences, but he was always hopeful that we would remain together.

For him, this was very important. He once confided in me that it was not so necessary to agree about everything so long as I always came back to their home on the edge of the forest.

When Jonathan had reached the mandatory draft age he had made a decision not to go into the military service. He told me privately that his country was responsible for starting both World War I and World War II and so he would never wear a uniform or carry a gun. Jonathan had to sign official documents stating why he volunteered to work in a nursing home in preference to going into the military.

His statement to the government in Bonn was very clear and explicit. He was not proud of the record of German military aggression and the terrible consequences which followed.

Jonathan was ashamed of the history of his country and if he could not escape this awful inheritance at least he could control his own destiny.

Jonathan put on a white uniform and volunteered to help the aged and infirm people of his country rather than be a continuing part of the military establishment, regardless of his personal consequences.

I am telling Jonathan's story because it is very important to know that there are many young men throughout the world who are committed to helping humanity. What a wonderful and sensational story it would be if the world's journalists could one day write this headline across the front page of every newspaper: "Today in Germany every eligible draftee has rejected the military uniform in favor of a white uniform of love and peace!"

Aquarius was not surprised when I became involved with Jonathan in several demonstrations against the awesome presence of American nuclear missiles throughout

West Germany. She also knew how unhappy and uncomfortable I was to see and hear American fighter jets screaming over her home every day.

How sad and angry I was to be sitting on her porch listening to the constant rattle of guns practicing on the target range in the forest.

One Saturday morning while we were enjoying breakfast I heard a very loud rumbling sound which caused the house to shake. I looked out the window and I could not believe my eyes.

A long column of armoured tanks was coming through the forest and was headed in the direction of Aquarius' home. It was incredible!

They were playing war games, only they were boys in uniforms conducting a mock battle against the enemy.

After Japan, Germany is one of the most densely populated nations in the world. Every West German is living on an American mock war battlefield.

Every German also knows they have five minutes to live once the U.S. and Russia launch a nuclear attack. It is the same in East Germany where the Russians are playing the same insane games everyday.

Every American should live in Germany for one month to learn how the American taxpayer's money is being wasted everyday on the madness of boys playing war games. Every American should also know that a peace treaty was never signed between the allies and West Germany.

West Germany is an occupied nation of over sixty million people. The American military has designated Germany as its private battlefield with close to one half million military personnel. Untold billions of taxpayers' dollars are supporting this insane madness.

By contrast, it makes Great Britain's military folly in Northern Ireland look like child's play.

If I came to Europe to expand my mind in cultural pursuits, I also had to be exposed to the ever present sickness of American "Rambo-ism" in Germany.

You should ask your congressman and congresswoman how much it has cost Americans to remain in Germany since 1945! The figure will stagger you! Also, your representatives in Washington will never tell you the truth!

One night after dinner, Aquarius and I went for a long walk in the evergreen-scented forest. We were very relaxed and quiet for a very long time before she asked me what I was thinking about.

I told her it was time for me to leave. I had remained in Germany too long and I wanted to take a trip to Russia.

The next night, when she returned from the hospital, she was very excited. She had called her travel agent and discovered there was a German charter flight leaving for Moscow in two weeks.

I immediately made contact with the American Ambassador, Arthur Hartman, in Moscow, advising him of my plans.

The fantastic memory of my first trip to Russia and the reception I received at the airport will always be one of the happiest stories I have ever told. I was the only American with sixty-five German tourists who arrived in Frankfurt for what would become my most unusual traveling venture.

24 / In Russia You Sit Where You Want

I could see the Russian insignia on the Aeroflot aircraft which was standing in the middle of the field. We all walked across the field and climbed the steps to enter the plane.

I was already smiling because from the outside, the aircraft appeared to be a World War II bomber. Once on board, I realized I was correct. This was a "no frills flight" and I was loving it!

I took an unnumbered seat in the rear of the aircraft and noticed the German group moving about the plane waiting to be told where they should sit.

Within a few minutes, after we had all boarded the plane, we were taxiing on the runway. There were no signs about safety belts, smoking, et cetera.

Finally, two Russian flight attendants emerged from the pilot's cockpit.

When the Germans asked where they should sit, the answer was for me the beginning of a fantastic "to Russia with love." "In Russia you sit anywhere you want to sit."

It may sound funny, but this crazy Aeroflot plane made me think of Charles Linbergh and his 1927 "Spirit of St. Louis" flight across the Atlantic. I can still picture the scene from my rear window seat.

From our Frankfurt, Germany take-off until our arrival at Moscow airport, it can only be described as the most romantic air travel I will ever experience.

I had the distinct impression that I could smell kerosene when we finally left the ground at the end of the runway. We never reached an altitude where I was unable to see the objects on the ground and our air speed was equally romantic.

When the pilot happily announced we were over Soviet territory I could see fields of snow and farm houses.

My heart was rejoicing! I was inside the Soviet Union and I knew the days and nights before me would change my life forever. It was the beginning of another lifetime!

Standing in the customs line, I was called by name and introduced to a young security officer who led me to another private room.

I was informed they did not want to detain me and asked if I had any reading material in my luggage. I told them I had two books and they requested me to please show them the books.

The young customs officer who was very short and stern looking took the first book, *Confession* by Leo Tolstoy, and, after quickly turning the pages, he requested that I produce my second book.

When I handed him John Reed's *Ten Days that Shook the World* he was grinning from ear to ear. In perfect English he smiled and said, "I hope you will enjoy your stay in Moscow."

I thanked him and then replied, "It is a great pleasure to be in Russia for the first time in my life." We warmly shook hands and I was led to a waiting driver and car.

A second Soviet official introduced me to my driver and told me that the driver spoke English and would be available to me throughout my tour in Moscow. He also added that in the event I did not require his services for any reason, my driver would understand.

Riding to my hotel, I was already thanking Senator

Alan Cranston and Ambassador Arthur Hartman for what was happening to me.

After I had registered and was given a security card for entering and leaving the hotel, I observed the German touring group coming into the hotel. The tour guide leader had been very upset by my swift departure from the airport and was very relieved to see me.

I informed him that since the guided tour of Moscow would be conducted in the German language, he should not worry about me.

I told him I had made arrangements for an English-speaking guide and I would be fine. He was apprehensive, but he understood my desire to travel independently.

My driver's name was Nicky and I could see he was very popular in the hotel and he would be a perfect guide.

Nicky introduced me to an Oriental receptionist who spoke English with a fantastic accent! She told me if I had any requests she would do her best to accommodate my wishes.

She could only guess what pleasure was already passing through my mind when I smiled and told her how happy I was.

My first request was to attend the world-renowned Bolshoi Ballet on my first night in Moscow. It was the opening night of the famous *Swan Lake* and it was a total sell-out however, she would try to accommodate me.

Ten minutes later, while I was unpacking my bags, the receptionist called and asked me if I could be ready in forty-five minutes. I would have a place at the Bolshoi.

A quick shower, shave and into my fabulous blue suit and I was on my way to the ballet.

Nicky enjoyed my insistence on sitting in front with him so we could enjoy a cigarette together. Before the day had ended, we had become understanding friends. He also quickly realized that I was not a typical tourist!

When we arrived at the ballet, he handed me a card of introduction and told me to pass the line and present the card at the door. I told him I did not want to jump the line nor do I enjoy other people moving to the front of a line.

He smiled, opened my door and took me to another stage entrance door.

Once inside the historic theatre, I was taken to a young man in formal tuxedo dress who gave me a program and small opera glasses. He told me the ballet company was honored to have an American guest and asked me to follow him to my seat in the theatre.

When we had walked up a flight of stairs, he paused and grinning very broadly, he pulled back a very heavy velvet curtain and said, "This is the Imperial Box which was reserved for the last czar of all Russia, Czar Nicholas and Empress Alexandria.

"We hope you will enjoy the *Swan Lake* performance." I was astonished!

I had read Robert Massie's *Nicholas and Alexandra* and I was familiar with all the events which led to the tragic massacre of the entire royal family at Ekaterinburg on July 16, 1917.

Even before I sat down in the ornate gold gilt imperial chair, I was dumbfounded with memories of all the events which led up to the Communist Revolution of 1917.

When I sat down to await the opening curtain I could feel hundreds of tiny opera glasses trained on the Imperial Box.

I will always remember the opening scene on the stage. I was blinded by the spectacular sight of marble white, statue-like motionless figures.

Gleaming thin white arms extended with their elegant fingers pointing outward. Dressed all in pure white satin, they all stood motionless with a slight bending of their knees and tiny waists.

When the conductor raised his baton for the opening note it was enough to take your breath away. The entire cast in unison made a perfect pirouette and the *Swan Lake* ballet performance had begun.

I could feel my eyes filling with tears of rapture. I am certain my heart and pulse rate increased because my joy was overwhelming.

Never in my life had I ever witnessed a ballet performance so magnificent as the Bolshoi in Moscow.

When I was leaving the theatre I realized something very wonderful was happening to me in Moscow. I also thought of John Reed and his brief life here in Moscow where he died at the age of thirty-seven.

Warren Beatty had produced, directed and starred in the true story of Reed's *Ten Days that Shook the World*. Beatty's portrayal of John Reed in his film *Reds* won international acclaim.

John Reed may have been the last of the really outstanding idealistic journalists in the twentieth century. When John Reed died in Moscow, Lenin declared that Reed's reporting on the Russian Revolution earned him the right to be buried with honor in the Kremlin.

Nicky was waiting for me and when he saw how happy I was with the performance he was also filled with pride. I asked him to drive me to the most elegant restaurant in Moscow.

Nicky could tell I was in rare form and I wanted my first day in Moscow to be perfect.

When we arrived at the restaurant, Nicky told me it was formerly one of the palaces which had belonged to the

Czar. I told Nicky I could find my way back to the hotel and I thanked him for a perfect day.

Entering the restaurant, I was amazed at the luxurious decor. Plush thick red carpeting, blue and gold velvet drapes covering windows and crystal chandeliers that looked extraordinarily expensive.

The whole extravagant restaurant looked like a scene for a movie. It was exquisitely elegant!

I also observed the waiters were all dressed in formal attire and after standing for a few moments taking in the splendor of the room, I was approached by an older gentleman who apparently spoke no English. He excused himself and went to find someone I could speak with.

As he was returning with another waiter, I observed a young woman intercepting them as all three approached me. The young woman had seen me entering the restaurant alone and was informing the waiters in Russian that she was inviting me to join her small party.

Before we reached her table she told me she was with the ballet company and she had seen me sitting in the Imperial Box at the Bolshoi Theatre. She had been a performer and now her work was in public relations.

Her guests were West Berliners who were doing a special documentary on the Bolshoi Ballet. The entire room had been reserved by the ballet company for their opening night celebration.

If you have never been to a Russian party, then you have not lived! Caviar, vodka and champagne were everywhere! There was much singing, dancing and laughter!

I suddenly felt very comfortable and as though I had lived in Russia a long time. It was a wonderful night, but for me it was only the beginning.

When the party was over Larissa asked me if I had a

program for the following day. She could meet me for lunch at 2:00 P.M.

It was already early morning and I was walking along the path of the Moscow River back to my hotel. I was ecstatic!

When Nicky left me at the restaurant later that day, there was a light snow falling.

At exactly 2:00 P.M. I saw her literally jump out of a taxi and rush into my waiting embrace. She was dressed all in white fur from her head to her ankles.

All I could see was a small smiling face, sparkling white teeth and shining blue eyes. She was absolutely radiant!

I brushed a snowflake from her eyelash and laughingly told her she was my Snowflake.

25 / Snowflake in Russian Is Che★nhka

Che★nhka she said is the Russian word for snowflake and that this name she liked very much in the wintertime.

She took my hand and told me she wanted to show me Moscow through her eyes.

There was something in the way she said it and the penetrating look at her eyes that made me realize why I had come to Russia. I squeezed her tiny hand and told her I wanted to see everything that was important to her.

Our first night together, she invited me to dinner to meet a small group of her intellectual, young friends. It was obvious from the moment she introduced me that my first real contact with the Russian people would become a permanent relationship.

They were as eager to learn more about America as I was to discover Russia. It was clear to me that they were proud to be Russian, but they also wanted to impress me with the fact that they were not members of the card-carrying elite Communist Party. This distinction was very important for them.

I explained that I was a democrat and in America my party has often been labeled the party of the working class. They were all very happy to learn that I opposed President Reagan and his Star Wars program.

Before our discussion had ended we had all become good friends and we made plans to see each other again before I left Moscow.

Hailing a taxi, Snowflake invited me to spend the evening with her. Before the taxi had arrived at her apartment, I remember she said, "John, you know I like you but tonight you are my brother!"

The following day I informed the hotel receptionist and Nicky that I had been invited by friends at the American Embassy to spend a few days with them.

Snowflake was waiting in a car with her best girlfriend two blocks away from my hotel.

The days and nights Snowflake and I shared together were like a scene from *Dr. Zhivago*. We were both very happy with each other and it wasn't necessary to talk about it.

It snowed the day we walked through the historic grounds of the Kremlin where I placed flowers on the grave of John Reed.

We went shopping in the famous window glass government department store where I witnessed hundreds of women patiently standing in line to buy material for a dress.

We rode for many hours on the most illustrious subway system in the world.

I told her that N.Y.C. could be the greatest city in the world and Paris is the most beautiful, but Moscow was the most romantic, cleanest and most dramatic city I had ever seen.

I also had a very favorable impression in Moscow and Leningrad of hundreds of young and old alike standing in long lines waiting to purchase a book written by an author from the West. Their thirst for knowledge of the Western world is unquenchable.

One night, Snowflake told me we were invited to a surprise party! When we arrived at her friends' home, the three rooms were packed with party-makers all having a Russian great time.

Standing in the center of the living room was the honored guest of the party. "My God," I said, "it's a washing machine!"

Hearing an American voice in the crowd, everyone turned in my direction and, as though I had told a very funny story, everyone roared with laughter over my discovery of the famous washing machine.

Snowflake informed me that her friends had two children and three years ago they had put their names on the waiting list to get this washing machine.

She was smiling at me and said, "I hope you are learning more about the Russian character and many other things as well."

"Yes," I said, "Snowflake and I also know I have an outstanding teacher."

The day arrived when the German touring group was preparing to return to Frankfurt. When they learned that I had been given an extended visa to travel to Leningrad they were flabbergasted.

It was very difficult for Snowflake and me to say good bye. We had become more than good friends! She had once called me her "Blue Dream" but we never had time to discuss this dream and perhaps it was better this way.

She and her girlfriend had driven me to the rail station where the train to Leningrad was prepared to leave. The woman conductor, at my request, took the only photo we ever had taken together.

When I had this picture developed I could not mail it to her because it only spoke of the sadness in our parting. I sent her a postcard from Leningrad and one month later, I had a letter from her which she had forwarded to Ireland.

I want to share a part of her letter to me so that the

reader will be able to see and understand the true character of Russia.

MOCKBA 25 May, 1986

Dear John,
    Thank you so much for your postcard from Leningrad.
    It was so nice to meet you.
    I hope you have a good impression of my country.
    In particular I hope also you have a good impression of the Russian people.
    John, I love the name you addressed me.
    Snowflake means in the Russian language *che★nhka* (pronounced Sneshinka).
    But I don't think I am a Sneshinka.
    Kahja and her husband send their best regards and my girlfriend Galina also tells you she enjoyed the time we spent together.
    I hope one day you will come back to Moscow soon and meet me again.
    I miss you.
With Love, Sneshinka
    P.S. This letter will take my girlfriend to East Germany. You know it is not so easy to mail from here.

    The train ride from Moscow to Leningrad takes nine hours. Since I was a child I have been fascinated by the romance of riding across the countryside in a train.
    I have traveled several times on the train from New York to California and I know I will do it again. I have also taken the train across Canada from Montreal to Vancouver riding throught the Rocky Mountains in a snow blizzard.
    Trains to me are always an enchanting experience.

Traveling from Moscow to Leningrad was another dream-reality which I had looked forward to with much anticipation. I was not disappointed!

If I had come to Moscow to pay tribute to John Reed, the great American reporter and writer, I had also come to Russia to learn more about Leo Tolstoy, the writer and Vladimir Lenin, the father of the revolution which shook the world.

Reed had called the Russian Revolution the only classic revolution in human history. It was a revolution of peasants, factory workers and soldiers.

The revolution to overthrow Czar Nicholas was finally led by Vladimir Ilich Lenin. Everywhere I would travel in Russia, Lenin's picture or monument was there also. He is Russia!

Even more than George Washington, who is called the father of his country, I had the feeling that even today Lenin is alive to the people of the Soviet Union.

Leo Tolstoy is also alive! His life and his writing from a century ago is still relevant today.

By the time Tolstoy had published *Anna Karenina* in 1877 he had been established as an international celebrity.

At a time in his life when he had achieved international acclaim, great wealth and was happily married with a family he decided he had to commit suicide. He was at the zenith of his career as a novelist and an intellectual, but he wanted to end his life.

In Tolstoy's personal *Confession* he wrote:

> I had not yet reached my fiftieth birthday and far from being insane or mentally diseased, I enjoyed on the contrary a strength of mind and body such as I have seldom met with among men of my kind; physically I could keep up with the peasants at mowing, and mentally I could

work for eight and ten hours at a stretch without experiencing any ill results from such exertion.

And in this condition I came to this—that I could not live, and fearing death, had to employ cunning with myself to avoid taking my own life.

And it was then that I, a man favored by fortune, hid a cord from myself lest I should hang myself from the crosspiece of the partition in my room where I undressed alone every evening, and I ceased to go out shooting with my gun lest I should be tempted by so easy a way of ending my life.

Tolstoy had been baptized and raised in the traditions of the Russian Orthodox Christian faith. He would ultimately reject the teachings of his church and would be excommunicated.

When he was dying in 1910 at the age of eighty-two, a group of church priests came to his home to ask him to recant his beliefs. He sent them away with the words, "Does two plus two still equal four."

Leo Tolstoy had found the answer to his own life-long search for the meaning of life and he died in peace with the knowledge that he had found the truth.

Throughout the seven year period of religious research and investigation, Tolstoy consulted leading priests, ministers, rabbis and clergy of every faith. He read all the writings of Solomon, Buddha and Schopenhauer.

He consulted all the available ancient manuscripts and with his expert knowledge of Greek he pored over the original gospels of Saint Matthew and the disciples of Jesus Christ.

Leo Tolstoy was convinced that the teachings of Christ held the answer to all his questions. Rereading the "Sermon on the Mount" when Jesus was addressing the multitude, he was astonished to learn anew what he had read from his childhood catechism!

The passage in "The Sermon on the Mount" which made a tremendous impression on Tolstoy was written by St. Matthew, Verses 38 and 39, "Ye have heard that it was said, an eye for an eye and a tooth for a tooth: But I say unto you resist him not that is evil. But whosoever smiteth thee on the right cheek, turn to him the other also."

Suddenly, as if he had heard it for the first time, Tolstoy now understood this verse simply and directly. That Jesus Christ says just what He says.

When the time came for Christ to die on His cross at the age of thirty-three, He rebuked St. Peter for lifting a sword to defend Him. "He who lives by the sword dies by the sword" were the words He used to St. Peter.

Giving His own life as an example, Jesus did not resist those men who wanted Him to be crucified. While He was dying on the cross His last words to His Father were: "Forgive them for they know not what they do!"

Tolstoy would have been very proud of two outstanding non-violent leaders of the twentieth century. Mahatma Gandhi in 1947 brought Great Britain to her knees and won freedom and independence for India, without the use of physical force.

In America in the 1960s, Dr. Martin Luther King also won a great battle over a racist society without violence or the use of physical force. Later, Dr. King would be awarded the Nobel Peace Prize.

After Gandhi and King, the rest of the twentieth century has been a case of madnesss and insanity which is what this story is all about.

A few hours after passing Vysnij Volocok, everything outside the train was covered with snow. A young man came through the train to announce that the dining car was open.

I joined a small crowd of Russian men and women who were enjoying hot borscht soup, black peasant bread and Siberian vodka. I was very happy!

The scene outside the train as we moved across the landscape made me think of the music and romance of Dr. Zhivago. It was all so wonderfully exciting and beautiful.

When I reached inside my jacket pocket for my billfold I discovered an envelope. Inside the envelope was a small pile of rubles and a note from Larissa.

"John, this is a small gift for you to enjoy Leningrad. Think of me! Love, Snowflake."

26 / Leningrad—a Five Star City

Upon my arrival in Leningrad, I was surprised to find a young Soviet official waiting to greet me. It was going to be the same as Moscow only in Leningrad they say "we can do it better."

My first impression of Leningrad was the one I had when I reluctantly left this great city. Leningrad is a five-star place with broad streets, magnificent palaces and luxurious colorful gardens everywhere.

The citizens of Leningrad are looking very proud and are also looking very prosperous.

On my first evening in Leningrad I was leaving the hotel dining room to go to my room, as I wanted to get up very early the next morning for a full day of touring the city. A large, middle-aged woman who had been observing me in the dining room followed me into the elevator. She invited me to her room for a "vodka nightcap." No sooner had she opened the door when she began to strip.

I must admit I was smiling because she was so big and looking very strong. She was also smiling and standing in front of a full-size mirror admiring her massive body.

Listening to English with a Russian accent in itself can be worth the trip to Russia, but when a woman tells you she wants you in three languages that is something unique!

Early the next morning, another driver was taking me on a scenic tour of Leningrad. I gave him my program for the day which I had worked on during the long train ride.

My first stop at the famous Lenin Museum could easily sum up all of my adventure in Leningrad. I met a young man of eighty-six who was one of the curators of the museum.

Boris was a former seaman with thirty years experience on cargo ships. He had visited every major port in the world.

His favorite stop was New York. Boris loved the American people although he said that American women are not so strong as Russian women, implying that Russian women are better lovers!

For two hours he talked to me about his family and their life in Russia. He was one of the most fascinating storytellers I had ever met.

He was only a young boy when his father introduced him to Leo Tolstoy. He remembered him as a giant of a man looking like a great bear with a full beard and a very powerful voice.

Boris was seven when he stood in a large crowd with his father listening to Lenin rallying the Russian workers at the moment in history when the Czar's government had collapsed. He also recalled how excited his parents were when the Communist party took over the government in Russia in 1917.

Boris had lived under many Communist leaders and when I asked him to give me his opinion of Chairman Gorbachev he smiled and said "Mikhail Gorbachev is a very young man! If the day arrives when every Russian can own a passport to travel the world then my opinion of his leadership will be very good."

Boris also could have added that if the world could meet the Russian people they would understand how much Russia wants to have peace in the world.

Before I left Leningrad and Russia I made a promise

to return. There are many reasons why I must return to Russia, but above all it is my desire to continue my friendly relationship with the people of this great nation. I also knew I would have to see Larissa again to learn more about her "blue dream" of childhood.

27 / Off the Beaten Track

When my plane arrived in Germany I phoned Aquarius and asked her if she could meet me at the railroad station in her city later that evening.

As the train was coming to a halt I could see her running toward the train. She was wearing her favorite grey felt hat which she only wore for laughter and love.

She had bought me a bicycle as a surprise for my birthday and we were now taking long rides on the bike paths throughout the sunlit forest to enjoy the magic of another sunset.

On weekends, I enjoyed sitting on her porch drinking a great German beer and watching her work in the garden. Next to practicing medicine, gardening was her favorite pastime.

To watch her in her flower garden was to know and understand the depth and devotion she had for color and beauty.

On sunny days when she worked in her bathing suit, I could only marvel at her figure. She was in her forties but her body was looking like a perfect thirty-six.

It was easy to joke with her about my feeling like Adam in her "garden of paradise."

There were days and nights when we were both totally out of control. It was the best of times for the two of us in the Spring of '86.

Returning to Ireland I had made a decision to spend a long summer on Peg Sayer's Blasket Island. Dan O'Shea reminded me that there was no pub on the island and he gave me about one week of island life before I would have to return to the mainland.

The usual stack of mail was waiting for me. I was now corresponding with over twenty persons and this would increase to over forty by the Fall of 1988 when I arrived in the White House in Kalamai, Corfu. When you are living alone, personal cards and letters are an integral part of your existence.

It became one of my greatest pleasures to receive letters and to answer them all as quickly as possible. One of the letters was from Maggie in Point Pleasant, New Jersey.

Maggie was making her first trip to Ireland and, after her two week holiday, I knew I could qualify as the number one tour guide in all Ireland.

Sometimes I feel very sorry for the countless American tourists who come to Ireland to only visit the so-called hot spots that are a major part of every tour of this interesting island.

The unknowing tourist rarely goes off the well-beaten track of popular places to visit small villages where the lifestyle is so much more delightful.

For these tourists, who have not had the opportunity to visit Ireland and Europe, I can only recommend that you take the flight and then get lost in the arms of local hospitality. This will be an adventure you will never regret nor will you ever forget. After all, it is only once in a lifetime!

Spending my time on the Blasket Island in the summer of 1986 was a magnificent decision. Mary and Paul were very happy to see me again.

The small guest house where Peg Sayers had lived was a perfect summer home. The same fireplace where Peg had warmed herself in the evening while telling her stories to the islanders was always a great delight in the evening hours.

Paul played the guitar and his knowledge of old Irish songs was absolutely amazing.

There were many evenings when young foreign campers on the island would gather in the guest house for an evening of music and entertainment. Paul was always the star attraction. He was always able to encourage everyone to join him in singing his favorite songs.

The island was an ideal environment for writing, reading and relaxing.

Both Mary and Paul were excellent cooks. They had a garden where they grew their own vegetables.

They also had goats and chickens that provided fresh milk and eggs for breakfast. The homemade oven bread and cookies were always in great demand.

Someone was always catching fresh fish from the sea and it was easy to realize how the former islanders could maintain a well-balanced food diet.

When I wasn't writing, I was taking long walks over the mountains and rugged cliffs, enjoying the sea air and observing the gulls who were always making circles over the island.

There were also many mainland sheep grazing on the island during the summer. Also, a small family of donkeys provided entertainment for everyone.

My greatest sea-pleasure was coming from a family of seals who lived in one of the island caves. There are many stories of island men venturing into these seal caves in search of food for the winter.

It was said that the male seal bull was a fierce fighter and a formidable opponent for even the bravest islander. The seals that I had the privilege of observing seemed to be just as interested in my movements along the beach as

I was in their water activities. It was a daily game we mutually enjoyed.

There were many days and nights when I was so happy singing and dancing on the beach that I felt as though I could embrace all humanity in my arms of love and music. There were some days of warm sunshine when I did absolutely nothing except lie on the white sandy beach and splash in the cool Atlantic surf.

On rainy days I enjoyed putting on one of my favorite hand-knit Irish woolen sweaters and curling up by the fire with Leo Tolstoy. I must admit that on these long and otherwise dreary, desolate days and nights of heavy rain, I had become a student of Tolstoy.

I wanted to learn about everything he had discovered in his many years of scholarly research on the religions of the world and in particular his final acceptance of the divine teachings of Jesus Christ.

In 1884 Tolstoy's *Gospel in Brief and What I Believe* was banned in Russia and he was excommunicated from his church. Despite all attempts to suppress his work, great numbers of hectographed copies were clandestinely circulated and smuggled abroad.

Finally, the first copies were published in Geneva, Switzerland, in 1888.

On hundred years later, not one single scholar, religious or otherwise, has come forward to refute the findings of Tolstoy's vicious and devastating attack on religious and government institutions. For me personally, his book came to me like a revelation with such force and impact that I could not put it down.

I wanted to understand everything he had learned in his seven year search for the truth which gave his life a new meaning and saved him from suicide.

It is not my intention here to give you a full account

of what I have gained from Leo Tolstoy. Nevertheless, Tolstoy's tireless efforts to learn the Greek language to enable him to examine the original gospel manuscripts was indeed profound.

He discovered that the church fathers in the fifth century inserted different wording other than the meaning of the divine words of Jesus Christ. For me and the world, this pernicious distortion of the true teachings of Christ is the greatest sin ever perpetuated against mankind in all human history.

And I will repeat, no Christian scholar or church leader has come forward in this century to refute Tolstoy's discovery. I also believe that two plus two equals four!

In 1921, Aylmer Maude, an English writer and critic, translated Tolstoy's manuscript. It is very interesting to read one of his footnotes regarding Tolstoy's *What I Believe*.

> Once accept the thesis that Jesus, by saying resist not him that is evil, intended to forbid any use of physical force to prevent anyone from doing whatever evil he likes, and that He was divinely and absolutely right in laying down that principle, and there is no logical escape from the ultimate conclusion that any government using force, all compulsory law, all police, and all protection of life or property is immoral.
>
> In the "Life of Tolstoy" in this series an argument is adduced—and one that nowhere has been refuted—to show that Christ's injunction admits of a different understanding from that which Tolstoy attributes to it. But be that as it may, Christ's injunction has till now been so little regarded, and reliance on it has been so generally the signal for scornful repudiation, that what Tolstoy

has to say in its support should not be overlooked or carelessly thrust aside.

The governments of the world systematically reject both Christ's injunction and Tolstoy's nonresistant theory, but while they have been doing so wars have become more and more terrible, till at last we are faced by the prospect, perhaps in the near future of defenseless men, women, and children, being massacred in the millions while our whole world crashes to destruction.

Aylmer Maude wrote this commentary in 1921, before Hitler and his "murder machine" had massacred six million Jews and 23 million Russian men, women and children.

Countless millions more were massacred by governmental madness and insanity in World War II, Korea, Vietnam, et cetera, and for all the sceptics who say a nuclear war is impossible I must tell them that my government unleashed the first and second atomic attacks on Hiroshima and Nagasaki in 1945, murdering thousands of innocent women and children in Japan.

It is never ending, but now, at the close of the century, the ever present nuclear menace is hovering over the lives of countless billions of unprotected men, women and children and the so-called leaders of government and religion are helpless to stop the inevitable Holocaust.

One evening after we had eaten dinner Paul told me we were going to be hit by a summer storm and it might last some days.

Late that night all hell broke loose on Blasket Island. Thunder, lightning and an Atlantic storm kept all ships in their harbors.

It was terrible and by the second and third day it was

still very bad. It was impossible for the ferry to make the three-mile crossing from the mainland to the island.

We were running low on many supplies and, for the first time, I fully realized how the islanders must have felt during the long winter weeks of total isolation from the outside world. Then, only the small fifteen-foot curragh was available for making this dangerous crossing. Made of lath and tarred canvas, this canoelike boat required great skill and courage during the winter season's unpredictable weather.

28 / Smitten by Blasket

Aquarius and her son Jonathan, who had come to spend two weeks with me on the island, were stranded on the mainland waiting for the moment when the lone ferry boat could make the crossing.

On the fourth day, the storm had ended, but there were still white caps on the ocean. Shortly after their arrival it was obvious that they also had fallen in love with the magic of the Blasket.

Sometimes I would take time from my writing to observe the two of them hiking up the side of the mountain, happily laughing and playing as if they were young children. It was so pleasant to see them together.

They both enjoyed an early morning swim before breakfast even when the air was cool. Watching them frolicking in the surf brought music to my heart.

They quickly became acquainted with Mary and Paul and enjoyed sitting outdoors drinking morning coffee and afternoon tea, talking for hours about life and living on the island.

Mary confided to me one day that she had never met anyone so interested in the history of the island or more sensitive to the people who had lived there than Jonathan and his mother.

Aquarius had many talents and her photographer's eye captured the splendor of the Blasket from sunrise to sunset. Her pictures were more valuable than a thousand words of description.

There have been many times in many places where I wanted to be able to follow her eyes to see objects the way she is able to see them.

One afternoon, we were in an art museum and I observed her concentration on a large marble statue. The ability of the sculptor to bring to life the perfect body form and the intricate details in the folds of marble clothing fascinated her vivid imagination.

It impressed me that I could learn so much from simply observing her reactions.

We had planned to take a trip to Paris for our third anniversary in September 1988. It was her first tour of Paris and she had told me she was waiting for me to take her to this extraordinary city of love and romance.

Before we left for Paris, we visited an art exhibit in Germany that was showing a collection of Toulouse-Lautrec and a Moulin Rouge film. During a dramatic moment in the film, when Toulouse was nearing the end of his short tragic life, I saw the tears streaming down her face.

I had seen this before when she was visibly upset in Portugal at the sight of a small girl begging on the street.

Aquarius sometimes gave me the impression that she could feel all the agony of the world and I loved her for this. I had also learned from her colleagues in the hospital that she always had a special relationship with her patients and their families.

Her reputation as a doctor went beyond her professional responsibility. Dr. Aquarius not only takes her work very seriously, but she demonstrates a mother's instinct in the care and treatment of all her patients and this is an extraordinary gift in today's computer society.

Perhaps what I am also saying is that if I did not have the fortune of meeting Aquarius, I may not have remained in Europe as long as I have.

The summer of 1986 was over and I was saying goodbye to my many friends in Ireland. I planned to spend a long time in Portugal, but this would be after some weeks of traveling in Scotland, England and finally back to the European continent.

29 / The Leather Connection

It was a full day's drive to the seaport city of Larne where I would take a ship to Scotland. Larne is a typical seaport town bursting with energy. It is also the only port connecting the north of Ireland with the port of Straneer in Scotland.

After booking my passage for the following morning, I found an Italian bistro that also ran a small pension which could accommodate me for the evening.

To my surprise, the dining room was crowded with many young Italians giving me the impression that maybe I was in Ancona, Italy.

The Italian food was absolutely delicious and my appetite was equal to the challenge.

Sometime later, the crowd began to thin out and I noticed four young men speaking in low tones and constantly looking in my direction.

It was obvious to me that they picked up my American accent and some minutes later the waiter presented me with a gift bottle of Chianti wine. The waiter pointed to the four young men who were smiling at me.

Their English was not so good, but neither was my Italian. Nonetheless, in less than one hour, we were all laughing and singing. It was "La Dolce Vita!" [The Sweet Life!]

All four men were looking like Rambo. I thought to myself that they must spend hours every day in a weight room building their tremendous muscles.

After the last customers had left and I was saying good night, one of the men leaned across the table and whispered that he had something upstairs that he wanted me to see. Everything was suddenly becoming very clear in my foggy brain.

I informed them that I had an early morning crossing and that I was very tired. I also informed them I was not interested in whatever it was they had in their room upstairs.

They were undaunted and began to laugh and wink at one another while my thoughts were picturing a woman waiting in their upper room.

The situation began to get tense and I glanced at the bar man who was closing down for the night. His knowing smile gave me the impression that he also was a party to this crazy game.

I was trapped! I wanted to leave, but I had already checked in and my bags were in my room. I decided I could handle the situation, regardless of whatever surprise was waiting for me upstairs.

When they opened the door to the large suite, there sprawled out on the bed were dozens and dozens of leather jackets. I began to roar with laughter! So long and loud was my laughing that soon they were laughing also.

I invited them to my room where I showed them my Canadian leather jacket with fur lining. They examined it very carefully and even put their cigarette lighter on fire to give my jacket the acid test.

After I told them I only required one jacket, they quickly changed their tactics from me to my family, friends, relatives, girlfriends, etc. Once again I was laughing, only this time I found their salesmanship irresistable. Today, Dan O'Shea is wearing an Italian leather jacket and everyone is very happy.

30 / Tatoo!

I had been to Scotland on several occasions and I know I will return again.

On one memorable trip with my family in 1963, we traveled through the remote, desolate and mysterious highlands. We visited the places where the Campbell and MacDonald clans had their terrible battles.

We had seen the eerie mist hanging over the locks where Mary, Queen of Scots, had so frequently ridden her horse to the delight of her subjects.

Now I was returning again to Ayr, the home of Robert Burns, the remarkable poet and literary hero of Scotland. My main objective was to attend the world renowned International Edinburgh Festival.

I found a charming B & B on the sea. My housemother was delighted that I had traveled so far to attend the famed castle performance known as Tatoo!

Tatoo is an annual gathering of top-class performers from all over the world. Every act has been rehearsed for one year in preparation for the Edinburgh festival.

On the evening I was leaving to attend the open air castle performance, my hostess gave me a Scotch plaid blanket to keep me warm. Smiling wickedly, she also handed me a very large flask of Skye High scotch. She laughingly said, "You will be the warmest spectator in the castle."

Every single international act was greeted with wild applause from the packed castle crowd. If you have never seen a performance of Tatoo, then you have missed one of the greatest shows on earth.

The highlight of the evening comes when there are 100 drummers standing at attention at one end of the huge castle grounds. At the opposite end are a like number of kilted pipers.

On command, the drummers, still at attention, begin to play. They are then followed by a rendition from the pipers. This is followed by an intricate parade march with both drummers and pipers playing in unison. You can feel the vibrations of their rhythm throughout the castle. It is simply awesome!

I have never heard two instruments come together with such musical force as the pipes and the drums. When I say there is magic in the air, I mean it is electric!

When their military arrangement has been concluded, there is thunder vibrating in applause throughout the international castle audience. If you are not prepared for this moment, then the finale can leave you dumbstruck.

Every light in the castle is turned off for the final act. Suddenly, from the highest castle tower, a single spotlight is shining on a lone piper. When he concludes his Tatoo salute to the audience, there is not a dry eye in the castle. Only chills are racing up and down your spine. This is Tatoo in Edinburgh!

Leaving Edinburgh, I pointed my Renault 5 in the direction of Hadrian's Wall which separates Scotland and England. Soon I would be in Yorkshire, the former home of England's most celebrated female writers—the famous Brontë sisters.

The Brontë country is something no travelers should miss on their tour of England. The Brontë sisters lived in a small parish home where their father was the village vicar.

Walking through the rooms where they spent most of their lives, you can feel the presence of their greatness. Only a short walk from their parish garden and you are standing in the moors of *Wuthering Heights*. It does not take too much imagination to see Heathcliff standing alone at the summit of the misty mountain.

After you leave the Brontë country, you are traveling south to Robin Hood's Sherwood Forest in Nottingham. You cannot help but notice the beauty of the English countryside. Even from the fast moving M1 highway, you have a panoramic view of the sprawling, colorful landscape.

England's history is filled with many fabulous places and people who will live forever. One such place is Stratford-upon-Avon, the home of William Shakespeare.

How difficult it was for me as a high school student to comprehend the language of one of the world's most renowned writers. Only later would I come to appreciate Shakespeare's genius and enjoy his haunting story of Macbeth.

Before you reach the exciting White Cliffs of Dover, you must first pay a visit to Canterbury. It was here in the massive cathedral that Thomas Becket, the best friend a king ever had, was murdered by his sovereign.

Standing on the very spot which is marked on the cathedral floor where Becket was assassinated, you can feel the very pulse of past English history.

I will always enjoy the ship's crossing from Dover to Calais. Now that England and France are constructing a new tunnel connecting the two seaports, I am afraid the romance of this trip is coming to an end.

Once you leave Calais, you see blue and white signs to Paris. Michele is living in the center of Paris and I wanted to say hello before I continued on my trip to Portugal.

We had not been together since she had made her first trip to Ireland.

31 / Café Society

Approaching the city limits, my French car gave a violent lurch forward in very heavy traffic and then quite unexpectedly, she stopped. After a few desperate attempts to restart the engine had failed, I put on my emergency flashers and prayed that the four lanes of cars would not converge on my small, yellow Renault #5.

In less than three minutes, a young man was offering me a push out of the traffic to an emergency exit. He recognized my foreign plates and wanted me to have a good impression of Paris.

I gave him Michele's address and shortly, we were ringing her doorbell. Jaques was carrying my luggage and I had a single red rose.

"Bonjour ma cherie." You could have knocked Michele down with a feather she was so surprised to see me.

The next morning Michele's mechanic put a new air filter in my car and we were on the road again. Michele is a fascinating and attractive woman. She knows how much I enjoy Paris and she invited me to spend a few relaxing days before I left for the south.

We walked all over Paris by day and night. She obviously enjoyed being my guide in her city.

Michele and I enjoy the same interests in life. We were never serious, but we are no longer strangers to one another. It is the kind of warm and friendly relationship that we have seen grow stronger with each passing year. We can never ask for anything more and we are both very happy whenever we can meet.

Michele also has a wonderful sense of humor and I always look forward to receiving her funny letters. When she learned I had become a grandfather, she sent me a card of congratulations. Inside the card she wrote: "In Paris it is not so bad to be a grandfather, only if you are married to a grandmother."

Saying *"au revoir"* to Paris and Michele with her promise to visit me in Portugal, I proceeded in a southerly direction to Orléans. Joan, the maid of Orléans who led the French army into battle and was later burned at the stake, will always be remembered as one of the INSPIRED heroines of French history.

After Orléans, I am enjoying the drive through the lush landscape of the wine regions of Château and Bordeaux. It is a perfect place to stop at a small village for some French bread, cheese and, of course, the village wine which always is a pleasant surprise.

My last stop in France before crossing the border was the city of Bayonne, which was the name adopted by my hometown in New Jersey. Bayonne, France is a coastal city with much charm and grace. It is also well known for its bull fighting.

At the start of every bull fighting season, the bulls are set free in the streets of Bayonne. On this day everyone becomes a matador and there is an air of celebration everywhere.

Crossing the border at San Sebastian, I was remembering Ernest Hemingway and *The Sun Also Rises*. Hemingway had a love affair with Spain and also his favorite sport of bull fighting.

His final book before he committed suicide was called *The Deadly Summer*. It was the story of the most famous family of matadors and the intense rivalry that brought them into the ring of death.

Motoring across from San Sebastian to Madrid and the Portuguese border was one of the most relaxing drives I have ever taken in Europe. In the early Fall season, most of the tourists are gone. Both the native people and the country return to a less hectic and more normal routine. There is virtually no traffic on the roads and the peace and tranquility surround you with natural beauty.

It is one of the best seasons to become better acquainted with the people and the village life.

Outside of Madrid, I met a young couple from Barcelona who were visiting their relatives. They invited me to join them for lunch at their favorite village eating place.

The owner was a former matador and the rooms were all decorated with dramatic scenes from his days in the arena. Emanuel was delighted to have an American guest and he provided me with a sample of the finest, spicy food I have ever enjoyed. For two days my stomach was on fire! Later he joined our small party and together we put away enough fine wine to keep me in his company for the entire evening which included the Flamenco dances and the remarkable Spanish guitar.

Before my new friends from Barcelona left, they gave me their address and reminded me that I must visit them in their famous city.

By early afternoon on the following day, I arrived in Lisbon, the capital of Portugal. I would return to Lisbon on several occasions and I would always be impressed by sharp contrast between the ancient city on the hill and the new city below.

The narrow streets of the old city resemble alleys where you are able to stretch out your arms and touch the ancient buildings to your left and right sides. The new city features countless sidewalk cafés where you can order a coffee or cappucino and relax for hours.

One of the most interesting aspects of European culture, in my opinion, is the outdoor café life. Rarely have I ever left a café without finding an interesting person to engage in conversation.

For me, this is one of the ultimate pleasures of the world traveler. For the small price of coffee, you have expanded your experience with new and sometimes lasting friendships. The sidewalk café is very definitely one of the most intimate social opportunities and should not be missed when you are traveling.

After a few days of touring the city, I visited the American Embassy to ask the ambassador if he could give me any advice about locating a home in the Algarve. Within one hour, he had made contact with an "old family" Contessa who had many friends in Vale du Lobo, called the jewel of the Algarve.

The following afternoon, I had an appointment with a real estate agent who I was told had several villas on the Mediterranean.

Martina Lisboa was a young attractive and very intelligent woman who spoke four languages fluently. We immediately hit it off so well that you would think we had been friends for years.

She told me the villa I had selected would not be available for several days. Travelling ten miles, I booked into a hotel in Faro.

Faro is more than the capital city of the Algarve and the location of an International airport.

While enjoying my breakfast on the roof of the hotel I was startled to discover how close I was to Sevilla in Spain. Also, I observed on my map that I was very close to Tangier in North Africa.

I called Martina in Vale du Lobo and informed her that I was taking a small trip. I would be a few days late in arriving to take the keys to my villa #96.

Martina was laughing when I outlined my hastily made program and told me to have a good time.

Sevilla reeks of beauty, culture and the sounds of Flamenco music. The major highway from Sevilla to the Spanish coast is breathtaking My spirits were soaring.

Miles and miles of citrus fruits of all variety and dazzling colors everywhere!

Arriving one evening very early at the port of Algeciras, I booked passage for a night crossing to the English "Rock of Gilbraltar"! The illustrious Rock is something everyone should see especially at night.

Glittering with thousands of jewel-like diamond lights it is from the ship one of the most spectacular sights in the world. Trapped between the coasts of Spain, Portugal and North Africa it becomes an exciting adventure in the life of every world traveler.

Early the following morning I was on my way to North Africa. It would be my first trip to the African continent and an experience which for a moment was a threat to my life.

Arriving in the port of Tangier I was met by a group of security and customs officials dressed in what appeared to be military uniforms.

They refused to let me enter their country without more identification for me and my car.

A senior official told me I would have to return to Gibraltar on the returning ship.

I was stunned!

I produced a picture of my family and pleaded my case.

Visiting Africa, I told him, was one of my lifetime ambitions.

After another stormy conference I was reluctantly granted permission to continue my journey.

32 / Memories in Tangier

Coming into Tangier is one of the great culture shocks you can never forget. The sights and sounds of Africa are totally foreign to the Western world. You are at once exposed to the Arabic and Islamic culture.

At sunset, from my hotel balcony overlooking the city, I was mesmerized by the sounds of prayer coming from the crowded streets below me. Hundreds of voices were raised in praise of Allah!

Before retiring on my first night in Africa my mind drifted back to the time I had spent in the service of my country. Perhaps it was the sight of military uniforms at the port security and the bureaucratic "red tape" which had upset me.

Now I was recalling the days of my military service.

It can be a traumatic shock when you are only seventeen and abruptly change the days of your childhood to manhood. Millions of young teenagers around the world would never be the same again. World War II did this to everyone!

In 1940, Franklin Delano Roosevelt became the first president in American history to be re-elected for a third term. His campaign slogan that year was telling America and the world: "I hate war, Eleanor hates war, even my dog Fala hates war . . ."

He also promised America that he would not send our boys over to fight on foreign soil.

One year later on December 7, 1941, the Japanese

attacked Pearl Harbor. Four days later on December 11, 1941, Hitler declared war on the U.S.

After the Japanese attack, I sat in our living room with my mother and father listening to the president on the radio. Roosevelt was telling America that the Japanese "sneak attack" on Pearl Harbor was a day that would "live in infamy."

The president then asked congress for a Declaration of War against the Axis Powers.

Almost fifty years later, President Reagan would fly to Bitburg, Germany and visit the cemetery where German S.S. murderers were buried.

Also, President Bush would fly to Japan to honor Emperor Hirohito, the last of the World War II leaders, who had initiated the attack against America.

Within six months after the war declaration, all my older friends had either enlisted or were drafted into the military service.

I remember my mother had left the room after the terrible war news and I heard her weeping in the bedroom. My father, who was a veteran of World War I, looked at me and we both knew why she was crying.

I broke my mother's heart when I enlisted in the service. In less than one year, her reddish-blonde hair became streaked with grey and new lines appeared on her face which made me realize how much she worried about me.

We all knew how many men died in war, but no one will ever know how many mothers died with their sons' deaths.

My barrack leader was a chief petty officer who had seen much action on board a ship and now he resented having shore duty training recruits. He was Polish and was called "Butch" and "Stasch" by his peers.

But to the "boots" as we were called, Stanley was a god! We respectfully referred to him always as Sir!

Sir was determined to make his company the best in the coast guard. Every morning precisely at 6:00 A.M., Sir would come screaming into the barracks always using the same language, "Drop your cocks and grab your socks; ten minutes to inspection time!"

You never in your life saw young men move as quickly as the men in Sir's company. The wild scramble to get into "the head" (W.C.) was unimaginable but somehow we always made muster in ten minutes.

By the moment Sir stormed into the barracks, it was perfect! Walking very sternly down the center aisle he and his aide checked every seabag, every recruit and everything in the barracks from top to bottom.

Sir always carried a shining silver coin in his hand when making the daily inspection. Heaven help you if he flipped the coin on your cot and if the coin did not bounce, you were put on report duty.

Your blanket had to be stretched so tight that there was no question in your mind about passing the "bed bounce" test. Failing this test or any other infraction of Sir's rules could mean a loss of weekend leave with an order to scrub the barrack floors and carry out a host of other unpleasant duties.

I hesitate to tell you the funniest story of my boot training experience at Manhattan Beach, but it is a vital part of my military profile.

One morning at the routine six A.M. inspection, Sir appeared with the company doctor. All the "boots" were standing at attention in front of their bunk bed. Suddenly Sir shouted, "Drop your drawers!"

Try to visualize one hundred teenagers standing at a nervous attention with their pants hanging around their ankles! Now picture Sir trying to hide a smile as the medical officer proceeded to make his "pecker check."

When he reached my bunk bed he stopped and said, "Skin it sailor." I did and he replied "all the way" to which I meekly answered, "That is as far as it will go!"

He turned to Sir and informed him that I was to report to the infirmary the very next morning to be prepared for a surgical circumcision.

Later that day Sir called me to his office. "Buehler," he said with a big grin, "some guys will do anything to get out of galley duty, but this takes the cake."

I also smiled and thought to myself—yes, getting up at 3:00 A.M. every morning for two weeks to prepare eggs and oatmeal for hundreds of young men is not so pleasant. I also realized for the first time that our Sir was, after all, a human being who could appreciate a very funny story!

Early the next morning I was being shaved in preparation for the operating theatre. I was informed that a full Commander was performing the operation and I should be honored!

At this point I must tell my European readers that today in America, every male baby is circumcised at birth unless otherwise instructed by the mother. However, in the year of my birth, my mother would not allow anyone to touch her precious infant let alone put a knife to her son's future manhood.

Anyone who has ever been shaved in the lower extremities will tell you that it is not so pleasant when the hair begins to grow back.

Sir had selected me for our barrack crew team and I will never forget the terrible jock itch I had the day of our rowing competition. It was like Dante's *Inferno* only I couldn't put out the fire!

When I was being released from the infirmary the

commander told me it was one of his finest operations and that, in years to come, he knew I would be very happy for his outstanding surgical accomplishment!

When I finished basic training I had qualified to go to Atlantic City, New Jersey, for six months' training as a ship's radio operator.

The allies had made a landing on Normandy Beach in France on June 6, 1944, before I was graduated as a radioman third class. Shortly thereafter I received orders to travel to San Francisco to join the Pacific fleet as a radio operator on the U.S.S. *Hutchinson*, a patrol frigate with an old crew of decorated veterans.

The first thing I observed upon boarding the ship were four Japanese flags painted on the upper deck, signifying four aircraft hits made by the crewmen.

I was the only teenager on the "Hutch" and my boss was a Canadian chief petty officer who would shortly give me the nickname "Buckets Buehler!"

From the moment our small ship passed under the famous Golden Gate Bridge and ran into foul weather I was deathly seasick.

Every radio operator had to stand four hours on duty and eight hours off duty. Seasickness was no excuse for not performing your assigned radio watch.

I was so terribly sick and suffered so much physical pain that I was certain I would never complete our first thirty day sea patrol duty.

When we had returned to port at the end of my first tour I had lost over thirty pounds. My chief, showing absolutely no sympathy, simply handed me a bucket with a rope to attach around my neck.

He painted "Buckets Buehler" on the side of my sick bowl. He also gave me stern instructions not to miss any messages and not to mess up the radio shack.

To add to my personal misery, there was a chief radar officer who stopped in to see me regularly, always holding a greasy pork chop. For many, many years I could not stand the sight or smell of a cooking pork chop.

How I survived those long touring months of Pacific sea duty only God can tell you.

This was but one small episode in my life as a sailor in the U.S. Coast Guard.

It was a magnificent chorus filled with emotional fervor! I will always remember my first red sunrise in Tangier and the chanting melody: Allah! Allah! Allah!

One of my great ambitions as a traveler is to gain a better understanding of the countless divergent religions of the world. I must say that while I have lived in Ireland, Portugal and Greece I have been able to learn more about the connection between poverty and God.

Also, while I have the advantage of Western civilization, my exposure to the East is still very limited. My brief trip to N. Africa and later to Egypt have at least opened my eyes to religions which heretofore I had only read about.

Later I will be talking about my invitations to Israel and Egypt where my young friends gave me a lesson in religion that has had a most profound impact on my life.

If more people from the East and West had the chance to meet, I know the world will be a better place for everyone.

Yes, it is true that people are the same everywhere. In all their shining eyes, I see hope for love, for music, for laughter and for peace.

Only government, religion and yes, the military establishments continue to baffle and deny the existence of a "common humanity."

After some days in Tangier, I made a special trip to

Casablanca, the city that Humphrey Bogart immortalized. Bogie, as he is lovingly referred to, was always one of my favorite film personalities.

I was not surprised while traveling throughout Europe to find large poster pictures of Bogie everywhere. I also admired Humphrey Bogart for a personal reason.

I had a very good friend in high school who later became a professional actor and lifelong friend of Bogie. Joe Hernandez was a short, thin, very handsome Puerto Rican who had earned the reputation of class clown. Joe always seemed to be able to do everything differently from the rest of our class. Even upon entering a classroom, Joe would never simply sit himself in a chair like everyone else. He could somehow manage to slink into his seat so artistically that it was fascinating just to observe his technique.

Joe was a born actor who could very naturally play the comic, mimic his teachers and sometimes create havoc.

We had an old English teacher who wore a hearing aid. During a lesson on William Shakespeare, Joe raised his hand first to answer a difficult question. He was also extremely intelligent.

When the teacher called on Joe to answer the question, he replied by moving his mouth without letting any sounds come out. The class waited and watched in amused silence as our teacher frantically turned up her hearing aid to full volume.

Once again she pointed her finger in Joe's direction for the answer to the Shakepearian question. Hernandez answered in his loudest squeeky voice, "MACBETH!"

Our teacher reeled backward and, leaning against the blackboard, she shouted for Joe to go to the principal's office "IMMEDIATELY!"

She had forgotten to reduce the sound of her own

voice and was forced to leave the room to recover her composure.

Joe Hernandez spent more time in the principal's office than any other troublemaker in Bayonne High School history. He was very proud of this achievement!

One day while I was working out on the high school track, Joe showed up in track shorts. He informed our coach that he wanted to earn a letter for sports before he graduated.

Later, when I went into the coast guard, I was surprised one day to see Joe turn up as a "boot" in Manhattan Beach. I began to regard him as my shadow.

He confided in me that he was very disappointed that he never received any mail from his high school classmates.

I wrote a long letter to our high school newspaper explaining how important it was for serviceman's morale to receive news from home. Some days later during our mail call, Joe Hernandez was pleasantly surprised when the mail caller continued to toss many, many letters in his direction.

After the war was over, I received a long letter from Joe. He was living in California and he would be appearing in a movie starring Humphrey Bogart.

He explained that he had been invited to a Hollywood party where he met Bogie. Bogie took a liking to Joe and from their first meeting Bogart never made a film that did not include Joe.

Joe had changed his name to Pepe Hern and I never missed a Bogie picture because I could always find my old friend Joe somewhere in the film even if he was only standing in the crowd.

This was just another reason why I came to discover the place where Humphrey Bogart told Hoagy Carmichael to "Play it again, Sam." "It's still the same old story," etc., etc.

Dressed in my favorite "Moscow Blue" suit and sporting a deep tan I was led to a small ringside table in the famous Bogie room. After ordering a bottle of red wine, I settled back to enjoy one of the finest exotic belly-dancing performances I had ever witnessed.

Following a half hour of preliminary entertainment by a small group of musicians, the star performer was brought out by enthusiastic audience applause. Little Egypt, as she was billed, was something else.

I know of no other dance form which so dramatically exhibits the beauty of a woman's figure than the performance of a top, professional belly dancer. Little Egypt had all the qualities of an exceptional performer.

Men and women alike were all captivated by her rhythm and the fantastic movements of her body on the dance floor.

It is obvious to everyone that Little Egypt was a skilled perfectionist. Every movement, every gesture, carried a message and the story of her dance was very inspiring to watch.

At one point in the performance the dancer singles out a few patrons for special attention. The proximity of my table to the dance floor and the fact that I was alone made me a perfect subject for the dancer's personal attention.

Needless to say I was not reluctant to become a small part of her performance. The closer she came to me with her twirling scarf, the more alluring she appeared.

I was completely fascinated by her attention regardless of where it might lead. I was enjoying every moment immensely and she knew it.

When her performance finally ended the applause

was like thunder. There was no doubt in anyone's mind that she had given an exceptional display of a dance form which is over seven thousand years old.

Some minutes later she appeared from backstage very colorfully dressed and carrying the rose which I had given to the flower presenter as a small token of my appreciation for her artistic performance.

She had seated herself at my lonely table and so naturally I invited her to share my bottle of wine. I could feel the curious eyes of many people focusing on the two of us. I could also feel my pulse pounding in my brain!

Her Nile-green emerald eyes were burning into my soul.

Little Egypt's English was not perfect but neither was my Arabic very good. We both managed to get through the preliminaries and I had the feeling we were both enjoying the exchange.

There came that moment in our communications when we had exhausted all the reasons for our being where we were. It was at that instant, which came suddenly and without warning, that she leaned across the table very close to my face and coldly whispered the most devastating words that I had ever heard.

"I am a terrorist, make love with me tonight or I will kill you!"

As a former controversial state senator from New Jersey, I was no stranger to death threats. Numerous anonymous cranks had made threatening calls to my office and my home.

I also received many anonymous letters which I promptly turned over to the state police. This is normal routine for many people in political life.

However, sitting at an intimate table in a very crowded

room with an exotic woman who obviously meant what she said, is another matter.

I remember this incident as if it happened yesterday! The room appeared to become very quiet as though everyone knew what was happening except me.

I remember leaning over the table and fixing my challenging eyes into her eyes, I remarked, "After enjoying the exotic movements of your body on the dance floor, either way I am dead!"

As I continued gazing into her enchanting eyes I was relieved to observe a small grin begin to form on her face. Soon, she leaned back in her chair and the smile became a quiet subdued laugh which was shortly replaced by outright laughter.

At the same time I heard the barman laughing and as if on command the entire room was uproarious. It sounded like New Year's Eve in Times Square. I also became uproarious.

The owner and manager, who were also a party to this game, approached our table. "You handled the situation exactly the way Bogie would have reacted, cigarette twitching in your mouth and all. The drinks and anything you desire are on the house. Enjoy it!"

I stood up to relieve my inner tension and asked them if it would be okay if I joined the band to sing one of my favorite songs, the theme song from *Casablanca*, Hoagy Carmichael's "As Time Goes By."

Leading my dancing partner to the bandstand, I also gave a brief performance that she would not forget.

The next day I returned to Tangier to catch my ship to return to Spain and Portugal. My hotel manager suggested to make a luncheon stop at a unique village where, for many centuries, women have carried on the ancient art of carpet weaving.

Getting lost has always been one of the truly outstanding features of my long traveling experience. Getting lost means getting help and this means making new friends.

For me, this is what traveling is all about and in Africa, this wonderful experience will live forever in my memory.

I stopped my car at a bus stop where many villagers were waiting. When I inquired about the direction to my lost village, hands were pointing in all four geographic locations.

On course I was laughing and when I was returning to my car, three middle-aged women wearing veils (one was carrying an infant), proceeded to pile into the Renault #5. Pointing straight ahead, they waved me onward while at the same time they were all laughing at my crazy car and perhaps the driver also.

They spoke no English and used sign language to indicate that they knew where we were going. Thirty minutes later, I was convinced that I was really lost.

We had left the main road and I thought to myself that I would never see the carpet weavers or Tangier this day and so I just relaxed and enjoyed the scenery.

I passed out chewing gum and began singing "Summertime" and "Old Man River." Now they were laughing and clapping their hands to the rhythm of my voice.

The women were even more exuberant when they saw how happy I was. We were having a party in my shake and roll car and it was fantastic.

From out of nowhere we came upon a very crowded village that made me think that I was stepping back many centuries in time—Camels, donkeys, barking dogs and everyone covered in clothing from head to toe.

It was a scene to make you want to cry. It was my first glimpse into the real Arabic culture and I loved it.

Sitting along the side of a dusty dirt road were women

of all ages weaving bright, colorful carpets. It was an awesome picture, but of course I could not take this photograph.

The women in my car were pointing to the village Arabic sign to let me know I had arrived in their ancient town. They had seen my camera in the car and when they stepped out they indicated they wanted me to take their photograph.

It will always be one of my best memory photographs to remind me how pleasant it is to get lost.

33 / The Wealth of Portugal

Returning to the "jewel of the Algarve" in Vale du Labo, I was astonished by the beauty and location of my Villa #96 on the Mediterranean. There was no doubt in my mind that I was prepared to live another lifetime in historic Portugal.

I had deliberately planned my long stay program in Europe with the intention of concentrating on Ireland, Portugal and Greece, the three poorest countries in the European Common Community. My objective was to learn as much as I could about the lifestyle, customs and culture of these nations of the so-called "poorest" people in Europe.

What I discovered after nearly five years of experience will be woven into the pattern of my story.

What first impressed me was the peace and tranquility among the countless people living in the small villages throughout these three nations. What they lack in material wealth is more than compensated for by their serene attitude, great appreciation of their native environment and their close relationships with their neighbors.

The level of tension and pressure which is so prevelant in the wealthier countries is not a problem in Ireland, Portugal and Greece. There is no question in my observation that love, music and closeness to nature are far more apparent in the poor nations.

If I must say it, then I will say this: "The poorer people

of the world may be after all the richest people in the universe!"

Also, for me personally, I have seen and felt the affections of so many people in these countries that I cannot deny they have all changed the direction of my life forever.

Yes, I had come to these countries as a foreign stranger but their warmth and friendship made me realize as never before that we are all a small part of one very large and important family.

This is a lesson that the world must learn. We must not be misled by leaders of government and religion who continue to deny the universality of our humanity.

My best friend in Egypt, who I will talk about later, once told me that people show their love by good deeds and not by big words. I think about this very often!

To put it more bluntly for all my friends who have urged me to say this—There is so much vocal bullshit in the world today from government and religious leaders, that it is reaching our eyeballs!

The famous Algarve is a 125-mile strip of cliffside sandy beaches with countless coves for private bathing and sunshine. Scattered along the cliff tops are endless numbers of secluded, quiet and peaceful taverenas serving delicious grilled sardines and magnificent Portuguese vintage wines of every variety.

To relax in this scenic friendly environment is one of the ultimate pleasures of the Portuguese Algarve.

While the Algarve is fast becoming an international hot spot, only thirty minutes inland from the ocean's breeze are the remarkable mountains of Moncheque.

During the winter season the perfume scented Magnolia tree looks like snow in the mountains of Roman Caldas de Moncheque. It is breathtaking at any hour of the day or night!

This view mingled with the fragrance of lemon and orange groves makes the whole experience overwhelming. But the most exciting feeling comes from observing the people in the villages scattered throughout the vast Moncheque mountain region.

You realize you are stepping back into the eighteenth and nineteenth centuries when you see the women kneeling by rivers and streams washing their clothes on large flat stones. Strong women carrying big baskets of fire wood perfectly balanced on their proud heads is a sight which is never seen in the affluent nations of the world.

Men work in fields with leather straps over their shoulders, attaching themselves to horses or mules while plowing the fields with their primitive tools. The technical "progress" of the outside world has not reached these people and perhaps the villagers of Moncheque are happier this way.

Of course, there is much history to be seen and appreciated in Portugal, a world leader in the sixteenth century. Everywhere you turn in Portugal, you see relics of antiquity.

In the year 711, the Moors from Africa swept across the sea and left their distinctive mark in villages and cities. Even the name Algarve comes from the Arabic "Al gharb" meaning the garden of Allah!

Your eye is always resting on the low, cool white houses with many of the fretwork chimneys that are a trademark of Portugal's past.

Just as in Spain, bullfighting is a very popular national sport, only in Portugal the bull lives to fight another day. The Portuguese enjoy the skill and grace of the bullfighter more than the drama of the killing of the bull.

As it was in Ireland, it did not take me very long before I had a wide circle of friends who would teach me all the things I had traveled so far to learn. But, just as it was in Ireland and as it would be in Greece, the centerpiece of my learning experience was the knowledge I would gain from the Portuguese people themselves.

After you have been living in one place for some months the natives no longer regard you as just another tourist. Once they appreciate your desire to adapt to their lifestyle, the door to their special world is opened.

For an American to say bon dia [good day] to every Portuguese he passes in the morning is very meaningful. The response is always very heartwarming and it does not take too long to increase this vocabulary of mutual respect and courtesy.

There were many personal events which occurred during my long stay in Portugal. All of my encounters with the Portugese people enabled me to get acquainted with their daily lifestyle as well as their aspirations for the future.

Martina Lisboa was much more than a real estate agent who collected my monthly rental fee. She became one of my best friends in Portugal. Whenever Martina came to visit me in the morning she always greeted me with a beautiful smile and said, "Bon dia, John!" She was always happy when I responded, "Bon dia, Martina" and we shared many pleasant hours together.

Martina was the first person in the Algarve to introduce me to the many people and places that made my stay so comfortable. She showed me where and how to shop, the traditional places to dine, where I could hear Fado music, et cetera. She was also a great dancer!

When I needed a writing table for my balcony it was delivered the next day. Martina was like this!

Angelo was another very close friend who made my stay in Vale du Lobo feel like a song. He owned an ocean front pub and restaurant where I spent many, many enjoyable evenings.

Angelo's Pub not only served good draft beer on tap, but his food was always delicious as well. In addition, he had an outstanding piano and organ player who worked several nights a week.

Angelo loved boxing and Mike Tyson was his greatest hero in the ring. We both enjoyed exchanging stories about who was the greatest heavyweight fighter in the twentieth century.

I told him the story of having witnessed my own hero, Rocky Marciano, the Brockton, Massachusetts, blockbuster, fighting in Madison Square Garden in New York City.

On this particular night, Marciano was fighting an up and coming heavyweight named Roland LaStarza. LaStarza could not answer the bell in the seventh round. It was obvious in the fifth round that he was having difficulty raising his arms to defend himself against Marciano's tremendous punching power.

Later, it was learned that LaStarza had suffered from broken blood vessels in both of his arms after repeated punches by Rocky Marciano.

Marciano was not a fancy boxer. His punching power, on the other hand, made him one of the most dangerous knockout fighters in the history of professional boxing.

When I told Angelo that Marciano was the only heavyweight who ever retired as a champion, he countered that it would be the same for Mike Tyson in years to come.

Angelo was also a music lover and many nights we would stand around the piano man with the bar men and entertain the guests with our fabulous harmony.

Carlos and Louis were two of my favorite barmen and we all shared in a mutual admiration society. When business was slow we enjoyed exchanging stories about everything.

They were as hungry for knowledge about the U.S.A. as I was to learn about Portugal. Their knowledge of the social, economic and political condition of their country was phenomenal.

They were my best source of information and they also had a wonderful sense of humor which never ceased to amaze me.

Carlos and Louis liked to joke with me about their success with the female tourists of the world who spent their summers in the Algarve. Based on their personal experience, the women from Sweden enjoyed the highest ranking.

The Swedish women were attractive, attentive, aggressive and, above all, they had the least inhibitions especially concerning summer affairs.

Before I left Vale du Lobo, Carlos and Louis gave me an all-night farewell party that was sensational.

At midnight they had fireworks which were accompanied by hordes of young people coming into my villa from all over the Algarve. It was a crazy uproarious party which lasted for two unforgettable days.

Other enjoyable evenings were spent at the illustrious five-star Dona Filipo Hotel which was close to the pub and ocean. Emanuel was an exceptional manager who attributed his success to an efficient and hard working staff.

Emanuel is in his forties and is very handsome and always impeccably dressed. He speaks five languages and is married to a very young Italian woman who recently gave birth to their first son.

While his opinions were usually more conservative than those of my friends at the pub, I also recognized his tremendous sense of pride in his Portuguese heritage.

Emanuel took particular delight in my interest in his country's history and culture. He also enjoyed watching me dance with the Portuguese folk dancers who came to perform at the hotel every weekend.

Returning from the beach one afternoon, after a great day of jogging and swimming, I had an urgent message waiting for me at my villa. "Please come to the hotel reception immediately" signed John, the hotel receptionist.

John had worked at the hotel for twenty-four years and he explained to me that he could be fired for violating one of the hotel management's rules.

A middle-aged English couple had checked out of the hotel and were taking a tour in the mountains before leaving later that evening. They asked John if he would take care of their luggage until they would return later in the day.

John nervously explained that he had consented to their request although he knew it was against the rules.

Included in their luggage was a large golf bag which contained a carefully wrapped, priceless antique statue of St. Francis. The hotel busboys had mistakingly taken the golf bag and loaded it in into another car which had gone to Faro airport earlier that morning.

Coincidentally, before I had gone to the beach I had driven an English golfer to the airport and I had a vague recollection of the golf bag. In fact, when I said good-bye outside the airport entrance I had observed the bag sitting on the curb as my friend disappeared into the airport terminal. Everything suddenly fell into place.

While John and I were talking, the smiling English couple returned from their wonderful tour of Moncheque. I quickly ushered them into the bar and invited them to have a drink.

John was as white as a sheet! I thought he was about

to faint. I asked him to call the airport security police to inquire about the golf bag while I explained the dilemma to my new English friends in the bar lounge.

Shortly, John, pale faced, timidly walked into the bar to inform us that the airport lost and found department had a number of bags that they were holding for people to identify and claim.

We told John to relax and we left immediately for Faro International Airport. After the police had received a complete description of the golf bag and its contents, they were able to find it and a very relieved couple were fondling St. Francis in the backseat of my Van Gogh yellow Renault #5.

John's facial expression as we entered the hotel with St. Francis defies description. He looked like he wanted to laugh and cry at the same moment.

We all returned to the bar for a drink on St. Francis' return to Vale du Lobo.

One Saturday morning Martina invited me to go to Loule which is a small village in the mountains.

Every Saturday is open outdoor market day and the mountain people come from everywhere to buy and sell everything from A to Z. By the time we arrived, all the stalls had been set up and the market square was in full swing.

The colors and activities of a typical Portuguese market day celebration should not be missed. It looks like a carnival atmosphere with pungent odors of fresh fish, many brands of cheese, salami, et cetera.

Women, wearing colorful dresses and balancing baskets on their heads, come and go, smiling and laughing all the while.

Martina could see how happy I was and she also was wearing a very big happy smile. We sat for some time at a sidewalk cafe in the center of the square from where we were able to observe all the activities of the market.

Children were running through the streets carrying their new balloons and hucksters were pitching their wares while the tourists were snapping pictures everywhere. It felt good to just sit there in the center of Portuguese activity and realize how wonderful life can be especially when you are at peace with the world.

Loule market day became a regular Saturday morning ritual for me. I would always buy my week's supply of fresh fruit, vegetables and fish.

One Saturday, however, when I had returned to my villa I discovered I had lost my wallet. Martina reported the loss to the police and for a few days I heard nothing.

I had told several of my friends what happened and one week later Angelo informed me that he located my lost wallet.

We drove to Loule where we would meet a woman in the village real estate office. She was quite old and was dressed in black from head to toe. She also spoke no English but her friend in the office would be the interpreter.

After I described my wallet and all of the contents she turned to the interpreter and told him to ask me if there was anything else in my wallet. Angelo was whispering something about stamps and suddenly I realized I had one stamp in my small change pocket.

As soon as I put one finger in the air and uttered the word stamp the old woman smiled and produced my wallet. When I offered her ten thousand escudos for her honesty she shook her head and told the interpreter it was too much.

After some minutes I slipped the money into her large shopping bag and said thank you in two languages. She bowed her head in gratitude and left the office.

In less than five minutes, while I was talking with Angelo and his friend, she returned carrying a large box and a bottle of Portugese wine explaining to the interpreter that I had been too generous.

Angelo was grinning when I explained that I would only accept the cake and wine if we could all share the gift. Now everyone was laughing and a small impromptu party was underway. This is the way it was in Portugal!

At Christmastime I had a huge pine tree decorated with many cards from my family and friends from America and Europe. I called it my tree of peace and love!

Aquarius and Michele had come to spend the holidays with me and even in March the tree was still decorating my large living room.

One day my cleaning woman asked me if allowing the tree to stand so long was a custom in America. When I replied that it was not a practice in America, I added that in Portugal I feel like it's Christmas every day!

The next day she came to my villa with a bouquet of roses and a smile that was worth more than a million roses.

She had also spread the word about my Christmas tree story and so my reputation as an American who was having a love affair with Portugal became well known.

In Monchique, the intoxicating air was filled with the aroma of lemons, oranges and the magnolia. How I enjoyed the winding roads which led me to my favorite places in the mountains!

I always made a late afternoon stop at a taverna close to the summit which had a splendid view of the village below and the distant sea. It was spectacular!

One Sunday I met another John who was born and raised in the mountains, just as his father and grandfather before him. John was an extraordinary man. I had never met anyone who was as attached to his environment as John.

He invited me to visit him the following Sunday. John owned a small hotel and restaurant. He also owned the side of a mountain which he told me he would never sell at any price.

The next Sunday I arose early to a brilliant sunrise. Little did I realize when I left the villa that my tour of Portugal might be coming to a tragic end.

My traveling speed in the climbing mountains was very slow because of the dangerous, narrow, winding roads which were barely wide enough to accommodate two cars passing from opposite directions.

Half way up the mountain, as I approached a hairpin curve in the road, I suddenly saw a speeding motorcycle directly in front of my car. We both hit our brakes, but he lost control. His motorcycle slid under my car and his head went smashing into my left front headlight.

The impact was like an explosion! I sat stunned for some seconds, repeating the words, "Please God, do not let this man die!"

When I stepped out of my car, there was absolute silence until I gently touched his shoulders. He let out a low, painful groan and I knew he was alive. I gently lifted him to his feet and thought how fortunate he was to be wearing a strong crash helmet to protect his head. His lip was badly cut and was bleeding profusely. I gave him my towel which I had brought for a swim.

I managed to get his motorcycle from under my car and left it on the side of the road. It was obvious we were both in a state of shock and I simply said "Hospital!"

He pointed the way and fortunately we only had to travel a few miles to a tiny village medical clinic. A young intern assured me that it was a routine incident and I should not be too upset. He encouraged me to meet my friend, John, and call the clinic from his hotel.

By the time I reached John's, I was trembling at the thought of what might have happened. John gave me a cognac and called the clinic to get the intern's report. When John returned, he informed me that the intern had put twelve stitches in the man's lip and he was released from the clinic. He admitted that the accident was his fault and wanted to pay for the damage to my car.

I was so relieved by the medical report that I wanted to cry. I told John that my friend, Dr. Aquarius, was coming for a holiday in a few weeks and I wanted her to see the Monchique landscape. He understood that I was too upset by the day's events and wanted to return to my villa and so we agreed to see each other very soon.

When Aquarius arrived, she was very excited about my plans to spend a few days at John's hotel in the mountains of Monchique. We always had fabulous times together but our days and nights in Portugal were pure poetry and it will forever remain that way in our memories of blissful love.

John was overjoyed to see us. He had cleared his schedule for two days so that he could show us his mountain paradise. How happy I was to see the gleam in Aquarius' eyes as we climbed over the mountain to explore the flowing streams and ponds filled with frogs.

John's knowledge of wildlife, trees, plants, rocks and the mountain people was an endless story of love and affection. His lifelong passion for open spaces was obvious from the start of our day's journey.

He owned a mountain "Garden of Eden" and he would never allow his place in the sun to be exploited.

Aquarius was spellbound by the natural beauty which surrounded her at every turn on the mountain. She has a special eye for nature's wonders and nothing escapes her vivid sense of color and landscape.

John and his Canadian girlfriend invited us to be their guests for dinner on the night of our arrival. John asked his chef to prepare a gourmet Portuguese treat. The assortment of food and wines could have been a banquet for the gods. The meal was served on the garden terrace surrounded by the scent of roses.

The view of mountain villages and the seacoast was incredible! Sunrises and sunsets are the magic hours of my life and to share them with someone who has the same passion is the ultimate joy in living.

From John's vantage point, we all experienced a feeling of peace and happiness which could never be touched in the world of normal reality. Even as the shadows of darkness and the flickering candlelight dimmed on our table, we all knew we had drifted into a sublime world unrelated to time and space. We were children of the universe.

Not long after Aquarius had returned to Germany, I received a long, whacky letter from my friend Dolcina. The letter was whacky because it was written in Portuguese. In order for me to answer this letter in Portuguese, I had to let Carlos and Louis do all the translating.

I would learn later that with the blessings of Angelo, my two translators made my response to Dolcina's whacky letter even crazier than her correspondence.

In essence, Dolcina wrote to tell me that she was living with her sister in Lisbon. She was working as a waitress in the Old City six days a week. On the seventh day, she would be happy to collapse in my arms. She was desperate to see me again.

In brief, Carlos told me that in my response to Dolcina, I expressed an urgent desire to see her dance again, but explained that it was impossible for me to go to Lisbon at this time as I was preparing to leave Portugal. Angelo had jokingly told me before I left Vale du Lobo that the P.S.'s at the conclusion of both our letters were so hot that they had to be put out with cold water!

34 / Once an Activist, . . .

Before I left Portugal, an incident occurred which triggered glorious memories of my past as a state senator and candidate for governor of New Jersey in 1980 to 1981.

In the seven months that I had lived in the Algarve, it had only rained four or five times. The weather of the Algarve is often compared in guide books to the weather of southern California, where there is very little rainfall.

However, in mid-March a heavy storm hit the Algarve with a vengeance. For twenty-four hours, thunder and lightning and extremely heavy rain, accompanied by gale force winds, played havoc with the coastline. Heavy sea and crashing wave action continued for several days. It was shocking to see the damage. The beachfront had disappeared into the sea.

As a former chairman of the New Jersey Beach Erosion Commission, I was familiar with this problem on both the Atlantic and Pacific coastlines. Only now I was living in the Algarve.

When I was finally able to survey the damage to the Algarve coastline, I could not believe my eyes. Tons and tons of cliffs which had formerly provided countless sunbathers with shelter had been washed away in the stormy sea. Many, many more cliffs were cracked and showed signs of plummeting into the sea at any moment.

I was very upset by what I viewed as a very dangerous situation for sunbathers who spent their days at the foot of these eroding cliffs.

By the time I returned to my villa, I had already composed in my head a statement regarding the dangerous condition of the beachfront. Only if you are an activist or political campaigner can you fully appreciate my outrage and how my blood was boiling. That is when my adrenaline is really calling for action.

Angelo and Emanuel, who had vested interests in the preservation of their beachfront, liked what I had to say. They translated my statement into Portuguese and mailed it off to the leading newspapers. Two days later, my story hit the front pages of the Algarve newspapers: "Vale du Lobo, the jewel of the Algarve, goes from 5 Stars to 1 Star!"

Before the end of the week, there were danger signs posted everywhere and a team of officials from the Algarve and Lisbon came to inspect the beach damage. It felt good to be back in the news and that night I allowed myself the luxury of re-examining my years in politics as a democratic senator from New Jersey from 1974 until 1978.

Also, in 1980 to 1981 I became a democratic candidate for governor of the State of New Jersey. Even when I was a teacher, I always provoked my students with the question, "Can one man or one woman make a difference?"

Following the tragic assassinations of John Kennedy, Robert Kennedy and the Nobel Peace Prize winner, Dr. Martin Luther King, there was a song that was being sung all over America. "Someone left the cake out in the rain, and we'll never get that recipe again!"

I also had the sad feeling, as did many people throughout the world, that something was happening in America. Perhaps everything was changing and would never be the same again. For me, liberalism and even idealism in American politics had ended. It is obvious to me that the Nixon and Reagan administrators turned their backs on the masses.

Even democrats became conservative in an effort to be elected to high office. There are no more liberal leaders in America or in Europe! World politics has changed and today the game is weapons before humanity.

When I decided to run for the Senate in New Jersey in 1973 I was a liberal idealist, as I always was and always will be. The year before I made my bid for the Senate I campaigned for George McGovern despite the fact I could not get enthusiastic about his chances to defeat Richard Nixon.

One day I had a call requesting me to meet Shirley MacLaine who was one of McGovern's star fund raisers. Shirley was coming to New Jersey to address a large group of Democratic women and I would be the master of the ceremony.

After meeting her, I was totally convinced that she would have done much better than George McGovern, had she been a candidate instead of a fund raiser. She is both brilliant and charming!

Also, like myself, Shirley MacLaine makes no secret of her sincere desire to put humanity as the highest priority with military weapons systems at the bottom.

Sitting next to her, prior to my introduction, I had the feeling she knew what America already knew. Nixon would be re-elected by a landslide victory over McGovern.

She looked very detached and so I decided to jolt her out of her seat. My introductory remarks were very brief and I concluded by saying that it gives me the greatest pleasure to welcome Shirley McGovern to the state of New Jersey.

Shirley's head had snapped in the direction of my smiling face and for a moment there was a shocking silence from the totally female audience. The brief silence was followed by peals of laughter when Shirley began to wave her finger at me, as a parent does when scolding a child.

It was the perfect way to relax everyone in a desperate campaign.

I was filled with positive energy on the night I appeared with several other Democrats hoping for the Senate nomination. To interview the candidates, the selection committee picked a well-known, oceanside resort and restaurant called Peninsula House in Sea Bright.

Every summer Frank Sinatra used to treat his mother, who was from Hoboken, New Jersey, for a vacation at this historic resort hotel.

After I made my presentation, I informed one of my supporters that I would be walking on the beach while the selection committee was making its decision.

I will never forget the Spring night air, the ocean spray and the stars on this night that would change my life forever. About an hour later I saw my friend racing along the beach shouting, "You made it, you made it!"

While it was only April, and the election would not be until November 6, 1973, I didn't want to lose any time organizing an effective campaign.

My campaign opponent, Republican Senator Richard Stout, was a household word in Monmouth County and was highly thought of as a future candidate for governor. He was a lawyer and the dean of the Senate where he had served for over twenty-five years. In addition, Senator Stout was highly respected and was well-liked by both democrats and republicans.

He would be a formidable opponent.

Dick Stout was also a personal friend of mine. He and his wife Nancy had six children and I had the pleasure of teaching some of them.

It would not be easy to defeat a man of his political stature and personal popularity.

When I went to my bank to request a $25,000 loan for my campaign expenses the manager almost fell off his chair. He politely informed me that, based on my teaching salary, et cetera, it was impossible for the bank to extend that much credit.

In order for me to receive $25,000, the bank would require four co-signers with good credit ratings.

I was in a daze when I left the bank, but I quickly recovered and by the time I had reached my home, I had four names in the back of my head—Charles Frankel, David Reznikoff, Bernie Karasic and Billy Poznak.

All four men had known me from my teaching as well as from my work as a township councilman. I invited them to my home to discuss my campaign and also to inform them about the problem of a bank loan.

Before I could relate the story concerning the bank loan, they all looked at one another and then asked me how they could help me.

After my election, not one of these Jewish friends ever asked me for a personal or political favor. They were simply very happy that they were able to help me to attain my goal.

Some years later when I was traveling in Israel, I sent them all notes to tell them that I had never forgotten how helpful they had been to me in my race for the Senate.

Once I had received the $25,000 in my campaign account, I very quickly became organized. I found an excellent campaign headquarters in the center of a shopping mall where hundreds of people were passing by every day.

Sylvia Asch, a middle-aged political professional, was hired to run the campaign office. In one week we were flooded with volunteers from twenty-two towns in two counties.

I also hired an outstanding public relations man and a photographer. In less than one month we had developed a well-oiled political machine. We were rolling!

I held a press conference to announce that I would be walking for votes in every one of the twenty-two communities in my 10th district. It was a page one story!

Everyday after school, a volunteer group of high school students would join me on my campaign walks. They would distribute literature and, at the same time, make a political pitch for their teacher. It was very effective!

On weekends, my campaign "Boost Buehler for the Senate" went to the supermarkets, bowling alleys, everywhere. In four months, we had virtually saturated the entire district. Voters in Monmouth and Ocean counties were beginning to see Buehler in their sleep.

Now we had name recognition and things were looking good. I had one key student, Mark, who was in my "Dirty Dozen" class. Mark became so personally involved in my race for the Senate that he arranged small neighborhood coffee parties where I could meet the voters in a more private forum.

Dressed always in a suit and tie, which I was surprised to see, he became one of my most reliable campaign managers. By the time I had arrived at these social gatherings, Mark had already distributed my literature and was prepared to deliver his "meet my favorite teacher" introductory speech. Mark was very proud to be a key member of my campaign organization.

I must explain that my "Dirty Dozen" class, which I had volunteered to teach, was made up of the high school's most incorrigible seniors. They were all potential drop outs who were on to every game in the book, including the drug scene. My staff of teachers gave them the name "The Dirty Dozen" from the film of the same name starring Lee Marvin and his criminal soldiers in World War II.

Sometime after graduation, Mark went out to California and became successful in the film industry.

Another student who was a member of my infamous twelve was Ted who was also active in my Senate race. Ted was a star runner on the high school track team which I coached, but his first love was auto mechanics.

There were days when I excused Ted from my history class so he could work with my friend, Al Courter, who was the auto shop teacher.

On graduation day, Ted won two awards. He was a champion cross-country runner and he was the state champion "Trouble Shooter."

The annual "Trouble Shooter" competition, which was sponsored by a national car manufacturer, recognized excellence in a student's ability to recognize and repair engine problems. The state award was given to the student who was the quickest and most efficient mechanic. The day Ted walked into the principal's office with a three-foot high trophy, he himself was standing ten feet tall. Ted opened an auto body shop in Point Pleasant and today earns more money than the highest paid teacher in New Jersey.

My philosophy of teaching was very simple and basic. Discover the interest and desires of the students regardless of their academic standing. Once you have established a personal contact with each student, you must help him or her to realize his or her full potential and then go for it!

The "Boost Buehler for Senator" was beginning to attract statewide attention.

New Jersey is one of the most densely populated states

in America with close to ten million people living in a small geographic location on the Atlantic Ocean. Our state is referred to as the bedroom state since many home owners commute to New York City everyday where they earn their daily bread, et cetera.

Articulate transportation systems have also been a big problem for New Jersey workers who must travel to New York. In 1973, the train system from New Jersey to New York became a major issue in my campaign.

In 1968, New Jersey residents voted in a special referendum to support a thirty-eight million dollar railroad improvement bond fund. From 1968 to 1973 virtually no action had been taken by the state to utilize this money for rail transportation.

It was a story which I would become very familiar with in the "bullshit world of politics." The people say "do it" and the politicians and bureaucrats milk it to death. In the end, the project hangs in suspended limbo.

Senator Richard Stout was the chairman of the Senate Transportation Committee. I decided to exploit Senator Stout's vulnerability as the chairman of transportation. If I could convince the voters that I would do a better job in the Senate, I could win the election.

Since my county had thousands of railroad commuters, I wanted to meet them all personally and learn about their biggest complaints on the rail system.

We set in motion a fantastic system at every train station in the district. Before I would go to school every morning, I went to town rail stations where my staff would offer coffee and doughnuts to the commuters. My public relations man had worked up a slogan picturing me on the trains talking with the commuters. My picture was saying "Buehler is not enjoying the Jersey train ride." In the evening, I would ride the train and meet the same commuters my staff and I had seen in the morning.

After several weeks we knew we were making progress because the newspaper ran a page one story concerning commuter problems on the railroad.

The Stout camp soon realized that he should not take my campaign too lightly.

Without dedicated political volunteers and efficient organization, it is impossible to upset a powerful incumbent. I had two individuals who were the backbone of my commuter organization. Jules owned a small trailer which he turned into a moving campaign headquarters. Every work day morning at 5:00 A.M. he would get coffee and doughnuts from an all night diner to bring to the train station.

Leo, his partner who later became my lover, was the one who distributed the early morning gifts to every commuter on the Jersey shore line. The three of us made a "dynamite team." Every commuter came to know us on a personal level.

When election day came, we all knew how the commuter was going to vote. If I was serious enough to board the trains every day to observe cars without drinking water or toilet paper and listen to complaints about hot cars in the summer, cold cars in the winter, et cetera, perhaps I could make a difference.

On election day, November 6, 1973, I visited every polling place in the county to thank all my many volunteer workers. By the time I arrived home, my wife was receiving the first early election returns.

Our campaign manager, who was monitoring all twenty-two towns, called to say the race was very close, but we were looking good. Then, while I was preparing to shower and get dressed for the win or lose party, I had a call that brought a big smile to my face. I had defeated Stout in a largely republican city.

Buzzy also became very excited by the news of our imminent upset of Senator Stout.

She had been a vital part of the campaign and had worked closely with Charles Frankel and her best friend Ester Karasic, who was in charge of campaign funds. My wife called down from our second floor bedroom that she was getting dressed for a victory celebration!

I knew it was going to be a happy party. When we arrived at our campaign headquarters, it was sheer bedlam in the best sense of the word. Cheering supporters had traveled from all over the county to congratulate their new state senator.

November 6 was also my oldest son, Warren's, birthday and so we had much to celebrate in our family.

On election night it was impossible to thank everyone for all the voluntary work they had done to make my victory dream become a reality. I made a very brief speech inviting everyone to join me in the state capital in January for the official swearing in ceremony.

Sometime later, as I was preparing to leave the celebration, Leo walked over to me to personally congratulate me. Her soft inviting kiss and my return was the promise of an attraction over which neither one of us had total control. For sixteen seasons of our life, four years together, we would scale the highest peaks and summit of a love relationship that never required any words. Often she would tell me that she enjoyed the golden silence of our love more than anything.

Leo was much younger than me. She looked like a twin to Jane Fonda only she was more voluptuous! She was also extremely intelligent. She ran my Senate office with the skill and efficiency of a political professional.

Working with her were two young attorneys, Matt and Paul, who were always sensitive to my personal ambitions as a state legislator. Their youth, intelligence and personal enthusiasm on my behalf were always a credit to the state of New Jersey. I will always remember those four years in the Senate as a time of great excitement and achievement.

Only two months after I was in office, the governor called to inform me that he was going to sign my $38 million dollar railroad improvement bill into law. I was invited to the law signing ceremony and had to be prepared to address the reporters, et cetera. It was the culminating act of my entire campaign and I could not have been happier or more proud than I was at that moment in my political life.

In the meantime, I had returned to the trains to thank all the commuters for their votes and for their confidence in me. They were astonished to see me again after the election. Some of them told me I was the first politician who ever returned after a victory to say thank you!

For me, it was a tremendous honor to be a law maker and representative of ten million people in the "Garden State" of America. It was also very gratifying to be the only teaching senator in New Jersey.

In most states lawyers dominate the state legislature. I quickly gained the reputation of a concerned law maker. I wanted to see and understand everything in my state that was related to the well-being of the people. After school and on the weekends I went to visit old age nursing homes, mental institutions, schools for the deaf and dumb, the handicapped and even our state prison in Rahway.

One afternoon, Matt came running into my office waving the local county newspaper. On page three in small headlines there was a lead to a story which started, "Buehler spends a day in prison!" He did not think it was funny.

He called the press and complained that some people only had time to read headlines. Matty was like that. The stories he did not enjoy kept him awake at night.

Several days before I went to the state prison, I called the warden for his permission. He was elated and told me I was the first senator to make such a request. The warden was a relatively young man who was winning a reputation as an innovator of prison reform.

Of course, all the prison inmates were told in advance of my desire to visit the prison. A small group of "lifers," who were serving ninety-nine years for murder, requested an opportunity to meet with me privately.

I was aware of the fact that the Rahway prison had recently made a film called *Scared Straight*, which won an Academy Award. The film depicted a group of men who were sentenced to life in prison. With the consent of the warden incorrigible juvenile offenders were invited to the Rahway State Prison to spend one day with the men who had been sentenced to life.

In that one terrible day the film accurately dramatized the ugliest events which take place in any "major league" prison.

For the so-called tough juvenile visitors to the prison, the public shower room can be a devastating experience from which one is unable to recover. This and other prison realities could shock the most hardened teenage criminal to tears of anguish and also great fear.

Prior to the young superintendent of correction's arrival in Rahway, the inmates spent their time washing institutional laundry and making automobile license plates for the state of New Jersey. He instituted a working program in cooperation with local industry to employ model prisoners.

Each working day the inmates were taken by prison

transportation to a local factory where they performed numerous jobs. The income from this work was used as a form of retribution to those members of society whose lives they had offended.

Before I left the New Jersey Senate, my personal friend and colleague, Senator John Russo, successfully introduced legislation to return the death penalty to New Jersey. The "electric chair" was taken out of moth balls and returned to New Jersey.

When I voted against Senator Russo's bill I was only thinking, "Judge not or you will be judged. Condemn not or you will be condemned!"

At the same time as Senator John Russo was winning statewide support to return capital punishment to New Jersey, another very close friend of mine in the Senate was looking for support to ban guns in our state. Senator Alex Menza, like Senator Russo, was a well-known lawyer.

Both senators were considered intellectually gifted, outstanding debators.

Senator Menza's gun control bill would forbid the manufacturing and sale of guns in New Jersey. I joined Menza as a co-sponsor knowing full well that we were fighting an uphill battle in what I believed to be a lost cause. Nonetheless, Senator Menza was determined to put his legislation before the full Senate for debate and decision.

A few weeks before the vote was to be taken, my office received a call from a New Jersey delegation of the National Gun and Rifle Association of America. They wanted to arrange a meeting with me prior to the debate on gun control. My staff was anticipating their call since many lobbyists frequently made similar requests on important legislation.

My staff and I set aside a Saturday morning for a

meeting in my office. Leo arrived very early carrying bags of fresh bakery rolls and a delicious variety of buns.

By the time the four lobbyists had arrived, she had made coffee and set up a small serving table in the conference room. I had already given my two legal aides instructions that under no circumstances were they to interrupt the lobbyists during their discourse. This was not so easy!

Obviously unaware of the fact that I was a history teacher, they launched into a series of arguments to support their position. The right to bear arms against the savage American Indian was guaranteed by the Constitution, which was written by the founding fathers, including George Washington.

After almost two hours, they drank my coffee, ate my rolls and buns and, continually staring at Leo, they brought their case all the way to Star Wars and Rambo!

I could see Matty and Paul were so tense that they were ready to explode. It was not very pleasant for any of us, but we also knew that our voices and our intense feelings on the subject of gun control were only a whisper in the winds of American thought and attitude. Like the handful of abolitionists who peacefully fought against slavery in America, we were outcasts in the twentieth century.

Leo left the room to make some fresh coffee. This was the signal that the lobbyist's time had expired and now it was our turn to respond. Paul, who had been one of my best students and who never had time to tie his shoelaces, opened our peaceful non-violent retaliation!

He asked if the founding fathers, including George Washington, would have approved of America dropping nuclear bombs on two cities in Japan during World War II. I saw their faces turning red with anger.

Matty picked up the attack by telling them that neither

Washington nor the founding fathers of the American Constitution ever intended to condone murdering hundreds of thousands of innocent women, and children, and old men in Hiroshimi and Nagasaki. Now they were livid with rage! I reminded them that "liberty, justice, and equality" were also a vital part of the Constitution and now it was our turn to explain the other side of the argument in favor of gun control in America and, indeed, throughout the world.

When it came my turn to sum up our strong objections to the manufacturing and sale of weapons, I thought to myself, *This is a dress rehearsal for the Senate debate which will also be fruitless!* I started with a very personal story and a general observation which I knew had great validity.

I told them that my oldest daughter Wendy's best girlfriend, Joanna, had her life shattered by a thirty-eight revolver. When Joanna and her husband returned from their wedding honeymoon, he presented her with a deadly and shocking surprise.

He was a traveling salesman and his job required him to be away from home for short periods of time. Unbeknownst to Joanna before their marriage, her husband had a license to own a revolver.

Before he left her on his first trip in their married life, he presented Joanna with his thirty-eight pistol. He showed her how to fire the loaded weapon and instructed her to keep it under her pillow when she went to bed each night when he was away on business.

Joanna was terrified! After he left, she called my daughter to ask her if she could sleep at her home. She described their long argument and her husband's stubborn insistence that she keep the gun handy for her own protection. Joanna never returned to her home or her husband. Some weeks later she filed for a divorce on the grounds of incompatibility!

Throughout the world of my travels and experience, most women have no desire to possess weapons of death and destruction. Conversely, it is my personal observation that most men legally or illegally own weapons for their personal satisfaction.

The lobbyists were not pleased when I gave them state and federal documents concerning the appalling number of deaths caused by the use of deadly weapons. I concluded my argument against weapons with a thought I will repeat over and over until the last breath is in my body.

Even if George Bush and Mikhail Gorbachev and their awesome military establishment eliminate 90 percent of their military power, they will still have enough nuclear power to wipe out the entire human race from this planet.

The U.S. today is leading the world in the manufacturing and sales of weapons systems. The sale and distribution of weapons is one of the largest economic enterprises in America and there is no end in sight. Any nation that must rely on weapons for economic survival cannot boast about being a peaceful and peace-loving country.

The American military will spend over two trillion taxpayers' dollars in the next five "Star Wars" years. When will the American people wake up and ask their representatives in Washington how long they must wait before our government will spend two trillion dollars on humanity!

During the term in the Senate, I became involved in issues which made national and international news. I had been elevated to Chairman of the Transportation Committee following my success with the railroad operation.

For several years, the French and English governments were seeking permission to fly the S.S.T. Concorde into J.F.K. airport in New York. New York and New Jersey share in a joint bi-state agreement to work together for the benefit of all their citizens.

I received correspondence from my Senate counterpart in Albany, New York asking me to join the state of New York in an effort to block the Concorde from landing at J.F.K. airport.

The New Jersey Senate charged me with the responsibility of holding a series of public hearings to get all the facts concerning the supersonic passenger plane. For several weeks I read everything I could obtain about the world's most sophisticated supersonic commercial aircraft.

I was very impressed by the outstanding safety record performance of the sixteen Concordes which have never been involved in an accident. To fly across the Atlantic Ocean in two hours at the speed of MACH 2 or 1500 miles per hour is an aviation accomplishment that England and France can be very proud of.

I had learned that the only serious objection to the Concorde's landing in New York was coming from people who said it was too noisy. I had discussions with experts in the field of environmental noise pollution. I learned that the 707 and 747 were just as loud as the Concorde on landing. However, while the Concorde was making more noise on takeoff, it was out of the air terminal space in less than ten seconds.

Even before the hearings, I received much hate mail, especially from New York.

Newspapers were even critical! One leading New York paper had me flying the Concorde in a funny cartoon. Only I was landing in New Jersey and not in New York. Apparently no one had taken the time to research the fact that the Newark International Airport runway was not long enough for the Concorde take-off.

It is no secret today that our planet's environment is

in danger. In 1976, I became involved in a perennial problem regarding off-shore drilling.

The Mid-East oil price game has prompted many nations to explore the depths of the sea in search of "black gold." Continuing oil spills have a devastating effect on marine life. Add to this the industrial and chemical toxic waste flowing into our rivers and streams, and you realize that we are living on an endangered planet.

The rape of our earth and its natural beauty is one of the greatest tragedies of the twentieth century. My many European friends who are members of the Green Party will take little solace from an American television commercial showing an American Indian crying over the fate of his once beautiful land of natural beauty and wonder.

When I learned that officials in Washington, D.C., had granted drilling permits to Exxon, Shell and Texaco oil companies to commence drilling activities fourteen miles off the coast of Atlantic City, New Jersey, I was in a rage. The government was conducting a hearing in Atlantic City to insure everyone that it would be of great benefit to the country and the citizens of New Jersey. I had a different opinion!

There was not much time to prepare a statement of factual evidence to express my opposition; however, Matty and Paul worked day and night to supply me with accurate research documentation.

When I arrived in Atlantic City, I soon discovered that most of the speakers were in favor of the drilling operation. I also learned that the hearings were being televised nationwide.

Similar hearings had been conducted in California where the bottom line position of the government was very simple and very legal. California did not have jurisdiction outside the international twelve mile Pacific Ocean limit.

Prior to my departure for Europe in 1984, I was visiting Santa Barbara, California where my surfing son, John, was contemplating going to college. Walking on the beach of Santa Barbara, which is trapped between the blue Pacific Ocean and majestic San Yancez mountains, can be a fantastic experience. However, when you leave the beach, you must scrape layers of tar from the bottom of your feet. Surfers' boards are covered with tar also.

But the worst damage has been suffered by the fish and wildlife. The sight of a beached whale is testimony to the severe damage caused by an oil spill. Oil spills, which were never supposed to happen, have become commonplace all over the world. Likewise, through propaganda, the public was led to believe that nuclear plants were perfectly safe.

Prior to my introduction as a speaker, I was listening to a southern governor who was extolling the virtues of off-shore drilling. He was very good! He was telling America about the economic rewards associated with the discovery of natural gas and petroleum. He also gave an emotional pitch for America's desire to be free from the Mid-East oil cartel which was strangling the American oil industry.

I could see his statement was well received by the exceptionally large Atlantic City audience. From past experience with reporters, radio and television commentators, I had learned that the first thirty seconds are crucial. I wanted to electrify my audience with a strong opening statement.

When I arrived home later that evening, my wife told me she had watched me on national television and there were many telephone calls for press interviews, radio shows, et cetera.

National television had focused its attention on the

statement of support from the southern governor. Following his statement, the TV commentator introduced me as a senator from New Jersey who was vigorously opposed to the off-shore drilling operation.

I had said that Washington, D.C., and the power brokers in the oil industry were committed to raping the state of New Jersey. Furthermore, the constitutional provision to protect the individual state's rights was being blatantly ignored by the federal government. It was one of the greatest crimes of the twentieth century!

As is typical in sensational stories, the news omitted the part of my statement which suggested several alternate sources of energy which are less hostile to the environment of America. I had mentioned, for example, that America has more than a thousand-year supply of coal resources. Western Europe and China are two of our biggest coal energy customers. If they can control the sulphur burn off, why are we concentrating on the high risk of drilling the ocean's floor??

As a result of appearing on national television as an advocate of state rights vs. the federal government, my office was flooded with telephone calls and mail, all very complimentary. I also received an invitation from a Philadelphia television station to participate in a debate against an expert in off-shore drilling operations.

While I was getting a cosmetic make-up treatment before going in front of the bright lights of the TV cameras, I was informed that my debating adversary had just arrived at the studio. When Sam Hudson walked into the make-up room, we both laughed and shook hands very warmly. Sam was my son Warren's father-in-law and so as you can imagine, it was a very unusual debate. We both jokingly agreed to call it a draw!

Two other major issues that I dealt with during my

years in the Senate also received national attention. One of these issues led to my downfall as a senator!

Atlantic City, New Jersey, is well known throughout the world as the place where the most talented and beautiful women from every state in the Union compete for the coveted title of "Miss America." Today, as a result of the action taken by the New Jersey State legislature during my term in office, Atlantic City is the number one legalized gambling center in the U.S.A.

When the bill was first introduced in the Senate by a group of South Jersey senators, there was a storm of protest throughout the State. My initial reaction was to campaign actively against legalized gambling casinos in New Jersey. New Jersey was already suffering from the odious reputation as one of the most dangerously polluted states in the nation. New Jersey has also been referred to as a "Mafia-controlled" state just waiting for the advent of legalized gambling as another base for underworld activity and ultimate control.

Once again, the lobbyists were everywhere attempting to convince the legislature that controlled legalized gambling would be of great benefit to New Jersey. The arguments for casino gambling were very strong.

Each hotel casino operation would provide five thousand new jobs for one of New Jersey's most depressed cities. In addition, the legislation provided for profits to the state which would be given to retired senior citizens to help pay for their home utility expenses (gas, electricity, et cetera). The prevailing evidence was overwhelmingly positive and my opinion was changing.

Even the Catholic Church became actively involved in campaigning against the Atlantic City legislation. While church officials never admitted that they were afraid of losing Bingo customers and much revenue, there were those whose believed this to be one of their main reasons for objecting to the legislation.

When the Atlantic City legalized casino bill came up for a Senate vote, I was voting in the affirmative. While the results have not been perfect, it has nonetheless been a major factor in the recovery of Atlantic City's economy.

In my first year in the Senate, the New Jersey Supreme Court threatened to close all the public schools in our state. The New Jersey State Constitution had a unique provision that every child should be guaranteed a "thorough, efficient and equal opportunity" in education.

There were many wealthy cities that were able to provide outstanding educational conditions for their children. The rich cities could attract the best teachers with higher salaries and better teaching conditions.

On the other hand, the poor towns were at a decided disadvantage. Many of these poor communities could not compete with neighboring cities.

Consequently, there was a large gap separating rich towns and poor communities. Ultimately, this situation was tested in a court case.

Parents with children in a poor community charged the state with educational discrimination. Using the New Jersey Constitution as their basis for legal action, the case finally reached the Supreme Court.

The issue received nationwide attention. Was it possible for a state to eliminate a class educational society?

In a landmark decision, the Supreme Court ruled that the legislature and the governor were mandated to correct the error and institute a new system for funding education in New Jersey. The Supreme Court, when rendering their judgment, gave the state a deadline by which to correct the problem. If the deadline was not met, the Supreme Court would close all public schools in New Jersey.

New Jersey and New Hampshire were the only states in America that did not have a state income tax. When the legislative battle was over, New Hampshire would stand alone.

As the only teacher in the Senate, I also served on the Education Committee. I became a co-sponsor of the bill that became popularly known as the "T & E" bill (thorough and efficient).

This bill, which was intended to equalize educational benefits for every school child, had to have a funding mechanism. This would be a statewide income tax!

It was the most intense political issue in New Jersey legislative history and the question was finally resolved by the democrats who could only find one republican state senator to support the new tax.

By this time, I had become a key member of the governor's leadership campaign to convince New Jersey citizens that we had an obligation to every citizen to make New Jersey the number one state in the nation in providing equal educational opportunities.

In several private meetings with the Governor, I had expressed my strong support for the T & E legislation, but I told him that I was the vulnerable senator in New Jersey.

The leading republican county newspaper was damaging my reputation on a regular basis with headline stories concerning my two incomes. The attack was vicious and my response was always lost on the wrong pages of the newspaper. Everyone in New Jersey learned that I was the highest-paid teacher in the state. My personal finances were public information. I was receiving a salary as a teacher and a second income as a senator. While this was perfectly legal, just as lawyers and everyone else had two incomes, my case became sensational page one headlines.

To make matters worse, because of my active support

for the income tax, I was receiving a lot of HATE MAIL. I was also receiving anonymous phone calls at my home and office. Callers threatened to kill me if I voted in favor of the infamous income tax! I had twenty-four hour protection from local and state police during the time of the long, long summer debate. It was not a pleasant time for my family.

When it was all finished, I knew I would be a one-term state senator! I was already thinking of my future. However, since I am unable to tell fortunes, I could not know the shocks I would receive in the next few years.

35 / On the Beach

All of my European friends will enjoy the story of another unusual adventure which I enjoyed immensely before I left the Senate. Because of my interest in the beaches of New Jersey, I was appointed chairman of the State Beach Erosion Commission. In no time at all, I managed to have the committee on beach erosion changed to the committee to study public access to the beaches of New Jersey.

Although New Jersey's 125-mile Atlantic beachfront cannot be compared to California's majestic 750-mile Pacific coastline, it is, nevertheless, one of the most attractive, sandy beaches in the world. Unlike, California, however, where beaches are all free and open to the public as are most beaches in the world, in New Jersey there is usually a beach admission charge.

In New Jersey, unfortunately, most of the beachfront property is privately owned. Also, with only a few exceptions, most of the beaches charge a large price to use the property. This includes all men, women and children. Fishermen, surfers, swimmers, even sun bathers, must pay a fee for any use of the beaches.

There are some things a senator is able to accomplish if he has the initiative and courage to pursue a noble cause. I decided to do something very dramatic!

Following six statewide public hearings concerning public access to the beaches, I called a press conference to announce that I was going to walk the entire 125 miles of the New Jersey coastline to personally examine every inch of beachfront! The story was a mild sensation and was picked up by the international wire service. My office could not handle all of the phone calls. Likewise, my mail was impossible. Thousands of letters both pro and con were dumped in my office for several weeks. I knew my beach promenade had hit a nerve center.

Do not ever let a politician tell you that he or she does not have a big ego! I deliberately timed my beach walk during the summer season when the beaches were packed with people from everywhere enjoying their holiday vacation. I was accompanied by officials from the State Department of Environmental Protection and the Attorney General's office.

I was mobbed every day by beach lovers and concerned public officials as well. Whenever and wherever I saw an illegal "no trespassing" sign, a private "keep out" sign or a fence, I had it taken down. I was determined to prove that anyone can use the beaches up to the high water mark, which is the point where the waves have washed up on the shoreline. Any obstruction up to this point I had removed. The public was cheering me, but the officials were boiling mad!

With many reporters, television cameras and radio people interrupting my beach walk, I was only able to cover ten miles each day. By the third day, I noticed people waving to me from the beaches and lifeguards were offering me cool soda and water to keep up my strength. No one was asking me to pay a fee to walk on the beach or to swim in the ocean. I was enjoying the walk and I was becoming very dark skinned.

I also had a surprise call from Bill Bradley who volunteered to join me for a few days on my beach walk. Every adult in America knew Bill Bradley! A former Princeton University scholar and All-American basketball player who went on to become a Rhodes Scholar and New York Knickerbocker Hall of Famer, Bill Bradley's name is like magic from New York City to Los Angeles. He was greeted on every beach by crowds of people who wanted to shake his hand or get his autograph. If he is widely acclaimed in America, I am confident that by the year 1992, everyone in the world will recognize the name of Senator Bill Bradley, the democratic United States Senator from the great state of New Jersey!

At the time of my beach walk, Bill Bradley had never held public office. Our discussions, as we walked along the beach, were very enlightening for the both of us. Bill wanted to help me in my campaign and of course, by appearing with me in public, he made no secret of the fact that he viewed me as a concerned legislator. He was also enjoying the walk and examining the conditions along the Jersey shore. We both knew also that he was testing the public voters for a possible future campaign as a United States Senator.

We had arrived at Manasquan beach and stopped at the boardwalk for a lunch break. The feature of the day was "Bradley and Buehler Burgers." We both joked about who was selling the most burgers that sunny day in Manasquan.

I did not have to explain the problems of the Jersey beaches to Bradley because he was already aware of them prior to our personal examination. The problems on the New Jersey beachfront were not new.

Beach erosion is only one of the serious conditions. Millions and millions of American federal and state taxpayers' dollars are spent annually to restore damage to jettys, bulkheads, boardwalks, et cetera.

No Jersey shore town could possibly pay for the excessive damage with meager local funds. Consequently, the legal question of private vs. public access to the beaches of New Jersey is for me very obvious.

Even if we do not want to acknowledge the right to walk on God's created earth, we must certainly recognize the fact that if every taxpayer is paying to maintain the beaches, then they should also be partners in the pleasures of the Atlantic coastline.

On the fifth day of my walk, I passed over the private property of many affluent Republican homeowners. The very next night, my oldest daughter, Wendy, was invited to a party in Bay Head where her girlfriend's parents owned a home. Wendy was very upset when she had to leave the party because the topic of conversation was her own father. Ignorant of my daughter's presence at the affair, everyone was at liberty to shoot her father down because of his insane idea to open up the beaches for everyone.

One day after school, I came into my office surprised to see Leo reading a letter with tears were running down her sad face. It was a letter from a North Jersey doctor who had recently lost his daughter in a moped accident.

The personal story in this letter was the saddest that ever came into my office. The doctor told the story of his thirteen year old daughter who requested a moped for her birthday. Fully aware of the fact that it was a motorized vehicle, he reluctantly granted her the wish which led to her fatal accident on her thirteenth birthday. He learned that I was the head of the Transportation Committee and was urging me to do something to prevent this situation from getting out of control. His closing remarks were to the effect that while it was too late for him and his wife to save their beloved child, he hoped and prayed that I could save other innocent childrens' lives.

I immediately mailed copies of his letter to every member of the legislature and the governor. In forty-eight hours, I had my legal advisors draft legislation to correct this problem which had been responsible for the death of a child.

My bill, which was signed into law in less than one week, established the minimum driving age at fifteen. The law also required the potential operator to pass a state written test and a road test. The operator was also required to carry insurance.

Some days later, I received a letter from the same doctor thanking me for my quick response and for restoring his faith in the democratic process. I will never forget his tragic story.

Being a member of the State Senate was not always work. There were so many social engagements and invitations to glamorous events that I could never manage to attend. All of the functions which I was able to fit into my schedule, I thoroughly enjoyed.

I had been a successful sponsor of a bill to increase the funding for the performing artists of New Jersey. Consequently, my wife and I always received complimentary invitations to all the main events.

One night we attended the opening night ballet performance. After the ballet, we were invited to a V.I.P. champagne party to meet the performers. The first person we were introduced to was Dustin Hoffman whose wife at the time was a ballet dancer. Before I had time to tell him I was surprised to see him in New Jersey, he was asking me how I enjoyed the ballet. I told him I was a ballet fan and that I had enjoyed the performance.

Holding his glass to his mouth, he floored me by asking how I enjoyed his wife's performance. Once again, before I could tell him that I wasn't even aware that his wife was in the ballet, he interrupted me with that world famous Dustin Hoffman grin from ear to ear. Smiling very impishly, he told me "she wasn't very good!"

I will always remember the night the governor asked me if I could attend a performance in Atlantic City that he was unable to make. The star performer was Barbara Eden! If there is entertainment in heaven, I hope Barbara Eden will be on the program.

Meeting her in her dressing suite after the show, I could not resist telling her that she was one of the most exciting performers I had ever seen. We became good friends immediately!

On one occasion, my friend John DeBella from the New York City District Attorney's office called to tell me he had four perfect seats to see Anthony Quinn play the role of Zorba the Greek on Broadway. John knew that Claire was a big fan of Anthony Quinn, as were we all.

Unknown to everyone, I had made arrangements to meet Zorba after the performance. I will never forget the look on my wife's face when Zorba wrapped his massive arms around my wife's shoulders and thanked her for coming to see the show. Even her meeting with President Jimmy Carter, who also put his arms around her, could not be compared with this meeting.

Even as a young boy, I remember walking along the water's edge, enjoying the feeling of the soft sand under my feet and the warm sun beating on my body. I was always building sand castles and dreaming of the day when I would be able to own a small beach cottage on the Atlantic Ocean. In the late 1960s, my youthful, utopian dream became a reality.

Anthony Weedo was a construction engineer from North Jersey who for many years owned a modest bungalow facing the sea. Over the years we became good friends. Anthony knew my heart's desire was to live within the sight and sound of the ocean.

One very hot and humid July day, he asked me if I would like to buy his cottage. He explained that he and his wife were getting on in years and he was retiring. His two sons had rejected the chance to purchase the cottage for their families.

I was flabbergasted! Anthony confessed that there had been a big family argument over his intentions to sell the cottage. He had grown tired of seeing his aging wife slaving in a hot kitchen every weekend preparing meals for their sons' families. He strongly felt it was time for his sons' wives to take over the kitchen and let his wife relax.

I could see how upset he was and I told him he should take more time before he made a final decision. He only smiled at me and asked me to make him an offer. Anthony Weedo knew I was a school teacher with a large family. When I gave him a ridiculously low figure, he extended his hand to mine and said, "You have just bought your dream!"

My sister Florence and her husband Dave had often told me how they wanted to own a beach cottage. When I called them they were elated. We formed a partnership!

After the summer tourist season is over, Point Pleasant Beach becomes very desolate, lonely and incredibly romantic. The countless days and nights of peaceful solitude which I enjoyed in the "Sandpiper" cottage were unforgettable hours of perfect bliss. Especially in the winter, I would sit for hours by my roaring fireplace listening to the sounds of the waves crashing on the beach. To watch an early sunrise out of the depths of the Atlantic Ocean horizon while you are enjoying your first morning coffee, is always a spectacular feeling. To share this moment with someone you love is the ultimate in sublime living.

I also knew how fortunate I was to be there. On dismal, foggy evenings there was a fog horn lighthouse to guide the fishermen through an inlet which was close to my bungalow. The lonely sounds of this mournful fog horn are unforgettable.

Years before I had purchased my "Shangri-la" in Point Pleasant, Eugene O'Neill, one of America's great playwrights, had lived there. He was also influenced by the constant droning sounds of the fog horn. You can feel the loneliness and isolation in O'Neill's autobiographical story, *Long Day's Journey into Night*.

O'Neill's tragic story of a mother who was a cocaine addict, his father, a frustrated aging Shakesperian actor, and a young dying brother suffering from tuberculosis, was many times portrayed on Broadway and in theaters around the world. Throughout the melodrama, the interminable fog horn reminds the audience of the awful reality of O'Neill's life with a dying family.

In 1965, I was selected for an academic grant to study at Princeton University. At that time, the university library was featuring an exhibit dealing with the writings of Eugene O'Neill. When I discovered that his wife was still living in Point Pleasant, I decided to pay her a courtesy call. Perhaps I was curious to meet the woman who had raised the two O'Neill children.

Shane was an unfortunate young man who died as an alcoholic. Oona, who now lives in Switzerland, was very young when she married one of the world's greatest silent film stars, Charlie Chaplin!

When I arrived at her home, I was shocked to see overgrown weeds and a dilapidated dwelling that must not have been repaired in years. I had to wonder what had happened to all the royalties from Eugene O'Neill's great works.

When Mrs. O'Neill answered the door, I was even more stunned by what I observed. Many cats came running out the door. Inside, books, magazines and newspapers were stacked from the floor almost to the ceiling. Mrs. O'Neill was living like a recluse! I realized immediately that she was totally incapable of engaging in any intelligent conversation.

Some months after my brief visit, there was a feature story in all the newspapers. Mrs. Eugene O'Neill was dying in the Point Pleasant hospital and Oona O'Neill Chaplin was flying from Switzerland to be by her mother's bedside.

There were many reasons why I was in love with Point Pleasant. I cherished my childhood memories. Later, when the daily pressures of being a teaching senator left very little time for my family or private personal moments, I could always run to my modest oceanside retreat.

Sometimes there were unexpected surprises. One night during the income tax debate, I left a meeting at the governor's mansion in Princeton and found my car passing my home in Monmouth County and then crossing over the Manasquan River bridge to another county and another world.

Perhaps it was all an illusion! As I approached my driveway, I noticed Leo's car and smoke rising out of the cottage chimney. Entering the cottage, my eyes rested on the glowing fire and the radiance of Leo's face. She had fallen asleep on the large sofa by the fire and there was a small note standing by a bottle of wine and two glasses. "Please wake me only if you want to make love!"

36 / Romance and Complications

Long before I left Portugal in the Spring of 1987, I was anticipating my long stay "lifetime" in Greece. How could I know that in the next year I would come close to losing my car and my life.

Everyone who has ever known me realizes that I do not like to say good-bye. It is always I will see you later and, of course, it is true for I will always remain in contact with my closest friends, regardless of where we are living.

My first stop was a brief visit to my friends Roberta and Fernando in Barcelona, Spain. They had wanted me to see the popular Pueblo Espanol which portrays the typical life in villages in all regions of Spain. It was a fascinating display that reminded me of Williamsburg, Virginia.

In the evening they invited me to join their friends at a coastal village fish fry. It was an enchanted night alive with stars and countless tiny lights coming from the offshore fishing boats. The enchanting sounds of musicians playing the Spanish guitar made the night complete.

My next stop was a special birthday gift to myself. Arles, France, is synonymous with Vincent Van Gogh. I wanted to spend another few days traveling on the same streets where Vincent had created some of his greatest masterpieces. While his tiny yellow house had been destroyed in World War II, I still found many places where he and Paul Gauguin had spent so much time fighting the maddening winds of the mistral and also fighting with one another.

I had written a postcard to *mon ami* (my friend) Michele in Paris apprising her of my visit to Arles, but I did not tell her where I might be staying.

Every Saturday morning is market day in the central square. I was sitting at a sidewalk café enjoying a late morning cappuccino and a croissant. In the distance I could hear many people laughing and shouting. Coming into the market square was a small locomotive on wheels. As it approached the place where I was sitting, I could not believe my eyes. Michele, engineer's cap and all, was at the controls.

When I jumped out of my chair and rushed into the street, she nonchalantly pulled over to the curb. She had a bottle of French champagne and two glasses. Hundreds of people were joining her in singing my birthday song. This was Michele's crazy surprise gift and the only way she knew she could find me in Arles.

The journey from Arles to Venice in Italy will always remain one of the most enchanting drives in Europe. The lush colors and spectacular scenes of the French Riviera are simply awesome. Arriving in Venice is another remarkable moment in the life of every world traveler. I love to recall the world famous Carnival of Venice which is held annually for two weeks in February.

There is nothing in Europe to compare with the color, excitement and entertainment centering at St. Marco's Square. Exquisitely costumed men and women are coming from all over Europe to participate in the ancient pagentry of Venice.

One dazzling night I was standing in the square with the famous four horses of destiny gazing down at me when suddenly two women grabbed both my arms. They were identical twins from Innsbruck, Austria. Their gowns were eighteenth-century royal Austrian. Their facial make-up included black beauty marks against their white, marble-like skin.

They told me I was the most fortunate man in Venice to be their escort for the evening. I could do nothing but agree with their statement!

Dr. Aquarius had spoken to me several times about the world famous Spanish riding school horses in Lipica, Yugoslavia. She was an expert rider and was very fond of horses. I recalled one occasion in Portugal when we had an opportunity to attend a competitive riding exhibition. She pointed out the riders who had a perfect understanding of horses and how the horse would respond to the commands of a rider who really knew how to ride well.

After crossing the border into Socialist-controlled Yugoslavia, I could not help but wonder what had taken place in the country which had once been ruled by Tito, one of the most powerful men in European politics. I also recalled that Tito was the first leader who stood firmly against the dictators of Moscow and for this action, he became one of the beloved rulers in Yugoslavian history.

Once over the border, Lipica is only a few hours' drive. After I had checked into a small, cozy hotel tucked away in the countryside, I decided to visit the stables to see the famous horses.

I engaged one of the English speaking grooms who took me on a tour of the stables and the fields where the horses exercise. This location would make an ideal location for the film industry.

The next day I purchased a ticket for the afternoon performance. The indoor arena was packed with tourists who had arrived in a bus caravan.

Over the years I have seen many horse shows, rodeos, and circus performances. Nothing could compare to the total riding perfection I witnessed in Lipica. It was obvious to everyone in the arena that both the riders and their horses belonged together.

After the stunning performance, I remained rooted to my wooden seat waiting for the crowd to leave the arena. After the arena had emptied and everything was very quiet, a young woman came riding into the arena on a white stallion. I moved up to the front railing and seated myself to enjoy the second solo performance.

At first observation, I had the impression that both the woman and the horse had just been introduced. They were both a little shy! The horse was jerking his proud head up and down while his rider was trying to assume control by gently tapping her small strap on the horse's shoulder. By the time she had commanded her stallion around the arena, I could see the horse's attitude changing.

This woman knew how to establish instant rapport with the animal she was riding. From that point on, the horse and the rider became one flowing motion. I was so happy I had remained in the arena and I knew both the woman and the horse were enjoying the fact that they had an audience. Riding without the musical background did not in any way distract from the poise and grace of their performance. I was enthralled!

Later she told me she was from England and had performed in competitions many times. However, this was her first ride on a Spanish stallion and she confessed to being nervous until she knew she had gained the respect of the horse. When I told her I thought she and the horse gave an artistic performance, I could see she was delighted. I will always get a tremendous thrill out of seeing someone really enjoying what they are doing with their life. Today, in the cold, unfeeling computer age, too many people have lost touch with the feeling world and somehow this phenomenon has become a destructive force in society.

Driving south on the Yugoslavian coast is a magnificent experience, but it is also a driving nightmare. With the rugged mountains on my left and the clear blue sea on my right, I would have been in heaven were it not for the single lane traffic which plagued me the entire trip to Albania.

In years to come, as Yugoslavia becomes a tourist hot spot, this main road will become suicidal. Unfortunately, the road is heavily traveled by huge trucks which make passing extremely dangerous since the entire trip is through winding mountains that are constantly twisting into sudden death traps.

I could not totally relax and contemplate the extraordinary landscape. I found myself continuously down-shifting behind trucks that were unable to maintain normal speed on steep grades. Both the Renault 5 and I were becoming very frustrated.

My next goal was to reach the historic city of Split. In A.D. 300, Diocletian established Roman rule in this famous city and made it his capital. I began to think that I could have made it faster if I had lived in Roman times and was using a chariot. Even my car must have read my mind because it started to balk.

I never panic or lose control when I am driving. But, when approaching the summit of yet another mountain climb, my car started to lose power, even at the lowest gear shift, I knew I was in trouble. It stopped dead in its tracks and with no time to dally, I immediately jumped out of the car and physically turned the wheel to push the vehicle in the opposite direction. I was also praying that nothing would come around the mountain turn before I could hop back in my car and coast back to where I had seen a small hotel less than a mile away. I literally rolled back in the direction I had just come from and braked at my unplanned destination.

The hotel manager informed me that the nearest service station was in Split some thirty miles further down the national highway. My car would be picked up the following morning. Early the next morning two young men who looked like Rocky I and II came to haul me and my Renault to Split. Sitting in their high trailer truck was another experience I will always smile about.

They did not speak five words of English and I had not learned three words of Yugoslavian. Nonetheless, they liked loud rock and roll music and so we all rocked and rolled our way into Split.

The next day I was told that I needed a new gear box and it would be a few days before I could have my car. Since I had planned on spending some time in Split, I was very happy to know that I still had a running car which would eventually get me to Greece.

Spending time in the center of the ancient city of Split is a very enriching experience. Once you are inside the walled city, you can feel the antiquity which is all around you. The Roman Emperor Diocletian knew what he was doing when he made Split the seat of his government, even though it did not last very long.

I also enjoyed the old world charm of my hotel with its magnificent flower garden and dining terrace. In the evening, four young musicians played popular ballads and also great jazz music which they knew I thoroughly enjoyed. When I was checking out of the hotel, the manager said he hoped I would return one day. Little did we know how quickly that time would come.

Driving my newly repaired car into a nearby petrol station, I observed a large garbage truck illegally parked near the gas pumps. Precisely at the moment when I was slowly approaching the pumps, the truck started moving in my direction. Blowing my horn was to no avail and before I could get out of his way, I felt the crashing impact of his massive truck slamming against my left side door, shattering my window and everything.

In slow motion, he pushed my car some yards before I was wedged between the truck and the gas pumps. Fearing an explosion, I quickly climbed out the driver's window on the right side and stood by in shocked, stunned and outraged silence. My car was finished!

In less than five minutes, there was a small mob surrounding me and my damaged car. Everyone, including two service attendants, were questioning the dumbfounded truck driver who was shaking his head and making all kinds of motions with his hands. When the police arrived, I was told that I had to give them my passport and go to the court house the following morning at ten A.M. I was not too pleased by the unexpected turn of events.

After the truck driver backed up his truck, I realized that structurally the car was in bad shape. However, the engine was unscathed. I waved good-bye and headed back to my hotel, looking forward to a cold beer on the warm terrace. What the hell!

Word quickly circulated around the hotel that the American with the funny looking car was back in town.

My son Warren's girlfriend was expecting a baby and I decided to call home to see if there was any news. "You're a grandfather again!" my oldest son happily exclaimed. "His name is Alexander and everyone is fine!"

This memorable night was midnight blue and full of songs they never heard before. When the quartet was taking their thirty minute break, I asked the piano player to give me a C note and I took care of the rest.

I gave the crowd "Flatfoot Fluggie," "A Tisket, a Tasket, I Lost My Yellow Basket" and a dozen songs which made everyone roar with laughter and enthusiastic applause. I was in rare form! The hotel manager offered me a summer job, but I told him my rates were very high. He laughed and told the waiter to bring a bottle of his best champagne for John and Alexander. It was a good night to be alive!

When I arrived at the courthouse the next morning wearing my international blue pinstripe, I was feeling very confident that I would soon have my passport and be on my way to Greece. I was advised that a judge would hear the case and make a ruling. I saw the truck driver dejectedly sitting outside the judge's chambers. He had not shaved and looked as though he did not get any sleep. He looked awful! I told him not to worry. No one was injured and so it was no big deal!

Of course he didn't understand a word I said. Only my smile and my warm international handshake made him realize I was his friend and that I was not angry.

When I was called into the judge's office, I almost jumped for joy. The judge was extremely attractive. I wondered what she looked like without her official robes on. I smiled and took a seat opposite her desk. An English-speaking interpreter heard my story as I continued to stare in the direction of the person who would give me my passport to Greece.

When the hearing was over, the translator read me the judge's statement. In Yugoslavia you must have two witnesses to an accident in order to place the cause of the accident. The judge was returning my passport along with an official document allowing me to cross the border and proceed to Greece. When the judge handed me my passport, we were both smiling at one another as though we were old friends saying good-bye. It was for me another fantastic memory never to be forgotten.

The driving distance between Split and the border to enter Greece is for me a full day of "light time traveling." Passing motorists looked at me and my crazy car in total disbelief. I was wearing a big straw hat, laughing, singing and waving to everyone. It was wonderful to be back on the winding, twisting road to historic Greece.

When I finally reached the border control, I decided to have a little fun. As if they had been waiting for me, four young security officials came to inspect my damaged car. After the officers held a brief conference, they decided to wave me back to Yugoslavia. When I handed them the judge's documents, they all had to read it to find out what happened to me and my casualty.

Crossing the border into Greece was another story.

37 / I Find Myself in Greece

I was greeted by three young, handsome men who were all interested in the awful condition of my yellow pearl. I stepped out of the car and handed them my Yugoslavian accident report and informed them that I was on my way to Athens.

I told them that my car and I were in an international rally for wrecks. In order to qualify for entrance into this famous competition, you had to present evidence of three bonafide accidents in the last year. They were delighted when I said that my car was one of the favorites in the race.

By this time dozens of curious people were surrounding us and snapping pictures. The young Greek men insisted on getting my autograph and wishing me good luck. They stamped my passport for one year in Greece. It was the friendliest border control welcome I had ever received in all my travels.

My first stop in Greece was the historic seaport city of Kaválla. I had a good feeling deep inside of me which told me that my Greek experience was going to be outstanding.

Somewhere in Greece, my inner voice told me, you will finish your manuscript and complete a very important chapter in your life. Of course, this voice has never disappointed me. When the drummer is playing a marching song, I always know it is time for another beautiful lifetime! When you are one with the world, there is no limit to the happiness you will always find. I have never been disappointed and I have lived many, many lifetimes.

On my first night in Kaválla, I met an extraordinary Greek fisherman. He at once reminded me of Hemingway's *The Old Man and the Sea*.

There were many fishermen selling their day's catch on the pier. The man I was attracted to, however, was unique. His small fishing boat was equipped with everything. He had weighing scales, wrappers for the fish which were on display and he had a song proclaiming that his fish were the best in all of Greece.

He was of medium height, very muscular with bright blue eyes and his graying, dark, curly hair was partially hidden under his typical Greek cap. He was without a doubt a very happy man.

Later he told me he had also been observing me watching his selling techniques. His name was Demitri! Demitri was over sixty years old, but he appeared to be in his forties. His wife died and he had two married daughters and three grandchildren. After his wife died, he said his lonely house had too many memories which made him feel very sad.

He decided to sell the home and buy a small cabin boat. It was close to the magic hour of sunset and I invited him to join me at a seaside taverena. I asked him to order a bottle of his favorite wine and some good fish. We had already become close friends.

While his English was not good, he told me he understood everything I said. He asked my why I came to Greece and how long I would stay in his country. A look of sublime joy covered his face when I answered his question and told him I might remain in Greece forever.

When he learned that I had a badly damaged car, he insisted on leaving the taverena to visit a friend of his who owned a body repair shop. Speaking with his friend in their native tongue, it was obvious to me that Demitri was driving a hard bargain, insisting that his friend repair my car for the lowest possible price. Finally it was settled, but it would take a few days to locate another door and repair the more serious damage to the connecting door lock which was badly mangled.

The following night, Demitri invited me to join him for dinner on his houseboat. My heart was overflowing with happiness and gratitude! I had only arrived in Greece, but already I had the intense feeling I belonged here.

Demitri's boat home was something special. While everything was very compact, it was easy to see that he had everything he needed to be happy and comfortable.

We motored out of the harbor and he anchored a few hundred yards off the coast. In no time his small stove was frying a fresh-caught delicacy. He also had a bountiful supply of homemade wine which he jokingly told me always gave him a good night's sleep.

The day I left Kaválla for the island of Thasos, I thanked Demitri for all his kindness. Suddenly he became very serious and as is the traditional European custom, he embraced me and kissed both of my cheeks. He said, "John, I think you are Greek and I know Greece will be very good for you." I remember replying that he was the richest man that I had ever met in my life and I would never forget him. There is not enough space in this book to tell you about a hundred similar encounters I have had in my two years in Greece, where this manuscript came to life.

The island of Thasos was recommended to me by a friend of Dr. Aquarius who knows a Greek restaurant owner who works in Germany, but who says that his heart and soul will always be in the place of his birth. So it is for every Greek man and woman!

There are more than fourteen hundred islands in Greek waters; however, only fifty of these magnificent islands have gained international tourist attention.

When my ship was approaching the island, I was shocked by the sight of an off-shore drilling rig belching smoke and fire. I knew immediately that my second island would have no such distraction.

Samos, Rhodes, Crete and Corfu are among the most famous "green islands" of Greece. I decided to start with the closest one which was Samos. My five months on the exotic island of Samos were a remarkable introduction into the life and culture of historic Greece. I wanted to find a perfect location to continue my writing and to learn as much as I could about Greece and the Greek character.

I spent the first few days in a sixteenth-century restored monastery in Samos City, the capital of the island. My guidebook informed me that Samos was the birthplace of the world famous mathematician, Pythagoras. Samos was also the place where Anthony and Cleopatra had made passionate love and they claimed Samos as one of their favorite holiday retreats.

One sunny afternoon while I was enjoying a sea view beer, I engaged a young Greek couple who were natives of the island. They knew exactly where I would find my perfect place of solitude and splendor.

Following their instructions, I left the main road and began what turned out to be a twelve-mile ride on the worst road my car had ever traveled. Halfway to the village of Nissi, I decided to turn around and abandon the whole idea.

Then, as so often happens, my inner voice said, "Hang in there—go for it!"

The last six miles were no better than the rocks, pot holes, et cetera of the first six miles. But the surrounding mountain and sea landscape made me realize that this was the place I was searching for. It was incredibly awesome!

Unfortunately, my Renault #5 was not enjoying the view or the bumpy, rocky road to my new haven on the sea. She was making new squeaks and noises I had never heard before. By the time I left Nissi, my car was asking me for an old age pension.

Nonetheless, the reward at the end of this hazardous road was exactly what I was looking for. Perched like an eagle's nest on the edge of a low hill, the pension stretched down to the sea. The unobstructed view to Asia Minor in the distance was sensational, especially at night when the lights of Turkey were turned on to remind Samos of their five centuries of domination by the Turks!

Fortas was the owner and manager of the modest pension and I was to learn later that he built his dream home with his own labor and Greek ingenuity. For several weeks I was the only full-time guest and this gave us a chance to become better acquainted.

Fortas enjoyed music as much as I and he was determined to teach me the more popular Greek dances. On rare occasions when there were many guests or mountain hikers who dropped in for a meal, Fortas became a master entertainer. After a few drinks, Fortas would jump on the nearest table and swing from the overhead rafters on the ceiling of his taverena.

I called him Zorba, a Greek folk hero who was synonomous with music, dancing and laughter. Also like Zorba, he was very powerful and daring. He was capable of any feat of strength and high adventure was just another challenge.

There was one true story I heard from one of his friends from Athens. One night, Fortas decided to take his speedboat to Turkey after a very late party. The man from

Athens said he was crazy enough to join Fortas in his wild, illegal trip to Asia Minor which was a thirty-minute run. Fortas had a Turkish belly dancer he wanted to see and so off they went into the black night with no running lights. Three sheets to the wind, Fortas and the man from Athens were passing a bottle of cognac from crazy driver to crazy passenger. In a blinding moment of madness, traveling at a speed that had the boat at a forty-five degree angle, they literally flew over a small fishing boat knocking the fisherman into the sea. Fortunately, the fisherman survived the accident and Fortas' sea venture was over.

Once every week, Fortas had to go to Samos City for supplies, mail, et cetera. Since my car was needing a rest, I always looked forward to these weekly surprises.

Everyone in Samos City knew Fortas. He was a legend in his own time.

We never left Samos City before sundown and by this time neither of us were feeling any pain.

Fortas' favorite driving game was to turn off the engine and allow the jeep to ride freely over the bumpy road from a high peak down into the valley below. It was always a raucous hair-raising event which we both looked forward to with sheer delight.

On one occasion, while we were singing, laughing and drinking a beer, he suddenly slammed on his brakes. My head crashed into the already smashed windshield and, in a second, I had a bump on my head the size of an egg.

He saw a baby bird crossing our path and did not want to kill it. For one hour he searched and searched trying in vain to locate the nest from which this chick had obviously fallen. That was the soft side of Fortas!

Fortas was also the first Greek man to introduce me to the dark side of the Greek character.

On one particularly busy night I could see Fortas was

becoming agitated with one of his hard working employees. Peter was a black belt karate expert and he was also Fortas' handy man. When necessary, he also filled in as a singing waiter.

Peter was very popular with the guests and on this particular night he was spending too much time socializing with the customers. Without warning, Fortas confronted Peter in plain view of everyone and, with a menacing look, he told Peter he was fired and ordered him to leave the premises immediately.

When I attempted to intercede on Peter's behalf, Fortas stared at me with equal venom and told me it was none of my business. After that episode there were other times when I observed his quick change of mood and I could not help but wonder what was going on in his mind.

38 / The Bliss of Being with Dr. Aquarius

The days and weeks of the summer of 1987 went rolling by like a beautiful melody. I had received a letter from Dr. Aquarius advising me that she was planning her first visit to Greece and I could expect her in July.

I always looked forward to her visits with exciting and wild anticipation. I knew she would fall in love with the place I had selected for our summer rendezvous.

My private suite was large and airy with a large balcony which extended out over the sea and the view was perfect. Before she arrived I prepared a grand tour of special places, including a boat trip to Turkey which I knew she would enjoy.

She worked so hard at the hospital and I knew she wanted a place that was peaceful where she could relax and forget all the pressures of her "life and death" work in the operating theatre. I also knew how much she always appreciated the perfection that I tried to bring into her life.

Whenever we were together it was obvious to anyone who saw us that we shared a unique relationship.

When she finally arrived I could see immediately how happy she was feeling. Her soft brown eyes had such a warm and wonderful expression of love and excitement.

She stood on my balcony and gazed out at the sea view. I heard her loving sigh of contentment which I had come to know so well.

Aquarius had an eye for perfection as no other person I had ever known and here in Samos she was in paradise. I told her I had discovered a well-hidden swimming cove not far from our pension. Before I could finish the sentence she was unpacking her bags to get her two-piece suit.

I watched her sensuous mouth curve into a smile when I told her she would not need a bathing suit where we were swimming.

As we walked through a silver-green olive grove with our arms around each other's waists we were both laughing and singing our favorite song of love. The bright sun was shining through the trees as we approached the small rocky cove far away from the eyes of the world.

When she saw the spot I had found for us she put her arms around my neck and tilted her face to meet my lips. While we were embracing and kissing one another, at the same time, we were unbuttoning each other's clothing for what we knew would be the most beautiful swim in our lifetimes.

Holding hands, we walked into the warm clear blue sea feeling the sun on our bodies. Aquarius plunged in ahead of me and swam some distance while I watched her graceful movements through the crystal water.

While she was floating on her back I swam to her side. I could wait no longer!

When I pulled her close to me we could both feel the pounding of the other's heart. We moved to a comfortable position in the cove and our tender embrace reminded me of something she had said a long time ago.

After we had made love for the first time, she wrote me a long letter. Her words, "If I never see you again I will still be happy for the rest of my life" were being relived again and we knew it was endless.

We had not seen each other for several months and

now we were touching each other as though it were the first time. Our passion was growing stronger with each caress and when we kissed our mouths and tongues were exploring each other in a brand new way.

When I took her hand to my manhood and entered her warm body we were both trembling with uncontrolled lust for each other. We could only hear the sounds of the water rippling all around us as we climaxed together in wild passionate love.

We remained together locked in each other's arms still trembling in the aftermath which would arouse us once more until we were both ready to collapse in blissful exhaustion. It was the most beautiful act of love we had ever shared and our eyes were glistening with tears of joy!

When we finally emerged from the sea I reached for the place in the cool water where I had put our bottle of Samos wine. The sun would be going down and our magic hour of silence and wine was always reminding me of how fortunate we had been to find one another. We touched glasses and kissed!

Now the sun was a gigantic ball of brilliant orange and we put out heads together reclining on the beach mat. I was gently caressing her breast which we both knew was the most sensitive part of her exquisite body.

She reached for the back of my neck to bring my face close to her. Her eyes closed when I began to kiss her hardening nipples and in a few moments we were both aroused as never before.

I knew she had already experienced a multiple orgasm even before I entered her warm inviting body. We were together again and once more our bodies were entwined and out of control.

Late that night we enjoyed a candlelight dinner of fresh fish and extra dry white wine. There was music in the background and all around us was the golden glow of love.

When we returned to our suite, very late that first evening, we were amazed to see the sky covered with stars. We held each other on the balcony, thrilled by the necklace of diamonds sparkling across the sea in Asia Minor.

Before long, we followed a majestic comet streaking through the silent night. We tightened our grip on each other knowing we had made the same wish. Let this treasured moment last forever!

When we climbed into bed and felt the cool sheets against our naked bodies we were reminded of how long it had been since we slept together. Every whisper, every touch was a brand new sensation.

We were like prisoners of love locked in each other's warm and tender embraces. It was like this for three weeks of our lifetime together.

All of the great art, music and beauty of this world which we have shared culminated in our exquisite act of love. We knew in our hearts and in our minds that no two lovers on earth had ever shared in the bliss we had known.

39 / Heat Wave from Hell

Two days after Aquarius left Samos, Dante's *Inferno* descended on Greece. I had never known anything to compare to the oppressive heat wave that struck Greece in the summer of 1987.

For two unbearable weeks the temperatures remained over 120 degrees Farenheit. Athens was a death trap!

Day after day the death toll kept climbing. More than 2,000 innocent victims died in the furnace of the nation's capital.

The horror stories on television and in the press are too inhuman to repeat in my manuscript. Every world traveler knows that Athens is the worst capital in the world.

Massive ugly buildings have replaced parks and green trees. After one day at the Acropolis, the Plaka and the museum, it is time to leave this awful depressing city.

If Pericles and the classical Greek builders could return to Athens for one day they would command the total leveling of their once magnificent city of art and beauty. Athens is a disgrace!

Even the islands did not escape the intolerable hot and humid temperatures. On the island of Samos everyone was listless!

Even sidewalk cafés by the sea were crowded with tourists silently ordering cool drinks but too uncomfortable to eat.

The flies and huge summer crowds added to the misery of this moment in Greek history which would always be recalled as the hottest summer in the century. Also adding to the problem of heat was the shortage of water.

There were days when there was no water for washing and people began to wonder why they had come to Greece for a holiday.

On Samos that summer, there were several terrible fires which were raging out of control for days. There was no water to fight the fire. It was a nightmare!

Even the bathing water was warm and offered little relief from the blazing, tormenting summer sun.

In my room at night, sleep was impossible. I could feel the torrid breath of Africa blowing in my room. I tried to concentrate all my thoughts on the most perfect summer I ever knew!

In the summer of 1966 I received an academic grant to study for six weeks at Wisconsin State University. Attached to the grant was a large stipend for my family and me.

We found a small cottage on a lake called Beulah Lake. The post cards we sent to all our friends were very funny!

When my university program was finished we drove to California. It was the first time my wife and children had seen the fantastic Rocky Mountains.

It was also the first time my children ever enjoyed having a snowball fight in July.

We visited my father's home in Salt Lake City, Utah where his twin sister Florence welcomed us with loving arms. My children will never forget their unusual swim in the Great Salt Lake.

The concentration of salt is so heavy that they were able to sit motionless in the water and sing the song I had taught them so well. "By the sea, by the sea, by the beautiful sea. You and me, you and me, oh how happy we'll be," etc., etc.

After Utah we visited the Grand Canyon and Yellowstone National Park. While Europe and Asia have a rich cultural history, there is no place in the world that can compare to the natural beauty and wonders of America.

From the Atlantic to the Pacific, you are constantly spellbound by the sights and sounds of an incomparable nation of endless surprises. While I am an East Coast man I must admit California is, after all, the most spectacular state in the U.S.A.

My family will always remember the 750-mile drive along the magnificent California coastline, especially the trip from San Diego and La Jolla (the jewel) to San Francisco's "Golden Gate."

How many places in the world can you swim in the ocean in the morning and ski in the mountains in the afternoon? That is only a small part of the Californian's unique lifestyle.

Visits to Big Sur, Malibu and Monterey are golden experiences in every traveler's memory!

I have many other golden memory summers which I will never forget.

For example, there were wonderful summers in Canada with my two youngest sons David and John.

During the years I was in the Senate, my sons and I could hardly wait for school to close in June. For weeks and months David and John were busy making preparations for our annual holiday on the Rideau Lakes in Ontario.

They read every book they could find on the best places to catch trout and perch. They purchased special lures to bait the fish and every day they talked about their summer plans.

I always allowed them to invite their best friends to accompany us on our holiday.

On the day we left my, car was packed to capacity with enough fishing equipment, et cetera, to open a store. I must also confess that I was as excited as they were and I could hardly wait to cross the border and drive over the fabulous Thousand Island Bridge to Ontario, Canada.

Roy, his lovely wife, and their two daughters and son were always waiting for our arrival. They were a wonderful family who owned a group of lakeside cabins and a number of small fishing boats.

They really enjoyed their summer guests. When we arrived they always invited us to join them in a family cookout.

The setting was idyllic, especially on one occasion when we happened to see the unreal "Northern Lights of Canada." Sweeping like giant land clouds, they came rolling into the camps like gigantic waves of color and light. It was a rare phenomenon of nature.

Once you have witnessed the dramatic Northern Lights you know you have been in the northern wilds of Canada.

How overjoyed I was the year David was old enough to drive my car to Canada. There is no greater reward for a father than to see his sons grow into manhood. David and John grew into manhood during our many summers in Canada!

David and John, as well as Warren, Wendy and Laurie, never knew how happy and proud my wife and I were watching them grow into adulthood. They were never tempted or threatened by the curse of drugs and ignorance so prevalant in the American youth of their generation.

If July in Greece was a glimpse into hell's fury then August was a return to Paradise. It was also a reminder to me of the awesome power of the forces of nature.

If nature is still important to the architects of the

world, then this is the dramatic moment in history when everyone should be concerned about the fate of our world's decaying environment.

All the great words are soundless in the ugly face of the twentieth century's rape of nature's environment. When you destroy nature to build monstrosities you must be prepared to receive nature's response to your outrageous ignorance.

40 / Among Gods and Goddesses

August was full of wonderful surprises! A large group of Athenian gods and goddesses arrived one afternoon and completely changed my future life in Greece.

Prior to my arrival in Samos, I had read Henry Miller's outstanding book, *The Colossus of Maroussi*. It is the story of Henry Miller's experience in Greece. The main character of his story was a Greek man named Katsimbalis.

Katsimbalis was an exceptional storyteller and a character of monumental stature with an intelligence to match his dynamic personality. After I had known my new friends from Athens, I often thought of Miller's Katsimbalis!

My new acquaintances were unique in many ways. Four intellectual middle-aged men with four equally exceptional wives and their children became a large part of my profile of Greece.

Some day I hope to write a special story about this Cyclopean family of Athenian gods and goddesses. When they told me their families had taken their vacations together for the last fifteen years I thought the title I had given them was appropriate.

I had also learned that for fifteen years the men played cards together every Wednesday evening. Every week they rotated from home to home.

The women prepared the food and spent the evening catching up on the family news while the children organized their own games. It was fantastic!

The men were builders, engineers and businessmen.

The women, in addition to running their homes, were contract lawyers and one was a medical doctor.

Their children always wore the kind of smiles that only come from inner feelings of love and happiness. The parents were also exceptionally talented musicians, artists and gourmet connoisseurs.

After I had only known them a few days, they invited me to join their evening meal party which was an absolute delight.

Every day I was amazed by the manner in which they planned their daily program. It reminded me of the classical Greek period of Plato, Aristotle and Socrates when all citizens had an equal right to express themselves. That was the system the Musketeers used in making decisions. It was wonderful!

One day, they were all hiking in the mountains while the next day everyone was in life jackets preparing for a day of fishing, et cetera.

Every evening, the children were very excited telling me about their day's high adventure. I was reminded of my childhood English teacher's comment, "The fruit never falls too far from the tree!"

All the children were reflections of their mothers' and fathers' personalities and characters.

One evening, they had invited me to join them in celebrating Lisa's eighth birthday. A few days before the party, I had taken everyone to my favorite taverena in the cool mountains. An elderly couple owned a small garden paradise only a short walk from my pension.

Their Irish Setter had just given birth to five lively puppies. I knew the children would have a ball playing with the puppies.

The taverna was well-hidden in the verdant hills shrouded by a multitude of trees and colorful flowers. A narrow path led to a small outdoor patio which was covered by grape vines. The scent from the grapes was intoxicating.

I knew everyone was very happy to be there, especially Lisa.

When I observed her particular fondness for one of the puppies, I whispered to her parents that I would like to give the puppy to Lisa on her birthday. They looked at one another for a few moments and smiling at me they simply said, "Oh John!"

It was a wonderful birthday party and after Lisa had blown out the candles we all sang happy birthday in two languages.

I told Lisa I had a surprise gift waiting for her in my apartment. When she came running back to us with the puppy in her arms, there were tears of joy running down her excited eight-year-old face.

When their vacation was coming to an end, we had a happy fare-well party. During the festivities they told me they had an opinion about me and they wanted to know if I also had made an opinion of them.

Jokingly, I answered that I did have an opinion, but they would have to wait until the *Snowflake in a Blizzard* was published in New York. Everyone laughed and Kostas began singing "We are the Five Musketeers"!

On the day they were leaving, they asked me where I was going after Samos. I told them my next two stops would be Santorini and Crete.

They all looked at one another and Doctor Ann said they all wanted me to spend some time in Kifisia as their guest before I continued with my travel plans.

41 / Eli and Isabel

Less than a week after my friends had left for their homes, an attractive young couple arrived at the pension. On their first night I asked Fortas to please give them a bottle of the famous Samos white wine. They thanked me for the nice surprise and asked me to join them at their table. Eli and Isabel Waxman had worked together on a kibbutz where they met and fell in love. Later, they served together in the Israeli army where they became engaged. Now they were on their honeymoon. It was a fairy tale story!

They had picked the island of Samos for their honeymoon after reading stories about Anthony and Cleopatra selecting the island as one of their favorite holiday resorts. They also told me it was their first trip outside of Israel. It was so good for me to see the look of love which was written all over their faces and in their sparkling eyes. Romance was in the air once again on the island of Samos!

Before I left Samos to accept my invitation to visit my friends in Kifisia, the Waxmans also invited me to visit them at their home in Beer-Sheba. Ann, who was a pathologist at the Athens University Hospital, and her husband, Kostas, met me in Athens. Kifisia is in the suburbs which is a thirty minute drive into another world. Tree lined, broad streets in an elegant neighborhood quickly made me forget the dismal capital city.

Their home was a virtual mansion, swimming pool and all. It was obvious they led a class life far away from the maddening crowd. While they were working, I passed the hours relaxing in the pool and going for long walks. Every night, we were visiting a different family for a late evening party.

I remained with Ann and Kostas since they were the only couple who were unable to have children. Dr. Ann had told me she had several miscarriages and her doctor had told her it would be dangerous if she continued in her efforts to have a child. She and Kostas were one of the most happily married couples I have ever known.

On weekends they all had planned special trips to their favorite mountains and sandy beaches. They gave me such a feeling of warm friendship that I was overwhelmed with joy. They were also very happy to tell me everything I wanted to learn and understand about their historic country.

In the days I spent with them, I came to appreciate the fullness of Greek culture. Their knowledge and love for Greece was boundless. They wanted me to understand everything about ancient stones, the healing powers of herbs, poetry, even the gods and goddesses of Homer's *Iliad* and *Odyssey*.

They bestowed upon me all the accumulated wealth of knowledge I had yearned for since my arrival in Greece. They were more than my friends. They were my first teachers in Greece and I was a most satisfied and fortunate pupil.

When I was preparing to leave, they decided to give me an impromptu birthday party even though they knew it was not my birthday. They all laughed and reminded me that I should always have a birthday party when I was feeling like another birthday. At the conclusion of the party, they gave me the keys to my next home in Santorini and a personal contact in Crete. I was dumbfounded!

Santorini is described in the guide books as the most dramatic island in Greece. But it is much more than that. Santorini is the greatest unsolved mystery in Greek history. Plato referred to Santorini as "Atlantis, the lost continent." No one has been able to explain what happened in Santorini during the period of tragic volcanic earthquakes and tidal waves that reached as far as Crete and Egypt. I for one could feel the mystery of this strange island even before my ship reached the harbor. Unlike the green islands of Greece, Santorini is a monstrous black volcanic rock which stands like a gigantic tomb to remind every visitor of what happened here.

My Santorini key opened the door to a cave on the side of the mountain. For two months of my life I was going to live the life of a troglodyte and I would love every moment of the experience.

After I had settled in and had an opportunity to explore the island, I found many artists sketching and painting canvases all over the island. On closer examination, I also observed the colorful layers of green, brown, orange and red lava imbedded in the ancient stone. It was an amazing study of geological wonder.

My cave villa was located on the north end of the island in a small village called Oia. There is only one very narrow marble stone path leading through the village. Over the centuries, the marble has become so smooth that you can slide on it.

Small intimate cafés are leaning out over the sea, leaving you with the sensation that you are cut off from the rest of the world. Sunsets on the island of Santorini are the most spectacular you will ever witness.

Every night, I would take a bottle of wine on my balcony and wait for the magic hour of sunset. I was never disappointed. The reflection of the sun hitting the volcanic mountain turned the sea into the most dazzling colors of red and orange that I had ever witnessed. The whole effect would send chills down my back. It was inspiring! Many evenings I invited my closest friends in Oia to join me in a wine and cheese party while enjoying the greatest show on God's earth.

Patric was a French African and his wife, Renée, was a Parisian. They told me their story of coming to Santorini ten years ago on a holiday vacation. When their holiday had ended, they had a long discussion with their many friends on the island. They were very persuasive! They tried to convince me as they had been convinced to make my life in Santorini permanent.

Nickos was another frequent visitor that I always enjoyed. He was a handsome, young bar owner who prided himself in being Santorini's number one playboy. On one night occasion he invited me to join a group of his friends in a session of all Greek music and dancing. Little did I realize that Nickos was the most popular dancer. At 3:00 A.M., which he told me was his best dancing time, Nickos gave the audience ten minutes of his famous Greek Eagle Dance. It was unbelievable!

For reasons I will never be able to explain, I started to feel very ill after six weeks on the island. I began coughing and had no appetite for food. I also noticed I was losing my energy.

I knew there was a light film of cave dust on the floor every morning, but I never realized that perhaps I had been inhaling the nightly fallout from the cave's ceiling. In any event, after two months I decided it was time to move on to Crete.

42 / Crete

I am sure all Greek island travelers have their favorite islands. For me, this island was Crete! I will always remember my stay on this exceptional island with a promise to return.

There is an expression which every Greek understands whenever you talk about the people of Crete. They will tell you in Crete that they are Greek, but first in their hearts and in their minds, they are all Cretans! This is only one of the countless reasons why Crete is unique among all the islands of Greece.

By the time my ship had arrived in the east coast port of Sitia, I was feeling extremely weak. I called my Cretan contact several times and finally learned that he was on a holiday and would not return for two weeks. Once again my guardian angel was guiding me and my springless and rusty Renault #5 to a place where my life would be saved.

Off the main road I observed a sign to a pension in the village of Palaikastro. Eleanor and John were more than the owners of a modest pension. They were the cure for my illness and for this I am eternally grateful.

They could see immediately by the haggard look on my face that I was not feeling well. While they could not speak English, they had a twelve year-old son who was studying English and he became our translator. They called their doctor in Sitía and I had an appointment the next morning.

After a very brief meeting with Dr. Dimitri, I knew

I had an excellent doctor. Since his knowledge of English was limited, he had his fifteen-year-old son Alexander waiting in his office to be our translator. When he finished his examination and had asked me several questions, he gave me my first shock! "If you were in America, your doctor would have you in the hospital immediately!"

He told me to return to my pension and remain in bed until the following morning. He would call the hospital laboratory to make arrangements for an early morning blood test. I was to bring specimens number one and two when I saw him the next day.

When I asked him what was wrong with me, he informed me that he would have to wait until he had the results of my specimens and the blood test. I had the feeling he already knew my condition and only had to have a confirmation from the laboratory tests.

The next morning the doctor's office was packed, but when Alexander saw me I was requested to see the doctor. Holding specimen one up to the light he exclaimed that it looked like cognac. I was not smiling! When he opened specimen #2, I detected the first small smile I had seen on his face.

Through Alexander, he said if specimen #2 had been the color grey, I would have to go to the hospital. Alexander rode with me to the laboratory and he would continue to be my guide, translator and friend throughout my long ordeal.

The next day the lab tests confirmed the doctor's suspicion. I had infectious hepatitis! I should go to the hospital for treatment and cure.

We had a very long discussion. I felt sorry for Alexander. I had to convince Dr. Dimitri that I would recover much faster in my pension environment. I told him that my balcony suite had a relaxing view of the hills and the sea. Also, I knew that John and Eleanor would help me with my diet, et cetera.

After some deliberation, he agreed only on the condition that I follow all the rules he would give me for my recovery. Strict diet and total rest! We shook hands and I thanked him for his professional help and his understanding.

After one month of Eleanor's wonderful cooking of special soups, vegetables, chicken, fish, et cetera, I was on my way back to gaining full strength. At the end of six weeks, I came to his office for more blood tests and a complete physical. A few days later, he informed me that all the tests indicated a marked improvement, but that I must not rush my recovery.

Dr. Dimitri was surprised one day when I announced that I was flying to Israel for Christmas. I had just lifted him in the air to demonstrate how strong I was feeling. When I put him down, he also lifted me in the air to tell me how happy he was that I had recovered. My illness had brought us together and we both knew our new friendship would be everlasting.

43 / Christmas in the Holy Land

Eli Waxman was waiting for me at the airport in Tel Aviv when my Olympic plane landed on December 20, 1987. He was very happy to welcome me on my first visit to his great nation. By the time we had arrived at his home in Beer-Sheba, he was telling me that there were three important streets he wanted me to see in Jeruselum.

Eli's wife had prepared a small banquet for my first meal in Israel. She was very happy with the Minoan gift that I had purchased for her in Crete. Our discussion about the Middle East lasted into the early morning hours and was full of answers I had been seeking.

Intellectually, they were blessed with knowledge beyond their youthfulness. They knew I was not happy over the fact that they kept their military uniforms and weapons in their closet.

We also had an interesting discussion about the three streets in Jeruselum: The Arab, Jewish and Christian paths. The Waxman's knew that one of the reasons I had come to Israel was to retrace the footsteps of Jesus Christ. They knew I would be in Bethlehem on Christmas Eve. They also knew that it was not going to be peaceful in Israel on the day that marks the birth of Christ.

Eli had managed to free himself from his job for a few days to be my guide. There were places he wanted me to see. He also wanted me to understand why his country would always be vigilant. Eli's knowledge of the history and culture of Israel and the Middle East was extraordinary.

We drove to Masada on the Dead Sea. Perched very high on a mountain, Masada was the place where thousands of Jewish men, women and children welcomed death rather than submit to enslavement by the Romans under King Herod.

Eli and Roberta were extremely proud to be living in one of the oldest places in civilized history. Beer-Sheba dates back to 4000 B.C. and is only preceded by Jericho in Palestine which goes back 5000 years before the birth of Jesus Christ.

He also took me to see and hear the faces and voices of the thousands and thousands of innocent children who were victims of the murderous Holocaust. I could not restrain the tears that filled my eyes and Eli knew that he had hit a nerve center by reminding me of man's inhumanity. I was also thinking of Anne Frank who would have been a great writer had she not been a victim of the Nazi murderers.

We did not have to discuss religion. Eli knew I would never accept the Old Testament's, "Eye for an Eye or a Life for a Life!" I also knew that Eli realized that in the twentieth century, the New Testament Christians were not turning the other cheek.

On Christmas Eve I called my family from Bethlehem. When my wife answered the phone in New Jersey, she wanted to know if I was okay. She told me all the television news broadcasts were painting a very ugly picture of Christmas in Israel.

44 / New Year in Berlin

Aquarius had sent me an airline ticket so we could be together for the New Year, as a Christmas gift. She knew of my illness and told me she personally wanted to do additional tests to assure me that everything was alright. When your lover is also a medical doctor, you can be assured that you will always have tender love and care!

Her blood tests, et cetera confirmed that I was regaining my health, but she also cautioned me about my constant diet changes as I moved from country to country. "Neither you nor your digestive system are made of steel and you are not getting any younger," she intoned.

With all her other attributes, Aquarius is also a sensational cook. Her kitchen, like her garden, is a place where she tries to reach perfection. Her super gravy and sauce alone could make me travel across a continent. She always enjoyed indulging me with the gourmet food that I adored.

Her son Jonathan was also very happy to see me again. He had several projects he was involved with and he wanted to know if I would help him. Jonathan and many of his friends from the Green Party were organizing a massive rally to demonstrate against the United States' nuclear weapons in West Germany. Would I join the demonstration? When I told Aquarius I would be away for a few days, she only smiled and told me to enjoy myself. I know she was very happy with the close relationship I had with her son.

The first thing I observed when we arrived at the

home of Jonathan's friends was the absence of any drugs or alcohol. They were all young intellectuals who had been active for several years in the fight to eliminate nuclear weapons from German soil. I was much impressed by their sincerity and tenacity!

The first day's conference was held in a rented public building where several eminent German scientists were addressing the dangers of nuclear weapons. The public had been invited to participate in the discussions and the attendance was far greater than anyone had anticipated.

On the second day, preparations were made for the march of demonstrators. Anyone who has ever been involved in a demonstration knows how important it is to maintain total discipline and control.

We would start in front of a U.S. Army base and everyone knew that we would all be photographed by cameras that would record for all time the individuals who were participating. This was no problem for me! As a senator and later as a democratic candidate for governor, I had led numerous demonstrations in New Jersey. If the cause is right, then the demonstration is important. I never enjoyed standing on the sidelines watching the parade pass me by.

Numerous well-documented pamphlets were being distributed throughout the march and at the speaker's platform. One leaflet in particular caught my attention. It had a very large headline which read, "Eleven former N.A.T.O. Generals stating that Space Weapons lead to War!"

Continuing, the article read as follows:

Let there be no illusions about space weapons! They are not for Star Wars but for nuclear war on earth. Space weapons combined with offensive nuclear missiles such as the MX, Pershing II and Trident II, destroy the enemies' second strike capability, thus making possible a first strike. A first strike capability leads with certainty to war. We resolutely demand: Let us not continue the insanity of the arms race by extending it into space. Let us instead unite our creative energies in the struggle against hunger and poverty and for the reconciliation of humanity!

I was stunned by this profound proclamation of eleven retired generals who went on the public record in opposition to Star Wars and the dangers of a nuclear holocaust. Also, I was feeling very uncomfortable to learn that there was not a single retired American general's name on the list of N.A.T.O. signatures.

I was also painfully aware that my government under Ronald Reagan and President George Bush, with the consent of Congress, continues to move forward with the infamous multi, multi-billion dollar Star Wars program of madness and insanity! The United States, after all, is one of the leading nations in the world in the manufacturing, sale and distribution of weapons systems around the globe. We are one of the leading merchants of death and destruction in the twentieth century.

All those sceptics who say a nuclear war will never happen must constantly be reminded that America was the first country to use nuclear weapons against Japan in World War II. The terrible record of history cannot be denied or forgotten.

After the demonstration, I was invited back to the home of Jonathan's friends for a "rap session" to assess the fallout from the two days of activity. No one could know that what started out as a quiet evening's discussion would turn into a donnybrook!

The women had provided much good food while the men took care of the beer, wine and soft drink department. Since I was the only American in the group, I had the feeling that most of the men and women were pleased by my participation. Also most of Jonathan's friends were aware of my background and they were anxious to have me as a member of their group.

Every German is painfully aware of their country's causing two world wars in the 20th century. Every German also knows that America and the allies never signed a peace treaty with Germany after the second world war.

Germany is an occupied nation! Germany is also marked in every German's mind as the primary battlefield for World War III. In both the allied-occupied West and in the Soviet-occupied East, every intellectual German knows they will have less than five minutes to live once the nuclear attack begins.

The heavy concentration of men and weapons is located in Germany and so, year after year, from 1945 to this day, Germans must witness the daily military activity of the world's two most menacing superpowers. The United States in the West and Russia in the East have never for a single day left the German battlefields. Billions and billions and many more uncountable billions have been expended by Russia and America to make Germany the most deadly and explosive nation in the history of the human race. Even the current negotiations to cut back and reduce the military monster are not even scratching the surface of the imminent danger which threatens the universe every day of our lives on this planet.

Close to midnight, three American G.I.'s wearing their uniforms came to pick up three women they were dating.

When they were introduced to me, I could read their expression of bewilderment at my being there with all these young Germans.

I thought to myself that they looked like Rambo I, II and III. They obviously spent their free time in the weight room pumping iron. Their three attractive girlfriends, obviously, also thought they resembled the typical Rambo character.

When one of the Germans offered the G.I.'s a beer, they joined the growing party without hesitation. I could see immediately that they were curious to find out more about me and they proceeded to play the famous twenty questions game which I was in no mood to play. I am sure they never suspected that I detested military uniforms, but I know they were perturbed by the fact that I did not express any interest in questioning them about their activities.

After a few beers, the men in uniform showed no inclination to leave the party. In fact, they called their women from the kitchen to join them for what was beginning to look like an all-night party.

Without the slightest provocation, they took turns telling everyone how happy they were to be in Germany, defending the country against the possible threat from the East Bloc countries, namely Russia. I had heard this story a hundred times before and I am sure my friends were also very bored by this outlandish statement. Nevertheless, undaunted, Rambo I, II and III took turns wrapping themselves in the American flag as if they represented the saviors of the world.

Jonathan could tell by the expression on my face that I was becoming very annoyed. One of the demonstration organizers was also becoming agitated and he tried unsuccessfully to change the subject. The Rambos, now with their arms wrapped comfortably around the shoulders, et cetera, of their girlfriends, took off in defense of President Reagan's Star Wars program.

They hit my nerve center when they extolled the words that all Americans were behind the president and Star Wars. I could not tolerate another moment of my long, tormented silence. Interrupting their outlandish oratory, I informed them that I was one American who vigorously opposed Reagan's Star Wars. I also had many friends in Washington and around the country who opposed the reckless direction of our military games. Furthermore, I let everyone know that there was a growing fear in both the East and the West concerning America's military posture.

You could have heard a fly walking on the ceiling! The room became deadly silent! I could see the G.I.s' faces becoming very red, but I wanted Jonathan and his friends to hear the minority side of the American viewpoint.

I reminded everyone that there are countless thousands of young men around the world who prefer to wear a white uniform of peace. These courageous men have strong anti-military feelings and are much happier working in hospitals and institutions for the aged and the handicapped. These young heros of humanity are the future peacemakers of the world. There was a light sound of applause in the room!

I also wanted everyone to understand that the American military personnel were predominantly mercenaries! No government in modern history has spent so much money to propagandize the romance and glamour of wearing a uniform than has the U.S.A.

Every single day, millions and millions of taxpayer's dollars are spent on television, radio, press, et cetera to advertise the benefits on enlisting in the military. The enlisting bonus of $5,000 is the payoff price to keep America strong as the defender of peace in the world. I could feel the room becoming electric, but I was not finished.

Everyone in the world today is familiar with the image of Rambo being flashed across the film screen. This multi-million dollar propaganda film and many others of the same insane caliber portray the killer as a great war hero.

Man in my eyes is never a hero when he kills another man. Man is a savage beast when he is capable of murdering his fellow man. And he is not so brave as governments of the world like us to believe. He is not so brave at all!

For if a man had to experience a menstrual period every month, this brave hero would commit suicide! And if this brave, decorated hero had to carry a child in his body for nine months, there would be no more children born in our world.

The day is fast approaching when the decorated killers of the twentieth century will be reduced to crying children pleading for forgiveness for their crimes against humanity. That silent, magic and magnificent day will come when the women of the world close their legs to the men who wear uniforms and carry weapons of death and destruction.

Only when these brave men have burned their uniforms and destroyed their weapons will they hear the soft sighs of love and laughter. For only a woman who has lost a son, a brother, a father, a husband or a lover can tell the world about the feelings and suffering of a Snowflake in the Blizzard of men's fury and hate.

When man finally realizes how much damage and pain he has brought to the women of the world, then and only then will he cease to be used as a tool of his government. Look into the eyes of women who lost their men and you will see the soul of humanity.

When Jonathan and I returned to his mother's home, she told us she read stories about the demonstration, but she could not find our pictures with the demonstrators.

Before my return to Crete, Aquarius and I had some wonderful days and nights which never seemed long enough. It was the winter of 1988 and we could cross country ski in the peaceful forest and enjoy the scent of evergreen trees filling our nostrils. How we loved to play in the snow like children who would never grow old. In the evenings, we would sit by the fire for hours and hours listening to our favorite songs and sometimes dancing as though we were in a dance hall. We never needed anything to make us happy. We simply enjoyed the excitement of each other's presence.

There were days when we would get very excited about going to an art exhibit or attending a ballet performance and there were days when Aquarius would say "I want to dance all night!"

One day she came home early from the hospital and she was very excited. We are going to a masquerade party tonight! A few of the nurses in her hospital decided to have an impromptu party and we were invited.

It was a Friday night and Aquarius was not on weekend duty. I could tell she was in rare form, singing and dancing all over the house. I had a custom-designed tiger sweater that was a gift from Mark Nelson, and Aquarius decided that she would go as a CAT. There are cats and there are cats. But I can tell you there never was a cat that could match Aquarius even on Broadway. She was something else!

Later that night when she finally emerged from her bathroom, she was covered in skin tight black from her gorgeous neck to her polished toe nails. She read my lustful mind and let out a soft MEOW from her tantalizing, puckered lips. Every tiger who has ever lived in the jungle knows that she was saying, "Later John, later!"

45 / Getting to Know the Universe

On my return to Crete, both my pension family and my doctor were happy to see me in such good health. Spring was coming early and you could feel the warm breezes from Africa blowing across the island.

Every morning, I would drive a few miles to the fifteenth century Tapalou Monastery for a Greek coffee metrea and a stroll in the fertile green fields to observe the sheep and goats grazing in the sunlit hills. Afternoons would be spent at Via, the fabulous palm tree beach with its extraordinary hills and cliffs. Most of the time I was alone and I would find a comfortable place to read and listen to the sounds of the waves washing up on the shore. It was a special time for me.

One morning I left my pension very early after advising John and Eleanor that I would be traveling to the western side of the island and I would be gone for several days. They only smiled and circled a number of places I should visit. I knew I must visit all those places they had circled.

Knossos, Phaistos, Gortyna and Gournia are but a few of the famous places that reach back in history to over 2500 B.C. What happened in the fantastic age of Minoan life can only be described as uniquely beautiful.

Numerous internationally respected archaeologists have devoted their lives to trying to explain why this ancient civilization was so far superior to ours. The art, sculpture, engineering, sciences, everything, is incredibly awesome.

When you are standing alone (as I have often done) in the center of these ancient dwelling places, you are overcome with a feeling of peace and love and beauty. It is the knowledge that something unique happened here at a time when life was devoted to the search for truth and perfection. The priceless gold, silver and bronze treasures along with the artistic, storytelling pottery, which has been unearthed in Greece and Egypt, surpasses everything in history that came at a later period.

One month in the museums in Athens and Cairo will stun you beyond your wildest imagination. It will also make you realize how impoverished we are in cultural achievement compared to the greatness of Greece and Egypt.

It was not just the fine delicate jewelry that attracted my attention in these museums. I was astonished by their knowledge of medicine, science, astrology, everything.

Solid gold pitchers for pouring wine were not only engraved with artistic stories, but the handles and the spout were perfect in form and function. Frying pans had engraved handles in the shape of a man extending his hands as if he were making an offering to the gods. The ancient Pharoah's bed was contour in shape to allow for nightly circulation of the blood while he dreamed of the next world.

There were a thousand contributions to civilization which made me realize how much they gave to the Western world. Everything in the West would be a copy of the Eastern culture and ancient civilization. What happened seven thousand years ago in Egypt will never be equaled in our lifetime. What happened to twentieth century man is a question we should try to answer.

After my Minoan tour, my car took me to the Valley

of Ten Thousand Windmills! Driving very slowly through winding mountain roads, you are looking down to fertile plains where every farmer in days gone by relied on his windmills for energy to irrigate his crops. How sensible, how practical and how environmentally beautiful.

Descending down into the valley, my senses were intoxicated by the scent of lemon and orange groves. Occasionally, I would see banana plantations to remind me that Crete is the only place in Greece favored by the African climate and that they are able to grow a wide variety of citrus fruits and nuts.

My next touring destination was a brief visit to the site of the longest gorge in Europe. The Samaria Gorge which has been cut through the mountains after thousands of years of powerful waterfalls, extends for twenty-six miles and ultimately empties into the sea.

While I did not take this unusual hike, I did make a promise to return another day when I could do it with a companion. It is the kind of romantic walk that one should not take alone. It is a very special narrow walk through paradise that must be shared with someone very special.

There have been so many times when I have been driving my crazy, beat up Renault when from out of nowhere, I am confronted by a new surprise. Standing in the middle of a lonely road, I came upon a man who was frantically waving for me to stop my car. This was no ordinary hitchhiker. Panos was a typical and traditional Cretan mountain man. We had a terrible language problem, but after he learned that I was an American, he became very emotional and very animated. It was obvious he liked Americans. Using sign language and good eye contact, we quickly became friends.

He motioned me to continue forward and indicated with three fingers the distance to his home in the mountains. Panos looked to me to be about sixty to sixty-five years old. He was of medium height but very trim. He had curly, grey hair under his Cretan cap. He wore high leather boots up to his knees. Panos was a formidable looking, rugged individual. I would love to hear his story.

Approaching his small village, he asked me to stop the car when he spotted a group of his friends enjoying a Greek coffee and Nero (water) at a local taverena. He wanted his friends to know his driver and that his driver was an American. Later, I would learn that he had invited them all to come to his mountain top home.

Minutes later we arrived at the summit. The view from this vantage point was fantastic. He pointed one index finger at me and with his other hand he put his left thumb into his smiling mouth. In international sign language, you all know he was inviting me to have a drink of something!

His elderly wife was a semi-invalid. She motioned me to a chair by a small round table. The tiny modest dwelling was spotless and the open door and windows looked out on a spectacular view that would make you cry with joy.

While Panos was showing me many pictures of visitors he had met, his wife was setting the table with plates, cutlery, glasses, et cetera. Obviously, Panos intended to delay my tour and I was delighted. When events like this happen to a traveler, you know you are one of the chosen ones and it is something you can never forget. I was enjoying a wonderful meal of goat cheese, home-baked bread, garden olives and village wine. I was in heaven!

Before we had finished eating, ten men came singing up the mountain toward Panos' home. He had invited them to meet me and also to have a small party.

The men were all gathered around my car pointing to my red Dublin plates and the window bumper sticker which read: "MIKE DUKAKIS for President." When I told them I was a John Kennedy Democrat, they were absolutely wild with joy. It was going to be a very long party and I was the guest of honor.

The party moved outside the small house and into the garden. Panos was pouring wine all over the place. Everyone was singing, laughing and dancing. They made their own music!

Greek men do not drink unless they are eating food. Panos' wife set out small tables with more cheese, olives, nuts, bread and fruit. It was like Christmas!

Watching the sun going down, I was reminding myself that I never drive at night, especially if I am unfamiliar with the mountain country.

Before long, Panos, who was in great shape, came out of his home holding a large unmarked bottle in one hand and a sheet of paper in his other hand. He had written the number 69 on the sheet of paper and laid the bottle on the table in order to point to himself. I laughed so loud and so long by the revelation that he was 69 that in moments everyone was roaring with laughter.

I tried to tell Panos and his friends that to be 69 was one of my great ambitions. Then I took the paper and wrote the number 96. Pointing to myself, I tried in vain to explain my final lifetime ambition.

The joke did not go unnoticed. In moments they were going crazy. Two strong men took my arms and began dancing with me in a circle while the other men were vigorously clapping their hands to the Zorba tune.

Now Panos was tipping the mysterious bottle of pure white liquid. Everyone was looking in my direction as they raised their glasses. I felt the cool liquid enter my throat and then my chest. I could hardly breathe. The smiles I observed were the smiles of angels. The party was not over!

For all my American and European friends, I can only

remember thinking that tonight I am big enough to embrace all of humanity in my arms of love. I also remember that I suddenly could dance the special dance of the seagull which Panos had taught me on the island of Santorini.

As if on command, Panos and his mountain neighbors formed a perfect circle around me. Crouching low to the ground, they started to clap in rhythm as I moved with majestic grace and Greek style. I knew I was dancing well by the happy expressions on everyone's face. Whirling in circles and bending low with outstretched arms, I was flying!

The mountain was also spinning in my head and I had no desire to end this night of nights!

I was in love with love!

I was music!

I was laughter!

I was drunk!

Panos' wife had long since retired for the night, but she had prepared a makeshift cot for me in the living room knowing that I was not going anywhere. The following morning the little drummer boy was playing a song in my head that I had not heard in a long time. I tried in vain to calm him down with many cups of black coffee, but he was a tenacious little devil and refused to stop playing until I reluctantly fed him some cheese and bread.

Before I left, Panos took my hand and led me down the mountain to a small monument. All I could read was the date in the year 1941. Pointing skyward, he shouted the words, "BOOM, BOOM, BOOM!" Then he took my map of Crete and pointed to MALEME. He indicated that it was not too far away and I should visit this place.

Arriving in Maleme, I quickly discovered the reason why Panos wanted me to learn what had happened. In 1941, I was told by a Greek guide, Hitler ordered one of his generals to take Crete in two days. The Cretans have a motto which they have always lived by—"Freedom or Death!" Hitler did not take the island of Crete in two days. More than five thousand small white crosses on a field of green stand out on the side of a low hill in Maleme. When I walked through the rows of crosses, I observed that all these young Germans were between the ages of eighteen and twenty-five. I did not remain too long in Maleme. My imagination is too vivid for memories like this.

John and Eleanor knew that I was planning to move on to the Peloponnese, but they also knew that I would be returning to Crete soon.

There is nothing in the world so romantic as a cruise on a Greek ship traveling from island to island. There is no nation in the world that I know of that has so many men who are involved with ships. For me, it seems as though every Greek man has been a seaman at one time during his lifetime.

For centuries Greek men have traveled the world and their knowledge of seamanship is legendary. Whenever I am traveling on a Greek ship as I have done so many, many times, I feel as though I am in another world at another period of time.

My interest in coming to the Peloponnese was to learn more about Mycenal history which covered a period of over six centuries B.C.

I also came to the Peloponnese to learn more about Heinrich Schliemann, the German scholar who was an avid follower of Homer, the most famous writer in classical Greek history. Schliemann was convinced that Homer was more than a great storyteller. He believed that Homer's *Iliad* and *Odyssey* were factual tales that would lead him to the discovery of King Priam's Palace in Troy and King

Agamemnon of Mycenae. While Schliemann's excavations in Troy and Mycenae were controversial, he, nonetheless, proved that Homer was much more than a great story teller.

When I first arrived at the dead end street leading to the Lions Gate entrance to King Agamemnon citadel, I recalled Homer's classic story of the Odyssey. Agamemnon, the king of kings, helped to organize a massive army to sail to Troy for the purpose of returning Helen to the home of his brother. Some months later while I was living on Corfu, I would travel to Turkey in search of Troy and the face "that launched one thousand ships!" But this is another story.

That first afternoon walking through the ruins of Mycenae, it became so unseasonally hot that I decided to return on a more pleasant day. Leaving the citadel, I drove less than one mile to a small village and parked my car to find a cool spot and a cold beer! Only a few yards from where I had parked the car, I noticed the sign pointing to LaBelle Helene Hotel. Underneath this sign were the words, "The Schliemann House—1862!"

I was amazed by my accidental discovery of the place where the great excavator had lived while he was digging in search of the "golden death mask" of King Agamemnon. Inside, the owner was preparing for the reception of a large group of German and Italian tourists who were coming for lunch.

I asked him if I could have a beer on his front porch which looked like the coolest spot in Greece. He smiled and asked me if I was English. He smiled again and served me a large ice cold Amstel beer.

When I observed the delicious food that was being served inside, I asked one of the waiters if I could be served on the outside porch. "No problem" was his reply. In

Greece everything is "no problem" and that is why I love the Greek style of living.

After one hour had elapsed, the touring group quickly boarded their buses and the owner came out to join me for a beer. I had observed him earlier and I was amazed when I heard him speaking fluent German and Italian to his luncheon guests. His English was also perfect.

He was very powerfully built, but his most arresting physical characteristic was his massive head and thick neck. I thought to myself that here was the kind of man that Homer so often described when writing about the heroes of the Trojan War.

He told me his name was George and I said George in American means "all right." We both laughed and in that moment everything seemed to click into the position of instant friendship.

Without a doubt, George was the most energetic and enthusiastic Greek man that I had encountered. He gave me the impression that he wanted to become physical with every subject whether it was food or art, it didn't matter. He wanted to sink his large, white teeth into it and chew it to pieces.

I was anxious to learn more about this dynamic Greek character. George was interested in everything! But he was especially curious about American politics. He was also dying to learn more about the wild west. When I told him my ancestors were Mormans who had crossed the plains in covered wagons, I thought he was going to jump out of his skin. That was George!

We could talk with each other for hours and hours and never did we feel bored or at a loss for virgin discoveries in any field. George was also a living encyclopedia concerning Greek history and culture. If I came to discover Mycenae which was "rich in gold," I had also found a golden man of knowledge and strong character. Because of George and his wonderful family, I remained as a guest at the Belle Helene for over two months.

No one can adequately describe places like Epidaurus, Tiryns or the Mystras. You must go there to experience the overwhelming feeling of what happened in these places centuries before the birth of Christ.

You must stand alone in the center of the world's first healing place to fully understand how these men used herbs to cure people from all over the world. That was Epidaurus.

And when you are alone at Tiryns, even on a warm day, you will feel a cold chill in your spine when you realize that this is the place where true Cyclopean giants had lived for many centuries. This is only a small part of the great Greek mystery!

When I finally left George and Peloponnese to take the ship to Corfu, I knew I was fully prepared to complete my manuscript. During my long story lifetime in Greece, everything in my head had become crystal clear. I finally discovered the reasons why I had left my family and my country in search of my destiny. To tell this true story was very important for me.

When I arrived in the tiny cove at Kalamai Bay in October of 1988, I knew why I was the happiest and most fortunate man in the universe. To be alive to every new day became the greatest adventure of my life in Corfu.

From the moment I stepped out on my balcony, jutting out over the Ionian Sea, to enjoy my first cup of morning coffee, I realized, as never before, how much beauty there is all around us no matter where we are living. In these past five years, I had encountered hundreds of people from all over the world.

What I learned is that we are all a part of a common

humanity. My love for music, for laughter and for peace is the goal of everyone I have had the pleasure of meeting. None of these individuals can be deceived either by government or religious leaders who speak well, but act poorly in the cause of humanity.

The time is growing very short for all the misleading parasites who feed on the weak and hungry of the world. One day soon, all the military, all the bureaucrats, all the pencil pushers and panic button pushers will shrink from the sight and sounds of humanity. All these things are happening already throughout the world that I have traveled. The silent voices of yesterday will be tomorrow's voice of love and hope and everlasting peace.

This is the legacy of the twenty-first century—the century of the awakening mind in search of a better world without fear, without hunger, without war.

Before I left the White House in Kalamai, I traveled to Egypt, my gateway to the Eastern world. When I left the airport in Cairo, I was with my friend Edel, a twenty-six-year-old Egyptian man whom I had met on the flight from Athens.

"John, where are you going?" he asked.

"I am flying to Luxor to see the Valley of the Kings," I had replied.

"No, first I am inviting you to my home in Alexandria to meet my mother and my family. Before my father died he taught me an important lesson. It is not so important to use big words about friendship but to show your love by deeds and actions! John, I want you to see the Egyptian character before you see Egyptian history."

Edel is the reason why I will be spending the next five years of my lifetime in the Eastern world!

Epilogue

After almost five years living in Europe I returned to the United States in the Spring of 1989. I had completed my manuscript and delivered it to my publisher in New York.

My brother Warren and his wife Eileen, who were living in New Jersey, were making final preparations for their daughter's July wedding in Santa Barbara, California. I spent several weeks with my family at the Jersey seashore, and then I decided to drive to California for the wedding of the year.

When I arrived in Santa Barbara there were two letters waiting for me. One was from my publisher, telling me they were prepared to sign a contract to publish my *Snowflake in a Blizzard*. The second letter was from Germany: Dr. Aquarius would be making her first trip to the "Golden State."

I must admit I was the happiest man in the universe! Aquarius and I spent a few delightful weeks in Santa Barbara and Big Sur before we made our way to San Francisco to plan the return route back to New York. I had borrowed my sister in law's 1977 Ltd. Ford, which Eileen affectionately called her "ray of light." For me the Ltd. was also a "ray of hope." Together the car and I traveled in over thirty states, covering sixteen thousand miles during the fantastic summer of 1989.

Aquarius had happily agreed to share the return cross country drive with me. We made our first stop in Reno, Nevada, where Aquarius became acquainted with the "one armed bandit" slot machine. She was dazzled with the color and activity in the Golden Nugget gambling casino.

She was also thrilled to meet my ninety-seven-year-old uncle Herb Maw in Salt Lake City, Utah. Herb Maw is the oldest living ex-governor in America. He still has a bright twinkle in his blue eyes, especially when he had his arm around Aquarius, telling her about his World War I experience in Germany.

Yellowstone National Park, the Badlands of South Dakota and Mount Rushmore were just a few of the many highlights of our magnificent tour of America. Of course the main event was our arrival in the Big Apple, which I jokingly told Aquarius I would buy for her when my book became a bestseller.

We dined on Italian food and wine at Mama Leone's, went to the theatre to enjoy *A Chorus Line*, and danced the night away on the top of the World Trade Center's Windows on the World. It was a spectacular way to say *auf wiedersehen* (until I see you again) when I left Aquarius at J.F.K. Airport for her return to Germany.

On October 11, 1989, I signed a two-year contract with Vantage Press and departed for Germany the next day. I planned on making a brief visit to see Aquarius before I left for a long tour of Thailand, India, and China. When I arrived at her home she was in a state of great excitement. The West German press had page one stories of huge demonstrations in East Germany.

Something very important was happening and I had arrived at a special moment when history was being made in Germany. In Leipzig and in East Berlin massive demonstrations were calling for free elections and transit visas to go to the West. The momentum of these demonstrations was growing stronger with every passing day.

On Friday, November 9, Dr. Aquarius was invited to

attend an important medical congress in north Germany. She suggested we travel together in her car and go to her apartment in Berlin when the conference was concluded. "Tomorrow," she said, "Berlin will be the center of world attention and we must be there!"

The next day we were heading in the direction of Hanover and the Russian–East-German check point.

The Berlin radio reports were astonishing. There were nine holes in the infamous Berlin Wall and thousands of East Berliners were entering West Berlin without any military interference. Many more thousands were taking to the road in their cars to cross the border to West Germany.

The Iron Curtain was being lifted and freedom was in evidence everywhere.

After we had driven past the Russian security check point in East Germany and were following the signs to Berlin we began to witness a scene we would never forget. Approaching us in the opposite direction were traffic lines of old vintage cars wearing the German Democratic Republic DDR license of East Germany. For more than fifteen miles we passed cars which were packed with men, women and children waving their hands with the V for victory sign. I could feel the strong emotional vibrations coming from Aquarius as she waved across the road to her East-German neighbours. It was a tender moment mixed with feelings of love, peace and freedom. As an American I was also filled with many emotions.

Since World War II ended in 1945, the two superpowers Russia and America have occupied Germany. No peace treaty has ever been signed to officially terminate the war. For forty-five years close to one million Russian and American troops as well as British and French have occupied Germany with the most deadly nuclear military force that has ever been assembled anywhere in the world.

The result of one demented insane maniac who started World War II in 1939 has brought the worst humiliation to a nation of Germans in the entire history of civilization. Today sixty million West Germans have become Americanized and sixteen million East Germans have been Communized.

The insanity and madness of one man in 1939 has been accelerated by the madness and insanity of the superpowers, who after forty-five years are still playing war games every day in the forests and airspace of Germany. I would not want to be a second- or third- or even fourth-generation German living in an explosive armed nation destined for instant nuclear annihilation. All the "bullshit" multi-million dollar "summit meetings" and military conferences are an insult to every citizen of the world. When the leaders smile and use big words to talk about the reduction of men in uniforms and weapons they should know that the people of the world are not so dumb anymore.

Even if the superpowers agree to reduce ninety percent of their nuclear capability, the remaining ten percent still could mean death and destruction for the human race at any crazy moment in the future.

Five billion people throughout the world are becoming stronger and wiser and more sensitive to world affairs. A handful of misleading rulers and military fanatics cannot continue to deceive the total population much longer.

The demonstrations of the 1990s will call for a total ban and elimination of all weapons systems starting with Star Wars and nuclear missiles. The twentieth century belonged to the "power brokers," the wheelers and dealers of multi-billion dollar weapons systems who are also controlling the so-called superpowers of today. The twenty-first century will be remembered as the century when humanity won freedom with peace, dignity, respect, and everlasting love for one another.

As a student of history my arrival in Berlin had to be one of the greatest events in my life. All the main streets looked like a gigantic sea of humanity. There were no shouts, no loud noises, no violence—only dignified, peaceful, smiling faces. Somewhere in the distance I heard many voices singing in German and English. The song was, "We Shall Overcome."

I had heard this song before, but this time the candle lit faces of young and old alike impressed me and I thought that nothing would ever be the same again. This was a brand new day!

Humanity is responding everywhere. In Moscow thousands of demonstrators marched in protest against the national parade of military weapons on display in the Kremlin. It was fantastic! In Czechoslovakia one million demonstrators marched for freedom and justice. If one was listening one could hear the swelling voices of all the people on the planet singing "We will overcome"!

I could see moisture in Aquarius's eyes as she observed the remarkable picture of East and West Berliners kissing and embracing each other in the shadows of the famous Brandenburg Gate. She was a very young demonstrator at the Berlin Wall on August 13, 1961. She told me twenty-eight years ago a part of her died that terrible day when suddenly without warning she was living in a cage surrounded by unwillingly courageous prisoners.

We decided to follow a large crowd of East Berliners who were returning to their homes in the east sector of the city. The Russian check-point guard did not say a word as we illegally walked into the "no zone" for West Berliners and Americans who had no passes.

Returning some time later I observed the same security guard with a strange expression on his worried face. I could not restrain myself from asking him what was his problem? He told me that he felt ridiculous standing there and doing nothing! I laughed and reminded him that for forty-five years American and Russian soldiers were doing the same thing. I told him that perhaps he could find another job where he didn't have to wear a uniform or carry a rifle. We both shook hands and laughed, but there was no humour in our laughter. I wanted to tell him that in the future uniforms and weapons will be out of style. I also wanted to say that all the many millions of people who are marching for freedom and peace have no uniforms and no weapons and they are winning. They are the real force of the 1990s and their silent, disciplined demonstrations will not be destroyed by men in military clothes.

Before we left Berlin I purchased many international newspapers in order to learn about the world reaction to what would become the story of the century!

In particular I was interested in a story that appeared in the *Daily Telegraph*, a leading English newspaper. Chancellor Helmut Kohl made a statement that there is now less reason than ever to be resigned to the long term division of Germany into two states. In the same newspaper John Keegan, the defence editor, had a story that caught my attention. The headline was titled: "A Future That Frightens the Generals." Keegan reported that, "a reunified Germany would inherit the military infrastructures of NATO and the Warsaw Pact combined, an embarrassment of military riches, including an army of eighteen divisions and eight hundred combat aircraft. At a stroke Germany would leap to a clear third place in military force in the industrialized world. Diplomatically newborn, it would also be free to develop nuclear weapons if it chose."

The ugly irony of this true factual story is that neither the East or West Germans wanted anything to do with uniforms or weapons after the Hitler disaster. The American and Russian military governments forced it down their throats like a bayonet—with devastating consequences.

One of the heroes of my story is Jonathan, the young German who refused to wear a military uniform. His decision to put on white clothes and work in a hospital is one of the main reasons why I believe there is hope in our world for peace and love.

When I went to bed on my final night in Germany before flying to Bangkok, I had a magnificent dream. I saw many bright fires burning in the distance. As I came closer to the brightest fire I saw hundreds of naked young men and women singing and dancing. They appeared in my dream as though they were nymphs of Greek mythology. They were beautiful and they were happy. I noticed the men had taken off their military uniforms and along with their weapons fueled the fire to a blazing glory of a newfound freedom.

When I awoke I smiled because I knew in my mind, my heart, and my soul that this dream is happening all over the world. We are finally peacefully marching out of the dark age of the twentieth century into God's brilliant Enlightenment of the twenty-first century. Peace and love to all mankind!